THE RED-HAIRED BRAT

Plots, suspicion, danger and death surround the young Princess Elizabeth almost from birth. Fear and misfortune serve to strengthen her courage and spirit, to develop her political acumen, while love for her country becomes the guiding force of her life. She learns patience and the art of dissimulation, how to see ahead, to learn from the mistakes of others, yet remains wholly human, witty and humorous, and fully conscious of her own faults. She is brave, proud, hot-tempered, hot-blooded and very cool-headed. Her emergence as Queen Elizabeth I is triumphant.

D1612945

JOANNA DESSAU

THE RED-HAIRED BRAT

Complete and Unabridged

ULVERSCROFT
Leicester

First published in Great Britain

First Large Print Edition
published 1999

British Library CIP Data

Dessau, Joanna
    The red-haired brat.—Large print ed.—
Ulverscroft large print series: general fiction
1. Large type books
I. Title
823.9'14 [F]

ISBN 0–7089–4098–6

Published by
F. A. Thorpe (Publishing) Ltd.
Anstey, Leicestershire
Set by Words & Graphics Ltd.
Anstey, Leicestershire
Printed and bound in Great Britain by
T. J. International Ltd., Padstow, Cornwall

This book is printed on acid-free paper

To my darling DEBBIE
With very much love
From JO-NANA.

x x x

Prologue

WHITE HALL

January 1603

It is Twelfth Night and the revels are done. I feel ill and chill, with a strange heaviness about me as I ponder upon the coming year and what it will bring. I think mayhap, it will bring for me the grave. It is a presentiment that hangs upon me and will not shake off, although Doctor Dee tells me that I am in good health and looks for a lady of my years. Well, so I am, despite the beginnings of a rheum in my head causing me to sniff somewhat. Few live to my number of years, and those who do fail to retain their powers as I have done . . . But Nature will have her way. She can outrule the greatest monarch and set her quiet hand on the chiefest beauties of man, causing them to crumble and decay as I am doing, sweet Jesu aid me.

I know it because I have lived all my life at a gallop, and now, struggle though I may, the pace is slowing to a walk, even to an occasional stumble. In all my long life I have never faltered or stumbled, so the signs are clear to me. If the swift horse of my life should fall, I should fall with it, never to rise again, for my days will be ended.

I shall have reached seventy years, come

September, if I live. Ay, this is the very face of the worm that eats away my peace of mind and lightness of heart. It is the worm of death, and the terror of it has marred my life and womanhood. Now it stares at me close, close, paralysing me, shrivelling me to ancient mortality, making me at one with all others, and this I have never been, except at the moment of birth which is common to us all. I would not have had it otherwise. My father a King, my mother — ah, my mother. She knew the face of the worm of death full well. For her, it did not slink in the shadows, but leaped forth one summer day and took her by the throat in all her pride and beauty. It is said that I never speak of my mother, and nor do I, for such thoughts rocked my reason, so I put them from me. Now she steals upon me oftentimes and I wish and wonder.

I have not looked into a mirror for twenty years, but now I do, and as I do, I see with a shock, the features of my father in his old age and sickness, for his cheeks fell in and his nose sharpened to a curved blade before the end. There too I see the look of haughty dominance shared by us both, but my eyes, though sunken now, are hooded and of an amber colour, while his were long and bright blue. My forehead, though lined, is high and round where his was wide and square, and my jaw is long with a pointed chin, like pictures I have seen of my mother. And I am thin. Willowy once, scraggy now, yet upright and erect as ever I was, and so will remain until Death overtakes me. It will not be long, I think. I have let forth his familiar spirit; he will not return to the cage wherein I prisoned him so long and I must live with him hourly until my days are spent.

So it is time to clear my mind and set my thoughts in order. Time to review my actions in the light of reality, and not as they may seem to others in the years to come, when I shall be judged in my absence. I have an increasing desire to be alone and quiet, and none shall gainsay me this, or any other thing . . .

1

OF MARRIAGE AND FAMILY LOVE

1536 – 1544

My first memory is of being somewhere high up and of looking down from thence. With my inward eye I can see a clear blue sky cut across by the dark block of a building pierced by rows of windows below which lay a courtyard. In it walked folk clad in gay colours, one tall fellow tossing a green ball, which he affected to throw up for me to catch. I leaned forward laughing, hands outstretched, but restrained from falling by someone's arms that held me. The arms were clothed in shining black and the hands were white and bejewelled. I turned my head towards her who held me, and could see a long rope of pearls upon a neck and bosom, the pearls ornamented by what I knew, even then, to be the letter B, all in gold with pearl drops. She always wore it.

Turning again, I saw more jewels; a veritable rainbow. I saw rich brown fur bands, scarlet sleeves, a gold chain, and gazing higher, the face of the god in my world. Red-bearded, hawk-nosed, with hot blue eyes that stared, not at me who worshipped him, but at her who held me. Her face I cannot recall, which is strange. Jesu, was she headless for me even then?

This I see with my mind's eye. The rest is quarrelling and the feeling of guilt and fear in my heart. They quarrelled about me — oh, I knew it. 'Twas because I was no prince to follow my father, but a useless girl, unworthy of his love. It seemed that my mother could not carry within her a prince for my father, and he railed at her because of it and because of me. I felt that I had caused him to hate her, and my cries were added to the quarrelling.

So I learned that girls were useless, and women fit only to breed boys. This was my first lesson in marriage and family love. It was not to be the last.

A day or so after this, I was sent from the palace of my birth, Placenta at Greenwich, to Hatfield, in the care of my Lady Mistress, Lady Bryan. I never saw my mother again, for while I and my entourage were on the road to Hatfield, she was arrested and sent to the Tower upon a charge of high treason. What followed all the world knows. My father had my mother killed with a sword on Tower Green and she lay headless in her blood for a whole long day before being taken up. Where she was interred, no one truly knows, not even I, her daughter, her only child.

I liked Hatfield, though I missed my parents. I liked visiting Hunsdon House, where my sister Mary dwelt. Dear Lady Bryan, how she indulged me while affecting to be stern. I loved her.

'See now, my Princess,' she would say, 'ladies of your rank must not scream and stamp when their wishes are denied, and never for such a paltry thing as a sweetmeat. Remember your toothache.'

And she would rub my hot gums with lotion from a bottle, which eased the pain greatly. Snatching the bottle, I would sniff greedily, for I have ever been sensitive to odours, and oil of cloves had a satisfying smell.

In those days, my sister Mary was designated the Lady Mary, while I was the Princess Elizabeth. No matter how she changed later, Mary was a sweet girl then, tender and loving to me, laughing at my arrogant baby ways, her unknowing supplanter as heir to the throne. My very presence must have been gall and wormwood to her who had been deprived of mother, of love, security and position, being treated with coldness and contempt by those who should have cherished her. She would give me toys, play with me and caress me, bidding fair to spoil me thoroughly. These were happy times, yet under the gaiety ran a thread of anxiety that gnawed at my stomach. It was something to do with the worried look on Lady Bryan's face when she dressed me, and when she mended my clothes. Before we had come to Hatfield I had worn a new gown each day, some jewelled, some of gold and silver tissue with velvet skirts, some of damask and satin. At Greenwich I had a little bed all of green satin with fringes. It was a gift from my mother, they said, as were my white and purple caps embellished with gold stitchery. Now I had but a few caps, all worn, and my gowns were fewer and plainer, fast growing too small. Sometimes the braiding hung loose and the seams gave way. This was when I saw Lady Bryan's dark eyebrows draw together in a frown. Her lips would turn down and all her dimples disappear. Then I would feel the gnawing in my belly. I thought it was a fox that gnawed as in the tale of the Spartan lad that Lady Bryan had told me. When I asked her about it, she wept and the fox gnawed harder than ever.

'Never mind,' I said stoutly to her, 'when I am grown and wear my father's crown, I shall have a new gown for each hour of the day, and you will not weep any more.'

This caused her to sob all the harder and I wept with her, for the fox was gnawing so mightily that I feared he would eat me up. So began the wretched discomfort in my belly that has plagued me ever since and for which I have never found a cure. Despite this, I was happy. 'Tis difficult to be otherwise at three years old.

I did notice the worn look deepening on Mary's face and how her rosary clattered when she told her beads. She was always at prayer and tried to make me pray with her but I had no wish to spend time muttering on my knees in a stuffy chamber, although the altar candles gave me pleasure for a short space.

'Little heathen,' she would say fondly to me, 'your mind is not upon God and His saints at all; it is upon running and riding.'

She was right. Physical exercise was ever necessary to me. Besides, she seemed a grown woman in my eyes, and an old one at that, with her sorrowful look and the lines about her mouth. Once she told me that she was twenty-one; I considered it a great age.

At Hatfield I learned another lesson. I learned

that those who were down could rise up, whilst those who were up could fall down until they felt that the friends of yesterday were the foes of today. It happened to me and in this wise. One day, the Governor of my Household addressed me as Lady Elizabeth. Surprised, I told him that I was Princess, but he seemed not to hear. Running to Lady Bryan, I told her of it.

'How haps it that yesterday I was Princess and today but Lady Elizabeth?' I asked her, puzzled and uneasy.

Dropping her sewing, she took me on her lap and sighing, told me that Mary was reinstated and had gone to London to take up her place at Court, that having done the King's bidding she was in disgrace no longer. I begged to go too, but Lady Bryan shook her head.

'Why not?' I cried. 'Have I now done wrong? Am I in disgrace? Ah, my father loves me not, for I am a useless girl. Did he order that I was to be but My Lady?' Wordless, she held me close and at last I went on: 'My father tired of Mary's mother and put her away and she died. He tired of Mary too. Now he loves Mary and has tired of me. Where is my mother, Lady Bryan? I have not seen her this long while and no one speaks of her.'

I trembled all over and the fox was tearing my belly to ribbons. I feared to vomit over Lady Bryan's gown. My head spun so that I did not hear her words and a great pain slashed through my eyes. When I came to myself, I was abed with the curtains drawn and Lady Bryan at my bedside. She told me that I had the migraine and that I must lie still and rest. But I could not rest.

'Lady Bryan, where is my mother? Where is she?'

She entreated me to be calm, to have a care, but I would not listen, imploring her to tell me of my mother, until for very anxiety she answered me, saying that my mother was dead and that my father had married a lady who was now called Queen Jane and who was pregnant with a new little brother or sister for me. I digested this in silence. Suddenly, a thought rising unbidden to my brain, I asked: 'Who was The Concubine?'

A great gasp was Lady Bryan's reply. 'She is dead too,' I said. 'She had her head cut off. My father loved her. Did he tire of her too, or did she have girl babies instead of boys? Was she wicked?'

'No, she was not wicked,' said Lady Bryan. 'She was frightened and unhappy.'

'Then why does everyone look foolish when I speak of her? It is strange and I do not like it.'

'Do not ask me, leave it be,' pleaded my governess. 'Do not ask.'

'Nay, I cannot leave it. I must know, for my head will burst else.' And so she told me as well as she could, that she who was called The Concubine was also my mother, adjuring me never to speak of it, and now that I knew it, to put it behind me. So I learned my second lesson in the art of marriage and family love.

★ ★ ★

My stepmother Queen Jane Seymour's baby was a boy. I had been recalled to Hampton Court some weeks before the birth, living there once again dressed as a King's daughter, but feeling unsure and full of hidden fears. I felt surprise at my stepmother, for she was not beautiful, and I had thought all Queens were beautiful. She had a great belly moreover. I stared at her belly more than at her face until Lady Bryan reminded me of my manners, explaining that the Queen had a great belly by reason of a baby within it and that all hoped for the birth of a prince. I felt I should like to see a prince and have a little brother. I watched Queen Jane narrowly through the days, expecting the prince to pop forth like a cork from a bottle.

It was at about this time that a new addition was made to my household in the shape of a merry young lady called Katherine Champernowne. She shared with Lady Bryan the task of caring for me, and as she was far more young and active, began to be with me much more often. I called her Kat, and from the first I loved her dearly, so that when my good Lady Bryan left me to look after my new little brother, I fretted far less than had been feared.

I saw my sister Mary almost every day at Hampton Court. She looked ill and very sad. She did not play with me nor pet me so oft as at Hunsdon, but sometimes she would snatch me up and cover my face with kisses, asking if I loved her. I told her I did and that she was pretty, which was true. Tiny and fine-boned, she had beautiful dark eyes, a little round nose, pink cheeks and a mass of red hair in springing waves. I did not know then that she had forsworn her religion and declared her mother's marriage to my father incestuous and unlawful, by signing a document to this effect. She had done this in order to recover my father's affection, indeed, in order to remain alive. I was the living shape of all her misfortunes, but I had no idea of it then, nor of how her miseries were slowly turning her against me.

My brother Edward was born on the twelfth of October 1537 at Hampton Court, and wild was the rejoicing. I was more interested to see if Queen Jane's belly were flat again than in hanging over the cradle, but she kept her bed as all ladies do after childbirth, so I could not really tell.

Little Edward's christening took place when he was three days old. I carried the chrisom, the cloth in which the baby was to be wrapped after his baptism. I remember the windows, black with the night outside, flashing into wavering flames of gold as the candles reflected their light in the glass. I recall the colours of the robes, the Archbishop's cope and mitre, the solemn chanting as the great procession wound its way slowly from Queen Jane's bedside to the chapel. My stepmother was carried on a litter, dressed all in gold tissue and emeralds and her eyes shone as green. For the rest, her face was pure white with a red patch on each cheekbone. I thought she looked as near pretty as I had ever seen her. She smiled greatly but seemed more wishful to sleep.

Kat told me that I should have been proud to be chosen to carry the chrisom and stay up late to do so. It was a signal favour, she said. But I was too occupied in stifling my feelings of rage and humiliation to enjoy the great occasion as I should, for as the procession began, I discovered that I was to be carried. There was no consolation at all in the fact that Queen Jane Seymour's eldest brother was to carry me. A Seymour, and a nobody withal! I clenched my hands upon the chrisom to prevent myself from casting it to the furthest corner of the Queen's bedchamber. I set my teeth and pouted my lips in a ferocious grimace to keep back the sobs, while the tears in my eyes blurred all the light and colours to a sparkling, shifting film. I glared at Seymour so furiously that he drew his head back in surprise. A poor fellow, I thought, to be startled by a four year old lady, and I liked him not at all, nor did I ever after that day. He may have been my brother's uncle, but he was none of mine, and let him remember it. So I turned my head away and twisted my body round, giving him a fine view of a crimson cap and the back-lacing of my gown, and that was all he had of me, save a kick on the shins when he tried to take me up again after the baptism. My sister Mary quickly stepped out of her place and took my hand, setting me to walk with her as if I were grown. I loved her for it and squeezed her hand hard, to tell her so.

Soon after this great happening, there was another procession in which Queen Jane was carried to the chapel. She knew naught of it, poor lady, for she was dead, and my brother but twelve days old. My stomach troubled me greatly at this time, for there was much to think on, touching the mysteries of men and women, and these thoughts brought with them a deep fear which I was at pains to deny. Yet at night, in the dark, behind the curtains of my bed, my dreams refused to deny the fear, and I rode the Night Mare. She galloped with me through shadowy caverns, through rivers of blood. She took me to a marriage bed, each post of which bore a woman's head, severed and bloody. She caused my father to appear to me as a monster full nine feet tall, with swords for teeth and an axe in each hand. She brought me before the body of Queen Jane lying dead, with her belly burst open like a ripe pomegranate while my father held my brother in his arms, shouting for joy. She caused me to look through a marriage ring as through a window and looking through, I saw Death.

From then on, I was always an uneasy sleeper. I formed the habit of calling for lights and setting my brain to the problems of learning. In this way I became so adept at Latin that I would speak it as easily as my own dear English. Greek too, I mastered, though never loved so well. French and Italian followed on, then Spanish. They were to stand me in good stead in later years.

The days were fairly peaceful, however, and I loved my little brother. When his toothless mouth widened in a smile for me, my heart filled with joy. He loved me, so how could I not love him? I, who had been laggard at my needle, quickly learned to set my stitches in order to make him a cap and a loop for his teething ring. I was jealous of Mistress Jackson, his nurse, for I wished not to share his love, but she persuaded me out of my humour, saying that I could help her to care for him, and so I was content. Little Edward grew and thrived, looking only to Jackson and me for love. Ah, he was clever, that little one. Words came early to his tongue. 'Mother Jack!' he would cry, and 'Sweet Sister! Come to little Ned!' And we would run, his willing slaves.

He had another slave in my father, the King. Naught was too good for Baby Ned, the prince so long a-coming. Yet Ned was a nervous child and shy; my father's loud voice and boisterous ways often made him shrink and turn his head away. In any other child this would have enraged the King, for he liked a child of his to be forward and gay, as well I knew, but Ned was his Prince, his Heir, his Son, and therefore perfect.

Because of Ned's avowed affection for me, I came under more notice from my father than I had enjoyed since I had lost his favour. When visiting the Nursery at Hampton Court, he would stare hard at me whilst petting his son. I would try to remain composed and smiling, showing no hint of the ferment of love and terror that raged in my small bony breast. Sometimes he spoke to me, and I would force my stiff tongue and dry mouth to answer in a way that might please him. I would school my eyes to a bright blankness, for fear the sick longing in them would turn his approval from me. It was hard, at five years old, to act a part and not fling myself at his feet, pleading for love. But to do this was to lose all hope of any for the future, so I played my part and grew accustomed to it, while he tolerated me, for did I not adore and minister to his son, that offshoot of himself? And seeing their little King-to-be so loving to his sister, once held in no account, the courtiers amended their ways to me somewhat and began to treat me with increased respect, which pleased me, although I mistrusted such veering friendship, even so young as I was.

★ ★ ★

So many Januaries and this is my seventieth. I may never see another. A dark door in my mind closes when I think of next Twelfth Night. There are those about me who would seek the rising sun, who would desert me to fly to his side, even as did those who sought me in the dreary drawn-out days of my sister's dying. When I saw this, I swore it should never happen to me, and so I have not yet given a name to him who is to follow me. I would have my creatures mine until I loose my hold, for there can be but one ruler of a realm. If this is in doubt, loyalty is lost and strength is severed.

Next January, will he who is to follow be seated on my throne? I must push my mind-door open and peer into the shadowscape thus revealed, though my heart pounds and my old flesh quivers. And if he is seated thereon — ah my love, my England, I can only pray to God to guard you, for he is an unworthy successor to whom I leave you when my hand falls from the reins. Well, I cannot help it, having none of my own to come after me. He is the obvious choice, and many people see that as clear as I do, but name him I will not, save only to mine own heart. Apart from possible disaffection caused by naming him, could I bear to see England's heart turning from me to another? Nay, never could I. Yet, if I grow infirm and incapable in body and mind, so will England turn, so must she turn. I would not wish to live and reign for one day longer than my life and reigning could do my dear people good. He whom I choose will unify England and Scotland at last under one ruler. It will set the account straight and redress the balance as nothing else could ever do, for the Queen of Scots, his mother, was born out of time, to her douleur and mine.

I will think no more of next year, but turn my mind back to the New Year's day when little Ned was two and I was six and half-a-year. In thinking of it now it seems but a few weeks agone instead of sixty-four years. I can see myself as I was then, as if looking at a picture . . .

Tall for my six years was I and thin as a scarecrow. Not pretty, but sharp and intelligent looking, and my hair was beautiful. Like fiery silk it was, falling down my back like a veil, already near to my waist. And my eyes were always good, of a colour like tawny ale. Sad eyes they were, and wary, as if ready for sudden disaster, while my mouth I kept close folded to restrain thoughtless speech.

My brother had had his own household since the age of one year, when he had been moved to Havering-atte-Bower in Essex, and it was here that we spent the New Year. The palace was old and had been first built by King Edward the Confessor five hundred years agone, and since added to in a hotch-potch of buildings that, to my eyes, made a pleasing whole. There were many complaints of the draughts and the damp, but my father felt it safer for Ned to be there while he was young, well away from the plagues and sicknesses that were always rife in London.

At Havering I saw dear Lady Bryan, who was now Lady Mistress to Edward, and she praised my manners and my careful ways. Careful indeed I was, for the King was to visit us and I had no wish to offend him. Mary came from Hunsdon, bringing gifts for us all, and upon seeing those for Edward my heart sank, for they were sumptuous. There was a coat of crimson satin all embroidered in gold, with worked sleeves, and a crimson jewelled hat with a white plume. She told me that they had cost her a pretty penny and I believed her, but my gift had cost little, since I had little to give.

I had made a shirt for Ned from some fine lawn cambric given me by Kat Champernowne, working the neck and sleeves in smocking, with gold thread on the neck part. If time were money, then my gift were as rich as Mary's. I had also worked a ball from scraps of coloured velvets joined with stitching in gold thread, and stuffed with wool.

Later that year, Master Holbein painted Ned wearing his crimson coat and hat and my cambric shirt. Right pretty he looked, with his round fat cheeks, pointed chin and little pink pouting mouth. So my work was on show for all to see, and glad was I that I had done it well and evenly.

New Year's Day was wet and wild and I could not ride outside. I stood staring out of the windows with their diamond shaped panes, scratching with the nail of my forefinger at the uneven greenish glass through which I could see great rags of dark clouds rushing across the grey sky and the rolling Essex countryside sloping away to meet the clouds. I thought of the dreadful whispers that I had lately heard, that although I was of a surety my mother's daughter, having come from her womb, I might not be my father's. I had heard it muttered that my mother had had many lovers and that I could be the daughter of a music master. My father had let these things be written and shouted abroad, so that all would believe her wickedness and his right to kill her because of it. So I needed a mirror in the cries of the people who shouted of my likeness to my father, as well as my own one of polished metal that I kept in my chamber and consulted many times a day. That little mirror told me that I was more like the King in feature than my sister Mary, or my brother Edward, and they were most emphatically of his begetting. The likeness between us was marked, and I showed promise of growing tall too. My father was of a great height; higher than any I ever saw. He was right proud of his similarity to his grandfather, the Plantagenet King Edward the Fourth, who had been a true child of his race in physical inheritance. Those Plantagenets had red-gold hair, hawk noses, fair skin, great height and a magical charm. They were the old Kings of England, and I too was like those Plantagenets. My mirror told me this and most people spoke of it, yet deep in my heart, in the most secret places of my soul, I was deadly afraid.

So on this New Year's Day I was cast down, and my stomach churned in sympathy with the gusts of wind as I thought of my father's coming. To raise my spirits I went to the table where stood my little clavichord, for music had the power to soothe me and raise cheer in me. This too was like my father who was a notable musician, and singer, writing his own sweet tuneable melodies and songs. I had been able to play since a babe, and did so today, sweeping myself so much afar that I missed the bustle of the King's arrival, knowing of it only when the door flew open and he stood on the threshold. My hands stiffened on the keys and I made to rise and curtsey, but he forbade me, ordering me to play on.

'You do well girl,' he cried. 'I would hear more.' With this, he came in and settled himself, bidding all his company withdraw. My mind had become empty and my hands turned to wax for I was feared that I would anger him by an unprincely show of cravenness. Turning towards him, I smiled brilliantly although my lips trembled.

'Give me but one moment Sire,' I said as coolly as I could, 'while I rub my hands. They are perished with the cold and I would not offend your ears by botching a melody by reason of stiff fingers.'

He rose and came towards me. Inwardly I quailed, but preserved a bold, fearless front. 'Let me have your hands,' he said and took them in his own. Ah, those hands were like heart's blood. They engulfed mine, rubbing and kneading them. 'They are like icicles indeed,' he remarked. 'I shall warm them soon enough. Is your brother well and healthy? Does he grow apace?'

'Indeed Sire, he is very well. He grows stout,

walking without a leading rein and chattering like a magpie.'

I pleased him with these words and he smiled down at me. I was happy, although the smile was not for me but for Edward's progress.

'I am most glad to hear it,' he said. 'I trust your words Elizabeth, for you are close to him and love him well.' He released my hands. 'Now play to me and dawdle not, for I would visit my son.'

By this time my wits had unlocked a little, and I chose to play and sing a melody of the King's own composing. It was called 'Pastance with Good Company,' and he had written it when a young man. After a moment, he joined with me in his beautiful bass voice, putting a harmony to my shrill treble. I felt my heart leave my body and lift towards Heaven. At the close of the melody, the King put his hand on my shoulder and gripped it. This was unusual, since he seldom caressed me by word or gesture. But his small interest had already left me. Turning with a rush of silks, he swept, a gorgeous, glowing planet from the room, leaving me curtseying unheeded to the floor, where I stayed bowed and sobbing with the release of emotions too confused and strong for me to endure with ease or composure.

The King stayed for several days and nights. I recall that he gave Edward a New Year gift of great richness. It was an equipage of silver-gilt, with dishes, mugs and porringers for his own especial use. I thought it a dull present for a child of two. Wandering from room to room on that dull, chilly

21

day, I sought out Sybil Penne, my brother's day-nurse. She was a kind, pretty woman; sister-in-law to Sir William Sidney, Edward's Chamberlain. I asked her if no one but myself had given my brother toys as a gift.

'Well,' she said, 'his uncle has given him a hobby-horse.'

'Which uncle gave him that?' I asked.

'Sir Thomas Seymour, poor Queen Jane's youngest brother.'

'Oh, I like him!' I said eagerly. 'He makes us laugh. I do not like his elder brother. He carried me at Edward's christening, and a poor, prating nodcock I thought him. What did he give Ned?'

'A hornbook to help him with his letters,' answered Sybil.

'He would!' I cried. 'Mayhap Ned will have the wit to use it as a bat for the ball I gave him. I tell you Sib, Ned will remember the ball and the hobby-horse, and the givers thereof, longer than he will remember gilt dishes and a horn-book.'

Laughing, she shook her head in mock reproof. 'You must guard that tongue of yours, or one day the devil will snap it off and fly away with it.'

'So, let him try!' I giggled, thrusting it forth before running off to find Kat for a game of chequers to while the time away.

* * *

Oh Thomas, Thomas Seymour. Even then I sensed your gaiety. Women and children adored you and men let you have your way while shaking their

22

heads at your unorthodoxies. To me at the age of six, you at the age of thirty were a male brightness rather than a person; a colourful warmth of song and laughter. How much more than that you were to become to me! Across a gulf of fifty-four years I look at you now in my mind. Tall and powerful, yet graceful withal. Hair of a golden-brown, slightly curling; large blue eyes always laughing, skin smooth and tanned. Your beard and moustachios were full and of a darker brown, but did not hide your curving mouth with its heavy underlip — a mouth ever curling to a smile and a flash of white teeth. I hear your voice, deep and caressing.

Thomas, you would not know me now, for I am old and all is dust and ashes to me. I am no longer the flame-haired sprite who stole the heart from your body and your body from dear Queen Kate's bed. The flame of my hair is white as ash and hidden beneath a curled wig. My tawny eyes are faded and hooded under wrinkled lids; their sharp sight is dimmed. My skin — like alabaster you said — is still white, but the yellow-white of old age and scored with lines which show, no matter how I try to conceal them with white fucus ground down fine and laid on thick with poppy-oil. My teeth, once so white and even, are almost all gone, and those that remain are but black stumps, so that I twist my lips when speaking that I may not reveal their ugliness. My hands, of which I was so very vain, are still long and tapering, but wrinkled, brown-spotted and aching with rheumatism. My movements, formerly so lithe and free, for I was never still, loving my own agility and lightness, are now stiff and slow. I still dance, Thomas, even yet. It raises my spirits and calms me. But now I dance in solitude, and not as I once did for others to marvel at. Indeed I am glad you cannot see me now, Thomas Seymour, my first love.

★ ★ ★

A year after Thomas gave Edward a hobby horse, Edward had moved to Hunsdon. I stayed at Hatfield, visiting Edward at Hunsdon and Mary at the manor of The More at Rickmansworth, once a home of Cardinal Wolsey. The King often sent to enquire of our progress, and once had his secretary, Sir Thomas Wriotheseley, visit me to discover my learning and accomplishments. This was a fox-faced gentleman who had raised himself by buying abbey land during my father's dissolution of the monasteries, and so having money, wits and lands, was fit to be considered as a person of some consequence.

I answered his questions gravely and showed off my knowledge; I danced for him, played and sang. He praised all I did, even my stitchery which fell somewhat short of the rest, and at the end, I verily believe he was sincere, for his look of haughty amusement had changed to something gentler, while the hardness in his eyes had altered to a look of kindness.

'Truly, Madam,' he said, 'if my own daughter be half as educated as you, it would be well enough for me. You bring credit to your august father and

24

do him, and all womanhood honour. I shall tell the King what I have seen and heard of you, and all of it excellent.'

Later he complimented Kat on her governance of me and on her knowledge of languages which she had taught me. His repetition to my father of the compliments he had paid me did much to sooth the awkwardness between the King and me, which pleased me well. Yet Kat and I derived much giggling from his name.

'Once it was plain Risley,' she said. 'Some of his kin still call themselves so, but when he acquired his lands, plain Risley was too plain for such a fine fellow, so he changed it.'

I laughed. 'Men are strange. Did you like his beard?'

'Aye, I thought it very jaunty.'

'I thought it bristly. Bristly Risley!' I cried, choking with laughter, for I dearly loved a nickname. 'Oh Kat, I thought of that while he was questioning me and near giggled. Methought he smiled too oft and was too fulsome.'

'He goes where power is,' said Kat. 'He will never break trust with your father, for where is there greater power than the King? The King made him, so he can break him. Sir Thomas does not forget that, you may be sure.' I did not forget it neither.

In the first week of 1540 my father married my next stepmother. She was not to his liking. I wondered when I should see her, or whether some disaster would befall her before this could come about. I spoke to Kat, but she told me to be quiet and hold my tongue. So I used my ears instead of my tongue and heard much of interest. I heard that Queen Anne of Cleves was big and graceless — a very man in woman's clothing, that she was pockmarked and covered in boils, that her voice was a corncrake's, uttering only in Flemish which none could understand nor wanted to. I heard that her clothes were hideous, that her table manners were those of a serf, that her breath was foul and she belched when she spoke. Hearing all this, I wondered that my fastidious father could be so gulled as even to dream of considering this lady as a possible bride, much less to wed her. Listening further, I discovered that she was almost an idiot, and cross-eyed also. I heard that she was still a virgin because my father could not bring himself to touch her, and that he had dubbed her The Flanders Mare. I could not understand this last morsel of gossip and asked Kat about it. She was horrified.

'God's grace, my Lady! What will you say next? Did I not implore you to keep a still tongue? You will bring us to trouble, sure!'

'I *did* keep a still tongue!' I retorted angrily. 'It is not my tongue that wags, stupid Kat. It is the tongues of others. I do but listen and keep mine own counsel. I have heard enough to send the whole household to the Tower if I repeated it to anyone important. I am no fool. What if I had run with my questions to anyone but you? Think about that!' With a flurry of skirts I flung round to flounce out of the room, but she stayed with me an arm about my waist. Angry still, I tried to

26

thrust her away, but she persisted.

'Nay darling, I am sorry. You are a wise little lady. Pity 'tis that your elders are not so wise that they babble gossip in your hearing. What is all this about a horse and the new Queen?' I repeated what I had heard and she shrugged her shoulders and put me upon her knee, holding me close in the way I loved so well.

'Since you have heard so much I will explain it or I will get no peace from you, will I? The Flanders Mare is the largest in your father's stable and the new lady is as big and gawky, so they say. Yet I cannot believe she can be so bad, for Master Holbein's portraits do not lie, so far as I know, being usually mirror images of the sitters. I saw the picture of her and pleasant I thought it. Not beautiful, but nor was Queen Jane, was she?'

'Oh no, she was plain and washed-out as a bowl of whey. Yet my father loved her and sired my brother on her. So why does he mislike this Queen?'

'Who can tell, my love? What one man will desire, another may mislike. It is so the world over. This poor Queen catcheth not the King's fancy and so he desires her not at all.' I remained silent, pondering this and she kissed me. 'Why so quiet, my chuck?'

After a moment I laughed aloud. 'I am making a vow, Kat.' I lifted a hand in mock piety. 'Before God, I vow that when I am a woman, all men shall desire *me*!' Jumping up, I ran giggling from the room before she could catch me and reprove me for blasphemy.

No disaster befell that Queen Anne. My father had wished to divorce her and had sent Sir Bristly Wriotheseley to her as his messenger. She, seeing in him a harbinger of death, had fallen down in a faint. When revived, she agreed to the King's wish at once and with great relief, for she had by now some small command of English. So she could not be such a halfwit, I reflected, having learnt enough of the language to understand and speak a little in barely three months. My father in his delight at her ready consent was eager to give her all she wished, for he was enamoured of another lady and desired to wed her as speedily as might be. The King was a marvellous hot-blooded man, said the chatterers, despite his leg which would have rendered a lesser man invalid.

I knew that he had a bad leg — who did not? It had been caused by a fall while jousting when I was a babe. My father, a giant of a man, more than six feet high, heavy of bone and muscle, had fallen from his horse when clad in armour and had burst a vein in his thigh, also the skin over it, resulting in a sore that never healed and often gave him great pain. The wound and its bandage were well concealed by the skirts of his doublet and many forgot its existence unless he was forced to limp, or rest his leg. This was not often, for he was brave and refused to acknowledge his discomfort. Yet he was forced to curtail the bodily exercise he loved so well, and this fretted his temper and slackened his great muscles, spoiling the appearance of which he had been most justly proud. In all my life I never saw any man to compare with him, for he was

28

the acme of manly beauty and strength. Nay, he was the sun in the heavens, invincible, all-bright, never-changing, second only to God Himself in the land. If he married this new lady she would be his fifth wife and my third stepmother. Most men seemed satisfied with one wife; but my father was a King, and Kings were not as other men.

Much have I inherited from him. I, too, was ever fretted by the urge for sports and exercise. I, too, inherited a weakness of the veins in my legs, for in my middle years, after a fall, I grew a sore which would not heal and which plagues me still at times. Like him, I am tall, broad-shouldered and straight as a wand; like him, I had red hair. Ah, proud was I of that, for it burned as bright as his, proclaiming me his own hotter than any speech. Were they blind who called me 'Bastard?' Sure it was but politic blindness, bred to please my father in his days of anger and guilt against her who bore me. Yet still the word has power to make me wince and feel as if a careless finger has touched a burn.

Some there were who said that my father's marriage to my mother was no true marriage, but he would not have been such a fool to have risked tarnishing a boy's name with the taint of bastardy. He even changed the laws and religion of his realm to force the union through, and got me for his pains. Yet even had I been a boy, the Catholics would have murmured, for in their eyes, Mary's mother was the King's only true wife. Indeed, they still do for the most part, long ago that it be she lived and died. Religious minds have long memories for that which goes against their creed.

* * *

My father married his new lady in the July of 1540, having had his marriage to the Flemish Princess Anne annulled. She, being a sensible creature, elected to stay in England in comfort and wealth, the King having given her a fat allowance, manors, jewels and rich dresses for being so amenable to his wishes. She had never lived so well in Cleves, a poor and insignificant duchy.

The new Queen was a little, young lady called Catherine Howard, niece to the Duke of Norfolk. When Kat told me this, it shook the blood from my lips and the colour from my cheeks as I tried to speak. Turning to me, she cried out that I was lily-pale! Was I sick, faint, feverish? Sure, the sun in the park was too hot and I was not in the shade as I should be with my fair skin! We would move under a tree, come my love! So she spake, so loving, so concerned. I answered so quietly that she had to lean close to hear me.

'Then this lady is cousin to me — to my — ' The parkland whirled and I was grievously sick into the grass at my side, a pain in my head thumped with the beat of my heart. Cradled in Kat's arms, for I felt too ill to move, I heard her answer.

'Yes, my pet, she is kin to some of your family.'

'My father's mother was a princess and a Queen. I was named for her, Kat. My other grandam was

30

a Howard, sister to the Duke.'

'Ay, lovey, think no more of it. Let Kat rock you awhile.'

'But Kat, what does she look like? Is she like — ?'

'Nay, not at all. She is tiny and plump, with dark red hair and a pink and white skin. I hear that she has little or no book-learning, being hard put to it to set pen to paper.'

'Nothing like, then,' I murmured.

'She has gaiety and a quick temper, they say.'

'Yes, I would think so. That is in the family. Will she like me Kat? Will she wish to see me?'

'Would you like that, darling?'

I hid my face in Kat's bosom, encircling her with my arms the while. 'Yes I would. Oh yes, I think I would.'

And I had my wish. The King and his new wife were wedded at the palace at Oatlands, returning to Hampton Court in September. I was sent for just after my seventh birthday. My sister Mary was also invited, but declined to go, saying that she would not bow the knee to one of that brood, who was nothing but a frivolous ninny and several years younger than herself withal. This comment reached the King's ears, with the result that Mary was deprived of two of her maids as a punishment for disrespect. My sister never did learn the art of compromise, to her eventual undoing.

I was only too eager to make the journey to Hampton Court. We spent several days travelling down the old Roman road through Barnet and Highgate to London, and although the countryside

31

was sweet, the passing through London was sweeter. The shouts of the Londoners were, to me, more musical than the purest madrigal, for their shouts were for me alone. I rode my white pony proudly, no hideaway litter for me, waving my hand and laughing with delight. 'King Harry's Own,' they called me, and kept up a roar all through the City and beyond the gates until we were fairly at White Hall and I munching a spice cake that an old woman had pressed into my hand. My new glove was marked, but what of that? I was filled with a joy sweeter than spice cake, more heady than hippocras. Here was the thing that made my blood race, my pale cheeks glow, my eyes to flash like the coloured glass upon the front of Nonsuch Palace. Even my touchy stomach, ever a-wamble, was stilled, and my frettish nerves were quietened. The Captain of my Guard spurred up beside me, all aghast.

'Madam, madam! We could not guess that the crowd would be so great nor the people so forward, or we would have surrounded you. As it was — they touched you, my Lady — your gown is dirtied! What can I say, except that I have failed in my duty to the King's daughter and deserve to lose my place!'

I laughed up into the dark, bearded face gazing so anxiously at me from under the polished helmet. 'Nay Sir Captain, I am glad it happened so. Never think again to surround me with your men when we shall pass through London, for I need no protection from those who love me so well.'

We rested that night at White Hall, and took

barge next day for Hampton. The weather was still glorious and folk passing along the paths at the riverside waved and called to me. It was pleasant to lie back on purple velvet cushions and listen to the splash and creak of the oars, to watch the gold fringing on the crimson awning fluttering against the blue sky, to note the trees on the grassy banks slipping lazily by. We passed Chelsea Manor, a lovely house with gardens reaching down to the river, its wooden landing stage jutting out into the water. My father was altering and enlarging it. Once it had belonged to Sir Thomas More who had been executed for refusing to comply with my father's wishes. He must have been a brave man, I thought, to have been so certain of himself as to hold out against my father. Those who did usually met calamity in the end, I reflected, even good men who wished him well. For that matter, so did bad men who wished him well, if they failed to carry out his really important orders. It was a great thing to be a King and answerable only to God. I felt I should like it very well for myself.

As we slid past Richmond, I bethought myself of Hampton which was still a-building. My father had had this palace from old Cardinal Wolsey a few years before my birth and was forever enlarging and beautifying it. I was looking forward to seeing the new additions, especially the astronomical clock made for the King by Master Nicholas Oursian and which was spoke of as a marvel of our age.

'Nearly there now,' said Kat, dabbling her fingers in the water. 'Hark, my Lady, I can hear shouting. God's word, it is for you! Listen to them!'

And indeed there was an uproar as my barge drew near. No bells rang, for the King would have taken it amiss, my standing being so uncertain. For all that, the screeching and tootling bade fair to have reached his ears anyway, had he been outdoors, for it was deafening. The good folk seemed wild with excitement, for all they had seen but little of me. I had the barge stilled for a short while, to receive and return their good wishes, despite Kat's admonishings, for like my father, I enjoyed my own way. I suppose it was my likeness to the King that wrought so strong upon them, for I was favouring him more in looks and ways with each day that passed, and he was loved throughout the realm as a god become human. I did not know it then, but it was the Plantagenet magic that he had inherited from his mother and grandfather that he had passed on to me, tempered and augmented by our Tudor blood working its spell in me. Also I was more of the people than any of my race, for my mother's great-grandfather had been a Cit — a Lord Mayor of London — with no royal or noble blood in him at all, being of true Norfolk yeoman stock. This side of my inheritance, deplored and ignored by so many, gave me instant entry into the hearts of the people, who saw me as partly one of themselves. It was the beginning of my greatest love affair, that between me and the folk of England. It will last until my death.

So we came upriver to Hampton and my heart began to pound as we neared the landing stage. I had not seen my father for many months and longed for the meeting in a frenzy of fear and yearning. Would he consider me improved? Might he even be proud of me? Then too, I would see the Queen, my mother's own first cousin, now wed to my father, she who had caused me to be brought here. This very fact warmed me to her, so that I was more than ready to like her without ever having known or seen her.

Up the wooden steps of the landing stage I trod, over the platform of solid oaken boards, across the towpath, through the watergate of the palace, then across a sweep of gravel to the bridge over the moat. Facing me was the great Gatehouse of Wolsey's manor, now wedged between two wings of my father's devising. I raised my eyes to the gilded weathervanes of the lead cupolas of the turrets. They scarcely stirred in the soft afternoon breeze. Through the Gatehouse into the Base Court surrounded by lodgings and apartments, through the next gateway decorated by the King in my mother's lifetime, then a touch on the arm from Kat. Staring up, I saw scaffolding at the top of the gateway between the towers, and behind it a gleam of gold and blue. I could see a large black dial hand, embellished with a golden sun, pointing across the clock to the left. It was working, telling us that it was past four o'clock of the afternoon, but I could see no more of its marvels for the scaffolding poles.

Returning to the gateway we mounted the stairs to the Great Hall, waiting in the screens passage while my escort announced me. The signal to enter was given and through the oaken screen door I went, sinking in a curtsey when fairly on the other side. Through eyes unfocused with excitement I saw the huge white and gold figure of my father standing by the hearth-place in the centre of the hall surrounded by courtiers. Completing the triple state curtsey, I sank at his feet. The warm tanned hand, its back covered with reddish hairs, stretched out and down to me. I took it, gazing into those long blue eyes, now smiling kindly into my own.

'Up daughter,' said the King. 'Up, and show us how you have grown. We welcome you to Hampton Court.'

There was a rumble of assent from those gathered there. So I rose to my feet and stood as straight and tall as I could.

'Why, Your Grace!' cried a feminine voice. 'She is your very image! And see, she is dressed in white and gold also. Is it not a sweet miting?'

I glanced round to discover the speaker, and there at the King's side, her hand through his arm, stood a little lady who, at first stare, seemed no taller than myself. She was dressed in a green satin gown, the sleeves turned back with red fox fur and her hair under the green caul was as glowing. Her red lips were full and smiling, her eyes a warm brown, large and sparkling with kindliness and a sort of innocent merriment that I was never to see the like of again. Catherine Howard, first cousin to my own mother and third stepmother to me, my father smiling at her as if she were the queen of Heaven.

'Your new stepmother, Elizabeth,' said he proudly. ''Tis because of her you are with us today. She is sweetness and kindness in all she does, the pretty rosebud.' Then, turning to me,

'Daughter, indeed you are growing apace. Are your studies progressing as Wriotheseley reported? Come, walk with me awhile; I would talk with you and see how you do. Leave us be, ladies and gentlemen.'

So wonder of wonders, taking my hand in his, he walked with me up and down the hall, all unattended, talking to me of my brother and sister, of Kat Champernowne, my studies, my journey, my looks and abilities, seeming well pleased. This time my tongue was loosened and my part in the talk came easily. Then we talked of Hampton Court and the alterations that were in progress. 'Have you marked the new clock?' he asked. 'The scaffolding comes down in a day or two and you shall see it in all its curious beauty. I helped Master Oursian with its designing,' he went on, 'for I told him what I wanted and he carried it out to perfection.'

As we walked I noticed how his limp seemed improved and I wondered if his leg pained him still, but he did not show any, and I thought peradventure happiness had cured him. So all was amity as we walked the floor of the Great Hall in the autumn of 1540, our feet kicking aside the rushes as we went. The rushes were fresh and mixed with herbs and dried flowers, giving off a pleasing perfume when disturbed. My father had the rushes changed once a month always and this pleased me, for I hated dirt and disorder, even at the age of seven. A heavy covering of rushes covers much more than the floor after a week or two, for few people are truly clean in their habits. I was looked upon as passing strange, for I showed my distaste at small actions such as spitting in the rushes, dropping or throwing food through carelessness or for the dogs. The dogs themselves were allowed to foul the rushes unhindered, more rushes being thrown upon the stinking place. Men and women blew their noses through their fingers, allowing the gobblets to fall to the floor, while after much drinking, men would piss freely and vomit also. No matter how oft all this was covered up, it stank, and any good disturbance released an odour to make me retch my heart out. Most folk, having grown up amongst such habits, were used to the stink and did not notice it, but I was born with a sensitive nose and detested all ill smells beyond reason, or so said others.

After I had spoke with my father, the Queen carried me off to her chamber to talk and watch her be dressed for the banquet to be held that night. She told me that she was to dine in public for the first time as Queen and that she was on the rack with nerves, not being bred to such a position and conscious of her shortcomings.

'Do call me Kate, sweeting,' she said. 'We are close tied in blood, you and I, and I would have you near me so that I can watch your elegant behaviour. I am woeful ignorant, Elizabeth. I know that you are right clever, even so young, while I am nineteen and scarce know one end of a pen from the other. I am hard put to it to scribe my own name!' Here she laughed, raising her eyes to the ceiling with such a comical twist of the features that I had to laugh with her. I could well understand why my father loved her. I loved her myself, already.

That evening we had our public dinner, and I,

little Elizabeth, passed over, pushed aside, with no place or rank of my own, occupied a place of honour close to the Queen. I glanced up at the roof with its great hammer beams and carved bosses, all painted gold, crimson and blue, displaying the arms of my father and mother. I could see their initials H and A interlaced, carved on the screen, and my stomach gave a warning throb. The King had begun work on this before my birth, and so impatient was he for its finishing that he had the men labour through the day and by candlelight through the night. It was completed in 1536, but by that time my mother was dead and Jane Seymour wife to the King. Best not to think of that if I wished to finish the banquet as a King's daughter and not as an hysterical babe who has to be taken out from an occasion that is too much for her. I drew a deep breath and steadied myself, for the Queen was looking to me as a model of elegant behaviour.

So passed the first of many visits to my father and kind new stepmother. Even Mary was forced to participate in the general lovingkindness, for the King and Kate took her with them next year on progress to the North especially to show the Northern folk that although the King had put her mother away, his daughter bore him no ill will. If Mary was not happy, the King was, while Queen Kate was on pinnacles of excitement at such a journey.

★ ★ ★

Alas, sweet Kate, it was not long to last. You loved too much and gave too much in your hunger for affection. You were too young, too gay, too unthinking, too slight in wits to hold the position you so heedlessly grasped. My father was forty-nine to your nineteen years, poor foolish one. He grew sick, as old men will, and the Court became dull. You wanted excitement, gaiety, youth and love. So you went a-hunting and found Tom Culpeper and untimely death. And you found it where my mother did, on Tower Green in a reek of blood and butchery. This was my last lesson in marriage and family love. I needed no other, for the pattern was set.

After Kate Howard's death my father was grievous sick and melancholy, but I was with him at Hampton and White Hall, and during my sojourns there, I consorted with the children of the Court. This was a new experience for me, having met but few of mine own age. At first I was wary, even hostile, but they were easy and merry towards me, especially the Dudleys, the large family of John Dudley, now Viscount Lisle.

I realise now that my father did not trust this man out of his sight, but fully valued his abilities as a henchman, being a sharp-witted gent with a head for administration. He and the King would play cards together and laugh a great deal once the pain of Kate Howard's defection had receded somewhat. I was glad of this, but could not look upon the new-made Viscount with unreserved favour. He was exceeding handsome; tall, elegant and very dark, with large brown eyes and winged eyebrows. He was unfailingly courteous and charming to me, and yet . . . Was it a certain cool aloofness, a calculating glance in the eye, a disposition to treat men as pawns upon a chessboard? Was it an indefinable air of ruthlessness, an icy detachment that chilled me as I harkened to the smooth sound of his deep voice and failed to be charmed? Certainly he charmed his family. His beautiful wife adored him, as did his children. With them he was a friend rather than a father. I had never seen this in a family, nor have I since. I envied them their warm closeness and lack of formality and enjoyed their company.

Mary Dudley became my friend; John, Henry, Ambrose, Robert and little Guildford laughed, frolicked, teased and played with me in a way that I had never known. It was Robert I liked best. We were drawn together from the first, and no wonder, for we were born on the same hour of the same day of the same year, and were star-twins, therefore. Even at eight he was taller than his elder brothers, his skin swarthy as a gipsy's, his eyes dark as night, his child's nose an infantile copy of the eagle-curve of the man. Bold, fearless, arrogant, passionate, tempersome, greedy, merry — I could chatter on about him like a green girl even now, old and weary though I am. He knew how to love, did my Rob; how to make a girl feel like a woman and a woman feel like a girl.

In those long-ago days we would often talk of our futures, of our childish hopes and plans, of wealth and marriage.

'I shall marry, of course,' announced Mary Dudley, 'for all girls must marry, but my husband will be rich and handsome and we shall love each other.'

'Ho!' hooted Ambrose. 'Do you want the moon as well as a man? Who marries for love? 'Tis foolishness!'

'Oh hush! Remember our father and mother!' cried Mary. 'Why the love between them is a byword. They dote on one another still.'

'It was happy fortune merely,' answered Ambrose. 'You know that, sister. One does not look for love in marriage. Mayhap you will be lucky and your lines will bring you love.'

'I shall be lucky,' said Robert confidently. 'I do not mean to marry without love, nor do I mean to marry without money. I shall wait until I find a lady in whom I can have both.'

Ambrose gave Robert a shove in the back that sent him tumbling on to the bearskin rug, where they rolled and tussled, grunting and giggling. 'Hark to the braggart!' shouted Ambrose. 'Nothing but a Queen will satisfy our Rob, eh, my Lady Elizabeth?'

The Lady Elizabeth thought in her own mind that none but a Queen would be suitable for so magnificent a fellow, but smiled and said naught, watching the two on the rug.

'By my head!' cried Mary. 'Will you two have done? You kick the furniture, you will tear your doublets, and you deafen us with your racket! My Lady here will think she has fallen among brigands!'

I laughed and disclaimed, but her words had an effect. The boys separated, grinning and panting.

Ambrose fell upon a stool and Robert rolled to my feet, stretching out a hand.

'Will your Ladyship give me a pull?' Taking his hand, I did so with a will, and he came to his feet with a bound to sit beside me on the cushioned bench. 'And what of your future?' he asked me.

'Why, she will marry,' answered Mary. ''Tis a woman's future.'

I shook my head and stared at the friendly smiling faces. 'I shall never marry,' I said quietly.

There was a silence. I had astonished the confident Dudley children by my statement. 'But you must marry!' protested Mary. 'You are a King's daughter.'

'Surely,' I said. 'But I shall not marry.'

'But my Lady, all women must marry,' spoke up Ambrose. 'What else can they do? And those of royal blood have no choice at all. They must marry for the sake of their country and its politics.'

'Maybe,' said I, 'but I shall not marry for all that.'

'Have you a plan then?' asked Robert.

'Nay, how can I? I have no true place but that which my father allows me.'

Impulsively, Robert took my hand in both his own. 'When I am grown I shall be a soldier. Then I shall be your champion and protect you from all hurt. Those who would annoy you will have to reckon with me!'

I let my hand rest in his warm brown ones, drawing much comfort from their hold. 'Thank you,' I said. 'It would be fine to have such a gallant champion.'

His dark eyes glowed as they met mine and my cheeks grew pink. 'I think you will grow to be beautiful,' he said consideringly, and my cheeks grew pinker still.

'For shame Robert,' called Mary, 'you make her blush!' Robert released my hand, and Mary went on, 'And all princesses are beautiful!'

At this we all laughed heartily. 'Oh Mary, such fustian as you talk!' gurgled Ambrose. 'The French princesses are hideous, and begging your pardon, Lady Elizabeth, what of your own cousin, the Marchioness of Dorset?'

This caused us much amusement, for my cousin was exceeding plain and very fat. She was of a grim disposition and greatly discontented by the fact that she had borne no sons but only two diminutive daughters, Jane and Katherine Grey. She had no time for either of them and 'twas well known that she was truly unkind to Jane, the elder, who, by all accounts, had a poor time of it.

So I spent the months between the Court and Hatfield or Hunsdon. My brother grew and thrived, and he and I invented our Secret Language, a mixture of Latin, Greek, French and English, so that we could speak our own thoughts to one another in private and in company, with none to understand or censure us.

I visited Mary too. She looked sadder and sicker than ever, poor soul, having much to chafe her spirit. I asked her why she stayed away from Court and she laughed humourlessly, her gruff voice sounding like a bark in the quiet room.

'I stay away because I am uninvited,' she said.

'Not like you sister. I had not the luck to be related to the fifth Queen and so win transient favour.'

The tears started to my eyes. 'Oh Mary,' I said, 'I cannot help my inheritance. Do not blame me for that.'

Impulsively she came to sit beside me on the settle and clasp my hands. 'Oh my dear, do not heed me,' she said contritely. 'I was not always bitter, indeed I was not. Nowadays I do not know what it is to be happy. My thoughts are black with hatred and envy and however much I pray, my mood does not lighten.'

'You are jealous of me,' I said flatly.

She nodded, the tears rolling down her cheeks. 'Ay,' she said. 'And shamed am I to be so. I cannot win my father's love no matter what I do, nor can I agree with his actions. Wicked it seems to be jealous of a child of eight and I a woman no longer young.'

'Do you not love me at all, then, Mary?' I felt inexpressibly saddened by her words, for she was my sister, my own blood, and heaven knew I had but few to be close to me.

'Oh I do love you, sweeting! You must believe that always. It is these black moods that come upon me. They seem to turn me awry, twisting my feelings and destroying my health — and my looks too.'

Indeed her looks were destroyed. At twenty-five she appeared ten years older, wizened, sallow, hollow-eyed and shrunken upon herself, her mouth twitching nervously, her fingers constantly picking at her nails and her rings. I bethought myself of something. Here was a princess who was not married.

'Mary,' I began, 'did you ever wish to marry?'

'Of course,' she answered, 'and why do you ask?'

'When I was at Hampton I was talking with the Dudley children — '

'That upstart lot!' she interrupted, snorting contemptuously. 'You will get no good from them!'

'Nay, but we were talking of princesses and marriage,' I went on, 'and Mary Dudley said that all princesses must marry.'

'So they must,' said Mary, 'and so should I have done. I was betrothed twice but all came to naught. Now my father means me not to marry, I think, for here I am still unwed. I am useful to him as a pawn to bargain with, for he is pleased for princes to offer for me as a means of keeping their countries friendly towards England. He does not mean to accept the offers. I fancy he intends me to wither in the single state. It is a miserable thought.'

'Why would you like to marry?'

'Because it is a woman's life, sister. I long for a proper home and little children more than anyone can ever guess. I pray for it night and day, but God has turned His face from me, it seems.' And she turned hers from mine, but not before I had seen fresh tears on her cheeks. Distressed, I sought to comfort her.

'Weep not dear Mary, for sure God will not turn His face from you for ever. Sure He would not wish so much sadness for you.'

Quick as a cat, she flashed round upon me. 'What do you know of God? Your God is not my God, your false creed is not mine. I am a daughter of true blood, of Kings on both sides, mark you that, and I need no heretic child of doubtful birth to prate to me of God!'

I fell back as if struck, too shocked to utter a sound, my eyes on her cruelly working face. I felt my cheeks go cold and a trembling shake me. I wished to leave her but could not move. Then I saw her look change to one of concern and she hurried to call Kat and fetch me a glass of wine. I drank the wine and felt better. Kat's arm was about me, my head on her shoulder, and my heartbeat steadied. Mary hovered over me in an anguish of remorse, berating her wicked tongue and spiteful speech.

'There, my Lady Mary,' soothed Kat, 'do not be in such a fret. Your sister knows they were but hasty words born of an unhappy heart. She will forgive and forget, will you not, dearest?'

I nodded, for I did forgive. Forget I could not quite, for her words had touched my raw place and had ripped a gap in the loose mesh of my hard-won security. I was conscious of a creeping fear of her that I was never to lose after this. When we left, she gave me ten ells of violet velvet and a gold fringe, also sweetmeats in a painted ivory comfit box and a little mirror with a ruby in the back.

Poor Mary, I feel sick and sad even now, when I think of her. How could she truly love me when I, by my very being, rubbed salt in the wound of her rejection? I bethink me of the yellow satin she gave me when I was seven that the thought of the gown it would make might comfort me in a childish illness. I remember how she taught me to play cards with her and how I won time and time again, she punctiliously paying me every penny I had won although her means were straitened almost to poverty. Ever generous, little pieces of jewellery from her scanty hoard became mine own, comfits and sweetmeats, even a wooden baby dressed in clothes like mine made by her own hand. She was born to be loved and cherished and knew but little of either. Her life was a tragedy from first to last and I cannot puzzle out how it can have been aught else.

★ ★ ★

My father suffered much all through that year. His temper grew more choleric, his girth increased and his leg became more painful although he fought it bravely. Melancholy grew on him, for he had no one to admire him in an intimate, cherishing fashion, no one to share his pain and uncertainties. In short, no wife.

He lost two valued friends in the autumn of my tenth birthday, which depressed his spirits still further. Tom Wyatt died of a fever and Master Holbein also passed away. Tom Wyatt was my mother's cousin and his death saddened me, for I loved my relatives as possessively as any miser, feeling them a bulwark against being unwanted, and in this I have not altered. Yet I ever preferred my mother's side of the family; mayhap to compensate for her ending, or because their natures were more in tune with mine own, I cannot tell. There were many of them and near in blood to me, like the children of my mother's sister Mary Boleyn, she that had been wed to Will Carey. This Mary had been my father's mistress, so that her children may have been my father's, making them at once my cousins and half-brother and sister, but none knew the truth of that.

The death of Holbein was a blow, for at this time he was engaged on a painting for the Company of Barber Surgeons, showing my father crowned and enthroned. It was thus never finished, and the proposed one of myself never begun. I truly regret this, for Holbein could catch a likeness and expression with such delicate exactitude that it was as if the sitter gazed into a mirror when he looked at his portrait. He was a handsome fellow too, and young-looking for a man of forty-five years. His self-portrait does not lie, nor did his work ever lie, not even the picture of poor Anne of Cleves. It would have been gratifying to have seen my young countenance come alive beneath his brush, for no one has ever done me full justice in a painting. Mayhap I should exempt Isaac Oliver from this charge, for he did me justice, but not in the way I wished. He painted me in my old age and made it as like as life, to my horror. So cunningly he wrought his tiny picture that one could not destroy it, but after seeing it I had the will to do so, believe me, and he did not finish it, neither. I thank God that it was in little only and not a large picture!

I enjoyed my visits to Court, even though its chiefest head was constantly in the mopes. He recovered in time for the next summer, evidently, for he married again. All were astounded at his choice and tore the subject of it to shreds with their tongues, for she was old, being just over thirty years.

'Dear heaven,' said Kat, as we walked in the park at Ashridge, 'one would think, by the tattling, that the lady is in her dotage.'

'Well, Kat,' I protested, 'she is near thirty-one. You cannot call that young. And she has had two husbands already.'

'What of it?' retorted Kat. 'Married to old Lord Brough at thirteen, to another ancient at seventeen, living with him for fourteen year in pious dullness — what more of virtue could one ask?'

'She has no children,' I observed. 'Think you she is barren?'

'Chance would be a fine thing, with two old men.'

I began to laugh. 'Now a third!' I spluttered. 'Mayhap 'twill prove third time lucky! I heard that she was betrothed to another before my father's eye fell upon her,' I added. 'Is it true?'

'Jesu!' expostulated Kat. 'Is there aught you do not hear? Ay, it is true. Lady Latimer contracted herself to Sir Thomas Seymour a short while ago, but he is out of the race now, see'st thou.'

'I like Sir Thomas,' said I. 'He is a merry uncle to Ned. What made him choose Lady Latimer, I wonder?'

'She is comely,' said Kat, 'and rich. Reasons enough.'

'I heard,' said I, grinning knowingly, 'that Princess Anne of Cleves would like to be in her shirt, she is so upset by this new marriage of my father's, for Lady Latimer is not near as handsome as she, and barren for sure, having no children by her two husbands!'

'Who said that? I would cut off these spiteful tongues, indeed I would. And to speak so in your hearing! It is too bad.'

'My sister Mary said it,' I replied, smirking, 'and she had it from the Imperial Ambassador Chapuys himself.'

'Being Ambassador he must notice these things, I suppose,' fretted Kat. 'But he is a great chatterer and so is — '

'My sister Mary,' I finished for her triumphantly. 'But then she has naught better to do, has she?'

Kat turned on me in exasperation, telling me that I was growing too opinionated and bigetty by far, that after pride comes a fall, and that children should be seen and not heard. She was ashamed of me, she said, for I had seemingly grown so hard and uncaring that I was not like her Pet at all. She wondered if I had learnt too many Court manners and would be spoiled for ever.

I flung my arms round her, kissing her rosy cheek. 'Nay, Kat,' said I, ' 'tis but a stupid pose put on to tease you, fear not.'

Smiling she aimed a thump at my backside. 'You are a naughty pack,' she replied, kissing me in return. 'I know not why I love you.'

And I found another to love me in my father's last and latest wife, may her dear soul rest in peace. Ah, a darling was Lady Latimer, born Catherine Parr, and when I knew her I knew why the King and Sir Thomas wanted her in marriage. Much has been said against Sir Thomas Seymour and much of it with truth, but I cannot believe that he wanted her only for her money. Nay, I am sure he was utterly catched by her, for she was sweet and right cuddlesome, with a real kissing-mouth as my father often said. Her eyes and skin were beautiful and her teeth were perfect. Never have I seen such teeth and this lady was past thirty! Would mine had lasted so well, but such was not my luck. She had no need to fear to smile by cause of black teeth and ugly gaps in the mouth. Ah, well-a-day. She was as warm and attractive as a fire on a cold winter day and large-hearted as Heaven itself. She was the only mother I ever really knew, and before God, I never meant to hurt her — I swear it.

She wanted us all to be with her, even poor Mary. She wanted us all to live at Court so that we could be with her every day, like a true family, and my father agreed. Mary wept herself nearly blind at the news, for she had memories of such a life. Dear memories they were, but by their very sweetness they caused her pain.

Apart from the short space of my first two years and the even shorter space of Kate Howard's Queenship, I had seen family life only from a distance, or as a benighted traveller peeps longingly through a lighted window, glimpsing warmth, light and love within, and is forced to pass on, chilled and sighing, yearning still.

Little Ned knew naught of such matters. He had no memory of his mother and saw his father only upon visits, being brought up by Mother Jack, Lady Sib Penne and an army of tutors. He was six years old now, a beautiful child, but quiet and remote, seeming unable to show his feelings, except to me. Mary often said that she feared for his spirit, having known no true love of parent and child, for his intellect had been over-stimulated at the expense of his heart. She feared that he would grow not to understand the meaning of love, of kindness, or even common humanity. She was right as it turned out. She should have had a brood of children at her skirts and a hot-blooded passionate husband to fill her belly with a new babe every year, for this is what she was made for and died longing and weeping for, before her time. Kate Parr understood her troubles and persuaded the King to take Mary with them on their marriage progress through the Home Counties, 'To make her feel she belongs to us,' she had said, so Kat told me.

'My father would not have thought of that,' I said. 'The new Queen sounds kind. I wonder if she will like me?'

Kat smiled. 'Of course she will. Who could not?'

That was a happy summer, for Ned arrived to keep me company at Ashridge, and little Jane Dormer who lived nearby came oft to play. She was much of an age with Ned who grew greatly fond

53

of her, saying that they would marry when grown, which gave us much amusement. To make times more lively yet, Mary herself joined us, appearing unexpectedly one afternoon, looking white and exhausted and lying in a litter. I jumped about her, plying her with questions.

'Mary! Why are you here Mary? Did the new Queen mislike you? Were they angry with you? Did they send you away?'

'Dear a'mercy!' cried Kat shoving me indoors. 'Will you be still? Your sister is unwell. Can you not leave her be for a moment?'

'Well, I wish but to know. Is she ill, fretting or angry? Is she in disgrace?'

'She is ill and has come from Grafton. That is the Queen's own litter that you saw. Dr. Owens has blooded her and she is very weak. Now be quiet and let us make her welcome in a fitting manner, or 'twill be said that you are wild beyond my control.'

Mary seemed pleased to see me and was kind and gentle towards me, telling me that she was taken ill on the road by reason of her Old Guest which plagued her every month, making her feel like to die. I cried hotly that it was unfair and that men had much the best of it to my mind, at which she laughed and said 'twas the way of life. She also told me that she had been in dire straits for money and even now could not think how she would be able to pay for the lodging of her people, Ashridge being too small to accommodate all her staff, but the Queen, on learning of this, had given her a goodly sum of money as a gift wherewith to aid her. I was impressed.

'The new Queen must be kind,' I said to Kat, when we were alone in my chamber, changing my gown for the evening meal. 'Perhaps she will wish us all to be with her. It would be a great thing, would it not, to be like a real family?'

'Ay indeed,' she said. 'Now that you are ready, my lamb, do you sit quiet and learn your book until the bell sounds to dine.'

Left alone, I leaned my elbows upon the table and gazed musingly out of the casement. I wished with all my soul that my new stepmother would make the King think to have us all at Court to live together. This longing was so ardent that it felt like hunger, with almost the same pangs. Sighing, I bent my head to my book, where the Greek characters awaited my learning. To stifle my yearnings, I conned my work well, resolving to get up my Greek in a manner that would astonish all. I resolved to pray also, for mayhap God would swiftly answer prayers of such deep moment. He did. Edward and I were bidden to Court when the Progress was over, and great were the rejoicings in my household, for everyone was wild for London and its delights. The journey was an adventure in itself, with all the baggage, the pack-mules, the litters for the ladies, the horses, their keepers and my escort.

For my part, I preferred to ride a-horseback. I always did, and always will while I live. Nor did I care for any wind or rain that might overtake us on a journey. Nor do I now. 'Tis but a challenge to stiffen the determination and raise the courage.

Upon this journey we had neither rain nor wind. The weather was fair and beautiful and I rode at the head of my straggling cortege, galloping free every so oft, laughing to hear the cries of: 'Wait my Lady!' 'Oh, she will be lost!' 'Forward to her!' and the like flutterings. Yet I always turned my beast to trot back to them, so that they would not fret overmuch. We came slowly towards London, making stops in Watford and Edgware, then on into Kylnbourne, where there are pottery kilns and a priory near the brook that runs through the village. There is a well at that place full of the clearest, brightest water warranted to bring long life and good luck to all who drink of it. So we rested there under the clustering trees, and I drank of the water from a brown earthenware cup brought to me from an alehouse beyond the brook. It was right pure and cool upon such a hot day.

The nearer we drew to Westminster, the larger grew the crowds, and once we had reached the Oxford Road where the Westbourne River runs into the waters of the River Tyburn, we could tell that folk had come right out from the City to watch us pass. All the ways were full of cheering people making holiday, whether permitted or not, and the press was so great that I feared we would never get through. Park Lane, usually desolate and lonely, was full. Picardilla, though broader, was worse, and when we reached the place where farmers sell their hay and garden produce, we were fain to halt. I loved it all, the cries, the press, the jangling bells, the gifts thrust at me, all, all. I could have screamed myself hoarse for very excitement, but tried to behave, in part at least, as a Princess should, although with indifferent success, for I exchanged wits with a farrier by the park fence of St. James, threw a posy to a laundress at Charing, lost both my gloves and one shoe, and blew kisses as one demented. We reached White Hall at last, having taken near two hours to struggle there from the Oxford Way through crowded lanes.

Galloping through the garden gate of White Hall, all aflame, with acclamations ringing in my ears, I checked suddenly in the forecourt, overcome with nervous fear, hanging back for Kat to come up with me.

'How now!' she cried. 'Has the firebrand turned craven?'

'Oh Kat,' I protested, 'do not tease! It is a hard step to meet yet another Queen, and I own I am a-quake with fears.'

She smiled encouragingly. 'Come my pet, up with your heart! We will go and fettle ourselves finely to make a brave show before Her Grace. You will love her, I promise you.'

But I needed a glass of wine in spite of my orange-tawney satin gown with its petticoat of cut velvet. My feet were cold in their russet shoes and the palms of my hands were slippery with sweat. It was growing dark and the torches were already lit along the Matted Passage as I clutched Kat's hand and marched forward as if to my doom.

Entering the Great Hall, after the herald had shouted my name, I was near blinded by the lights, but I made my three curtsies and rose to meet my father's eyes smiling warmly upon me. The tears rushed to mine own and I feared to weep, but the spasm passed and I smiled bravely back. Oh, but he was aged. This was all I saw at first. His face had sagged into jowls each side of his jaw, there were pouches beneath his eyes and the wide forehead was furrowed. Also, he was seated; he who was ever on the move. Seated and with his leg up on a stool. I was aghast, though I showed it not. Then I saw the look in his eyes and the expression on his face. Why, he looked happy. Not exalted or ecstatic, but quietly warmly happy. He looked more beautiful that day than I had ever seen him look, my adored, feared, wonderful father.

The greetings over, he said proudly: 'Well, daughter, here is your new stepmother. Love her well, for she is most dear to me.'

And there she stood, all smiles, her arms outstretched. For a moment I stood dumbstruck, fighting the desire to turn and see whom she welcomed so eagerly. It was all for me. Hesitantly I stepped forward to receive her kiss and embrace. She would not let me kneel, but held me at her side with an arm round my waist.

'My dearest child, I have so longed for your coming,' she said. 'Now I have two lovely daughters. Mary is with us and waits to greet you.'

As she spoke, Mary came forward in a flurry of silks and kissed me heartily. I blinked, for Mary attired in such splendour was a new sight to me. Purple satin jewelled, furred sleeves, and a glitter of rings upon her rheumaticky fingers. 'Elizabeth, dearest sister,' she said, kissing me again, 'right glad am I to see you and know that we are all to be together at last.'

A few days later Edward arrived, safe enough, but heavy with a summer cold. This was enough to throw my father into such a frenzy that he had thought for naught else, but the Queen calmed him and managed all with ease and dispatch. Edward recovered well, showing a cool, but decided liking for the new lady, but he was ever withdrawn and becoming more so.

Ned and I looked much alike at this time, his hair being of a reddish-gold, his skin pale, and at almost six years, promising to grow tall and slender, even as I. Folk said that we shared the intent, serious look that goes with much learning. Indeed, Ned was awesomely clever. At six, he was near as far on in his studies as I at ten, and a better Greek scholar than I could ever hope to be. He considered his words, seldom smiled, never lost his temper, and was as full of Protestantism as Mary was Catholic. I was surrounded by prayers.

I have always believed in prayer and many times have proved its worth, but never have I allowed religion to rule my reason or blind me to the needs of humanity. There is but one faith; the rest is dispute about trifles. This is my creed and I hold to it.

Mary called the Queen by her given name of Catherine, for that was her wish. Edward called her Mother, pleased to do so. For my own reasons, I could not use either name, so as ever, I compromised. I named her 'Ma Mie,' which is French for My Darling, yet sounding like Mama.

At this we were all satisfied. My father told me that I was his clever daughter to have hit upon something that gave so much pleasure, for the Queen was delighted and gave me many a kiss. I bloomed like a rose amongst this loving adulation. We were truly happy then, all of us.

Now that Mary was mistress of an adequate and regular allowance, she gave full rein to her hitherto stifled love of finery, purchasing velvets, satins, lace and ribbons in profusion, and some very costly jewellery. She bought on impulse, never heeding what suited her, loving brilliant colours and glittering braid. Childlike, I thought her very fine and felt gladness to see her gay in manner and dress.

It was the Court ladies who chattered. 'See how the Lady Mary grows more like a peacock every day!' cried one of the Protestant faction who affected to despise finery. Their scorn did not extend to their own apparel, I noticed, for they tricked themselves out as gaily as my sister; more so at times.

'Oh she is a very popinjay!' they would giggle when she was not by. 'I wonder she does not feel too old to deck herself out so fine. She is but an old maid, and growing ugly withal!'

'Hush!' another would whisper, seeing me in the window-seat. 'Do not speak so loud! There is one here who hears all and will tell all, no doubt.'

'I am no blab-mouth,' I said proudly on one such occasion. 'I have no reason to pass on hurtful gossip to those I love.'

'Deary me!' shrilled a dark maiden. 'How sharp-tongued is my Lady! You are too young to realise that we meant no hurt.'

'Mayhap,' I answered straight. 'Then you should make sure that I am not by when next you mean no hurt.'

At this, they all glanced at one another, raising their brows meaningly before curtseying and hurrying out of the chamber, silenced for the nonce, and there was no more tattling, in my hearing at least.

With Ma Mie as his wife, my father mellowed. She dressed his bad leg herself, allowing him to rest it in her lap, seeming truly devoted to him, while he responded by showing all that was lovesome and winning in his nature. Yet Edward remained aloof from his most endearing and fatherly advances, from his sudden tempers, from his true majesty. He watched the King with cold eyes, speaking only when spoken to. My father sought his son's smiles with anxious eagerness, but to no avail. Edward would allow himself to be placed on the King's lap, suffer his embraces, accept his gifts, reply to his questions, obey his commands, and give naught of himself at all.

If my father had treated me so — ! Mayhap it were better he never did, for sure it would have turned my brain and I would have laughed and wept like a zany to bask in the light of such a sun. 'Twould have been the surest way to get myself returned in disgrace to Hatfield, so I stifled my deep desires and tried to play the part of the perfect child, neither girl nor boy, neither wilful

61

nor humble, eager but not forward, and a mirror of learning withal. So, much as I loved him, I never felt free in my father's presence, for always I had to play a part if I wished to retain his chancy affection. Therefore I kept my counsel and became a quiet, learned young lady in the King's eyes, reserving my truer self for Kat and Ma Mie.

★ ★ ★

In the spring of 1544, the King was planning to cross to France with his army. All was being put in train when he suffered a reverse in health. His ulcerous leg, which had seemed better, grew suddenly worse, giving him great pain, so that he roared and shouted with it, raging like a lion in torment. Dr. Butts constrained him to stay abed for a se'ennight, and all was in turmoil, for he took it very unkindly indeed. He was in such pain and so feverish that Ma Mie had her bed moved to a small room leading from my father's bedchamber, so that she could be with him when he needed her. Mary thought this strange and informal behaviour for a Queen and said so in a censorious tone.

'Well, Lady Mary, my dear,' said Kat, 'it seems to me natural for a wife to wish to ease her husband's sufferings. Here at Court we stifle our feelings, do we not? The Queen is true to hers, and I honour her for it.'

'I too!' I cried, bouncing out from behind a curtain where I had been upon the window-seat, reading. 'She is a marvellous, sweet, warm-hearted lady and she brings my father great comfort. I heard him so say!'

'Beshrew me!' said Kat, hands upraised. 'We have another Imperial Ambassador here, Lady Mary. I shall tell old Chapuys that there is no need of him, for the Lady Elizabeth has her ear attuned to all secrets and can give account of all!'

'Oh well, well!' I cried angrily. 'Tease an you will, but Ma Mie is truly good and kind and Mary should be shamed to criticise her.'

'And you should be shamed to speak so of your elder sister. Where is your respect and consideration, Madam? I am the one who is shamed, for it seems that I have failed in my duty towards you.'

I glared mutinously from Kat to Mary, full of the zeal of partisanship, and stamped my foot challengingly. 'I am not shamed!' I shouted. 'No one speaks ill of those I love in my hearing without my protest!' And I threw my book to the floor with a slam.

So we stood, staring at one another, one red as a turkey-cock with temper, one blushing with dismay and one pink with ill-suppressed laughter. Into this impasse walked little Edward. Straight up to me he came.

'Sweet sister,' he said in his small fluting voice, 'I wish your company to help me get my Latin, for if I finish it quick, Mr. Cheke says I may play with Will Somers' monkey. So do come, Elizabeth.'

Mary and Kat both nodded permission and as Ned and I left the room, I heard Mary say to Kat: 'She is marvellous passionate and wilful. I envy her, having forgot what it is like to be so.'

Ned and I soon finished the Latin and ran to Will Somers for his pretty monkey. Will was the King's Fool, but no fool he. My father counted him wise, and his friend. We played up and down the Long Gallery for an hour, and a fine din we made, for the monkey ran up the hangings, pulling threads from the tapestries, dislodging wall ornaments and chattering loudly at Ned and me who were jumping and calling below, careless of the racket until Mr. Cheke came for Ned and Will for his monkey.

Later, Ned asked me why I had been angered at Mary.

'Would you not be angered if someone passed unfair judgment on Lady Bryan or Mother Jack?' I pressed him, when he seemed not to understand my explanations.

He raised his pale brows. 'Nay,' he said, looking mildly surprised.

'Would you not?' I cried. 'Then what if someone censured me unfairly?'

He considered this. 'I would ponder it,' he said. 'Then, if it were truly unfair I would know it to be so and would say so, but why should such a thing make me angered?'

'Do you not love *me*?' I burst out.

'Ay,' he answered calmly, 'but what has that to do with it? I do not understand you, sister.' At this I fell silent, having no reply to my small brother's reasoning.

In the evening, at our meal in the Great Hall, I sat beside Ned who took the King's place on the dais while my father and the Queen supped privately. We looked out from our table down the hall, where the lords and ladies sat in order of precedence and rank, and beyond them, the gentlemen and squires, down to the pages, valets and body-servants. There was always a great din. Sometimes the King had to call for quietness in order to hear the musicians, but this did not worry Ned, for he had less interest in music than any of our family. He was a hearty eater and gobbled with a will, whereas I, who was termed 'picky' by Kat, trifled with this dish and that, allowing my mind to wander, wondering how those who sat below the dais enjoyed being crowded and crushed up together on the benches.

'To have a place at Court is worth a mort of discomfort to most,' said Kat, when I spoke my thoughts to her as the raised pies and the fish were brought in. 'Your great nobles gladly suffer vexations here that they would never tolerate in their own homes.'

'It is worth something to be of our family,' I observed, 'even though we ourselves do not have all we wish at times.'

'Indeed it is, sister,' mumbled Edward, his mouth full. 'It is a good thing to be of consequence in the world. Do you think my father will die?'

I jerked upright at this question so suddenly shot at me. 'Why, nay brother, he is strong. How could you ask me this?'

'I should like to be King,' answered Edward simply. 'I should like to have my own way as he does.'

'Ned, you seem to be waiting for him to die!'

'I am,' he said. 'Then I shall enjoy myself.'

'Do you not love him, then?' I gasped.

'Nay,' replied Edward placidly, filling his mouth again. 'He is too loud, too big, and always handling me. Moreover, he treats me as a baby, which I am not, and gives me gifts that do not please me.'

Again I fell silent, chilled to the heart, and pondering the strangeness of love; how it was so often denied to those who sought it, and poured in plenitude over those who desired it not. Yet their were exceptions, I reflected, as in the family of the Lord High Admiral Dudley, where love seemed a thing to be joyed in. I hoped I would come to know that part of it in time . . .

I was jolted into the realisation that the sweets and subtlety had appeared on the table, by Kat's elbow in my ribs. Kat was allowed a place by me on the dais by Queen Catherine's especial request, to keep an eye on my poor appetite. The subtlety was all of sugar and marchpane in the shape of an oak tree, with deer at its base and a squirrel darting up the trunk. Edward, who was near as mad for sweetmeats as I, made a grab at the squirrel and stuffed it gleefully into his mouth. At this signal, everyone fell upon the sweets and the server divided up the subtlety amongst us at the High Table. I was guiltily glad that the King and Queen were absent that day and that Mary did not favour sweet things overmuch, for I was next in precedence after her, so there was a-plenty left for me. I remember I had two branches, all stuck with sugared cherries and angelica and a stag with antlers of cut almonds.

'Oh greedy!' whispered Kat. 'There will be but poor pickings for the rest of us.'

Grinning, I cared not, so long as my mouth was full.

My father was confined to his chamber for another week after his se'ennight abed. Edward and I felt strangely free, but Mary ran back and forth from the King's room like a lackey. The Queen remonstrated with her, but Mary would have it so, saying that it soothed her to feel needed and useful.

I romped merrily with the Dudleys and Edward joined us at times, but he found the Dudley children too boisterous. He knew no games, neither, being feared to disarrange his garments or to fall. He was happier seated on a stool, warning us of possible mishaps and probable retribution. He refused to accompany us out of doors, being feared of catching cold, for Mother Jack had warned him so oft against this disaster, that he thought of himself like a little old man.

'Oh, better he stays indoors!' cried Mary Dudley as we ran up the path by the Tennis Court on our way to the Wildernesse, there to jump in the long grasses and attempt to climb the trees. 'He is a real Doleful Dobbin and will spoil all our fun by his prosing. Leave him, Bess. He is happier so.'

'Ay, you are right. Poor little lad, he has never learnt the way of enjoyment. He knows naught of fun and frolic.'

'He is even afeared of Baby Guilford, who is a mother's darling himself and always tale-bearing. Come, let us sit on this branch and swing. We can push ourselves up and down by our feet on the ground.'

So we scrambled and clambered on to the branch, dirtying ourselves well in the process and rending our gowns in sundry places as we swung and screamed in concert.

'Hey, we go up, up, up!' I yelled.

'Hey, we go down, down, down!' shrieked Mary by my side.

And so we kept it up until we were scarlet-faced and exhausted. Robert found us sitting there, deep in giggling girl-talk, and gave the branch a mighty heave, upsetting us both, so that we tumbled headlong into the grass and tussocks below, miring ourselves from top to toe. At this, he went off into a fit of laughter, ignoring our cries of rage and dismay, rocking himself back and forth and hooting like a zany. Infuriated, Mary struggled to her feet and dealt him a worthy blow which checked his merriment somewhat.

'See, you great fool, you gowk, you wittol! See what you have done to the Lady Bess!' she screamed. 'Why, you might have killed her with your stupid antics. How do you know she is not injured or broken, I say?' And she fell to belabouring him again.

'I know because she sits and laughs, all a-mired as she is! Come, Bess, up with you; give me your hand.'

I did so, and he hauled me to my feet, attempting to dust me as if he were rubbing down a horse. I was near to die of laughing at the pickle we were in and at our sudden loss of dignity, and in a moment,

Mary was laughing too.

'Oh, oh!' I gasped. 'Think you if Edward had come! Only think!'

The Wildernesse rang with our shouts as we pictured it, holding one another up and stamping in our mirth. A fine upbraiding we got upon our return; the Dudleys for leading me into mischief and myself for being led. If anyone could lead me anywhere I did not want to go I had yet to meet that one, and so I said, still bursting with unrepentant giggles, as Kat stripped me of my filthy gown, threatening to lose me my supper. Yet I did not lose it, for dear Kat did not really mind. Methinks she was glad to see me carefree and childlike as I could so rarely be.

2

THE BREAD OF ADVERSITY

1544 – 1549

Such odd, small things stick in the brain. My fall in the mud, my dirtied skirts, Robin's laughter, dear Mary and I on the bouncing branch, these are as clear to me now, after nearly sixty years, as if they had happened but yesterday. Yet Mary and Rob are gone and I live on, full of years and majesty — and loneliness. No one now is left who knows my heart, or who remembers me as young and swift. Even those who recall me in my middle years are growing few. To most folk now, I am 'The Old Queen' who has seemingly reigned for ever and has never been young. Indeed, sometimes I wonder if I ever was truly young. In years, sure, but in my mind I was always old. Yet, there were some times of pure youth, and these remain bright with carelessness and laughter.

This was the year that my sister and I were restored to the Succession, enabling us to hold up our heads as Princesses in fact, if not in name. It was good to have a real place again and be acknowledged by the King as his beloved daughters in public. It was wonderful strengthening to the spirit. When the King finally left for Boulogne and battle, he stayed away for three months, naming the Queen as Regent in his absence. Happy times we had. My sister Mary smiled, Edward ceased to prose, and I ran and sang, glorying in the small freedoms vouchsafed to me. We became more close to our sweet stepmother, who loved us as if we were her own.

That winter died good Dr. Butts, my father's loved and trusted physician, of whom I was very fond, for he had treated my mother for the Sweat when all feared she would die of it. He had thus earned himself much gratitude and favour from my father. Now I knelt by his deathbed, filled with forlorn regret, for he had been a link with my mother. The King, too, was cast down and saddened by this death, becoming conscious of his mortality, fretting about his health and insisting that he had been far better astride a horse in France than bestriding the rushes in White Hall.

'It was a man's life, Kate,' he grumbled to Ma Mie. 'A-horseback in the fresh air, all taking our chance as equals, hard and free. Now here I am, for ever half-ailing; plagued with soreness of the throat, stomach gripes and aches of the back, not to mention my thrice-damned leg which hammers me with every heart-beat. And now Will Butts is gone. I miss him sadly, Kate.'

'I know it, dear heart,' she answered gently. 'Would you like me to read to you from the narrative of the campaigns of the Emperor Charles the Fifth? That is suitably warlike, methinks.'

'Ay, do so. Mine eyes itch and burn, and the words run together on the page when I attempt to read for myself.'

Ah, how the memories rush and jostle for foremost place in my reckoning. They illumine the dark stage of the past, each one like a lighted picture, gleaming clear and bright before giving place to another. I see the King, a book on his knees, peering at the pages through eye-glasses in gilt frames. I see Mary, a dice-box in her hand, dark eyes glowing, laughing at the antics of her tumblers, at Silly Lucretia and Jane the Fool. I see myself stitching, in secret, a gift for the Queen, pricking my fingers and pulling out threads that had gone awry.

I smile when I recollect how I struggled with the setting of that embroidery. The translation I made easily enough, out of French rhyme into English prose, from *'The Mirror or Glasse of the Sinful Soul'* writ by Queen Marguerite of Navarre. I joined the sentences together as well as I could and hoped that Ma Mie would alter the words if she found them to be clumsy. 'Twas the stitchery gave me the labour, but when all was done it looked well enough. I stitched K.P., the Queen's initials, in the centre of a diamond shape in blue and silver, and wrought flowers of heartsease in purple and yellow at the corners. She was delighted with it and gave me much praise.

It was a happy time, with promise of more to come, yet I ruined all soon after, and brought a year of sorrow and regret upon myself. My father turned against me, deaf to the Queen's entreaties on my behalf, and sent me from the Court. The thought of this still gives me a pang so sore as to pain me still. I caused my brother to fall and strike his head upon a stool.

My father called me 'Murderess' and 'Bastard', threatening to strike my name from the Succession, to send me to the Tower. He seized me by the shoulders and near shook me to death, shouting and raving like one run stark mad, while Ned wailed from the floor, and Mary sobbed in hysterics.

'Let be!' I shrieked. 'You are all crazed! Let be I say!' My father shook me all the harder, beside himself with rage and fear for his son. ' 'Twas an accident, a mishap! Let me be, I have done no wrong!'

Ma Mie and Kat came running in, aghast at the uproar, endeavouring to restrain my father, to calm Edward and Mary, to recover me, who by this time, was screaming. At last they separated us. My father fell back, purple and spluttering on the Queen's arm, while I collapsed, weeping, into a chair.

'Take her away!' roared my father. 'Take her from my sight! She is a danger to my son — careless, heedless, violent. Curst red-haired brat — I will not have her near me! She will leave tomorrow. It is my will. Mistress Champernowne, remove the Lady Elizabeth at once!' And I was removed, not to return to Court for a year.

It was a hard sentence to serve for nothing more than a trifle, and an accident at that. Sure, I had meant to push little Jane Grey, and push her I did. But mine intent was not that the stupid mammet should catch her foot in her gown and fall against my brother, knocking him to the ground. It was all in play, moreover. We were in the Long Gallery, for the day was cold, dark and wet. My father, his leg upon a cushioned stool, was seated slumberous by the fire, idly watching us through half-closed lids. Jane Grey, the eldest daughter of my cousin Frances of Dorset, was spending a se'ennight or two with us at her parents' wish. She was almost exactly Ned's age, and as much of a sobersides as Ned himself. He was my brother and a youngling, he had occupied a place in my heart from his birth, and so I could tolerate his odd ways and quirks of humour. Also, he was heir to the Throne, and this set him apart in a way that forced him to be different from others of his age.

But Jane! She irritated me beyond the bounds of reason. I think it was the combination of servility and arrogance in her that tore at my patience. She had a look about her like that of a dog who constantly expects a beating and so draws one upon itself. Certainly she had received many beatings from her parents and no affection. It seemed that they could hardly bear the sight of her, poor little wretch. She was pretty enough, too. Tiny and dainty as a doll, with small delicate features like her Grandam, the King's youngest sister, and with the Tudor red hair and white skin. Yet, with such prettiness came an insistence upon being always right and never wrong; a voice of carping rectitude that irked the feelings of others unbearably and caused them to tease and jeer at her. She was mighty proud of her learning and prated of it by the hour. Poor child, I see now that her learning was all she had. She and Edward chimed well together being full of book-love and empty of human love and gaiety. They seemed to draw pleasure from one another's company, and I was glad for my brother's sake.

On this unlucky day I had felt restless, my eager vitality curbed, and myself kept indoors by the rain. I had wished for a gallop on my new mare, but Kat and Ma Mie denied me, for I had a cold that threatened, and the damp, they said, would be enough to set me in a fever. So I persuaded Edward and Jane to play Tag with me. After much argument, they consented, and the very fact that I had been forced to persuade them lit a flame of irritation in me to think that such young children should be so mealy-mouthed and feared of frolic. We played at last, and Edward began to enjoy it. He laughed and ran, though soon made breathless through lack of exercise. When Jane's turn came to be Tag and to chase and catch us, she whined and protested.

'Oh, I cannot run any more! Oh, I shall fall! Oh, do not make me be Tag, I cannot do it, I shall never catch anyone. Oh, let us stop the game!'

'Nay, Jane!' cried Edward, dancing close to her. 'See, I am near. Come, catch me, catch me Jane!'

'Ay, catch him, stupid,' I snapped and pushed her towards him. In his downfall came mine.

That was a sad year. I kept my twelfth birthday at St. James' Palace and shed tears in spite of Kat's warning of the sorrows that lie in wait for those who weep upon the anniversary of their birth. I could not help it, for I thought of my family at Hampton, at rosy Richmond, at dear Greenwich, at grey old Windsor, at glittering Nonsuch, or at Oatlands, the palace that the King had rebuilt and enlarged, all in a hurry, for his bridal holiday with Ma Mie. I imagined them all gay and happy on this my special day, and I alone at St. James' in sore disgrace, like to stay there for ever for aught I could tell. My sweet stepmother had writ me many a letter in the preceding months and sent gifts too. Gifts and letters came in goodly number on my birthday, even a note from the King asking if I would become less forward and more biddable, as befitting a royal lady. This made me sob anew.

'What does he want, Kat?' I wept. 'Does he wish me to turn myself into an echo to prate only what he wishes to hear? Nay!' I cried, overriding her protestations. 'Nay, it is because I am too much like him in spirit, and too much like the son he would have Ned be! Yes, Kat, it is as I say, do not argue with me! Oh why was I born a useless girl? Why did God punish me so? My life is ruined and my happiness stillborn!'

In vain Kat sought to pacify me; I would not be calmed. I sobbed myself into a violent migraine that lasted for nigh on three days. Later, Kat suggested that for my father to write to me at all was a good sign and showed that he must be relenting, if only a little.

'Depend upon it, sweeting, the dear Queen has wrought upon him to bring this about. She will spare no pains on your behalf.'

'Ah, but Kat, is it not passing sad and strange that my father has no words of love to spare for me who adores him and a plenitude for Ned who cares not at all?'

Kate pressed her hands upon my shoulders, gently forcing me to seat myself on a cushioned bench by the wall. 'See now darling, you waste your time, your health, and your peace of mind upon something that cannot be altered. Will you not try to accept it just a little? If you can, you will be easier and less inwardly tormented.'

I sighed long and deep, clasping her hands in mine. 'Ay Kat, I will try, but it is so unjust.'

'Many things in this life are, my dearest, but if you spoil your beauty by so many sighs and tears you will have no one to blame but yourself for that misfortune.'

As always, the invaluable woman had struck the right chord. I gave a doleful chuckle and looked about for a mirror. 'Oh me, am I a sight? I'll wager my face is white and my nose red!'

'As a cherry,' nodded Kat.

'And my eyes are pink and puffy!'

'Indeed so.'

'And my lips droop, my neck is bowed, my hair in strings — go on Kat, let us have it all!'

'One can see that your Ladyship is weighed down by care. So sad, poor child, to lose your bloom at the age of twelve. Once gone, it can never be recovered. Sure, you will die young, your looks ruined, a lone, unwanted maiden,' groaned Kat in tones of direst gloom.

I laughed aloud, despite myself. 'Kat you are my jewel! But I tell you what; I will die a maiden, though neither young, nor careworn with ruined looks. I mean to live long, to keep my beauty, and never, never will I marry. That, my Kat, is the way to the grave.'

'Dear me,' she answered comically, 'then I am in a pickle, am I not?' At my look of surprise, she went on: 'I had bethought myself of taking just such a dangerous step.'

I gazed at her, horrified. 'Why — why — will you leave me? Kat, will you then leave me?'

She seized me, holding me close. 'Never will I do that, foolish one. Nay, I hope for a place for him here, with you.'

'Oh, gladly Kat! Who is he? Do I know him?'

'Well, he is a friend of Roger Ascham, the famous scholar — '

'No fool then,' I remarked.

She smiled. 'By no means. Did he not choose me?'

Laughing, I shook her by the arm. 'Nay, but who, Kat?'

'He is known to your tutor John Grindal; John Cheke, your brother's tutor, knows him too. And mark this, my Lady; he is related to you.'

'Related to me? How so? Undo me this puzzle, quick, quick!'

'He is John Ashley of the Boleyn family, my love, and as such, a cousin, of sorts, to you.'

I clasped my hands with pleasure. 'Oh Kat, this is happy news indeed. How foolish you must have thought me with my talk of marriage and the grave! I mean it is so only for me. This John is a link with those I cherish, and through him — why Kat — you will be kin to me. Think on that! Is it not

78

great beyond anything?'

She pinched my cheek, smiling fondly. 'Shall you mind having such a humble cousin, by marriage only, to be with you day by day?'

'Mind? Why, it is marvellous good! Bring your John, tell him I wish him to have a place in my household. Nay, rather I command it.'

'You will find that he loves you as I do, my pet. He has admired you this many a day, and is not a little proud of his kinship to you, though he does not boast of it.'

So I was cheered, and my days passed more happily thereafter. I grew very fond of John Ashley, and felt myself lucky in having Kat and him so close to me in loving kindness. Because of the blood bond I found myself less desperate at being parted from my family, and so dwelt less upon my wrongs, becoming happier thereby.

In the letters I received from Ma Mie, there grew a more hopeful note. She told me that she had never ceased to intercede for me with the King and that he seemed more willing to listen to her words upon my behalf, even to agreeing that I should return 'not yet, but soon.' My gratitude to her was unbounded, and to show it in some small part, I embarked upon a translation of her own prayers into Latin, French and Italian, writ in mine own hand and bound into a book. This kept me busy all through the autumn, for I wished the work to be perfect to show to Ma Mie how I had progressed. I finished it upon the second of December whilst at Hertford, and sent it off by fast messenger to the Queen, who received it with delight and much praise, showing it to my father.

When the messenger returned with letters from the Court, he told me of this, adding that the King said I wrote an excellent hand, found no fault in the translations, remarking that I took after him in my ability to acquire languages. On being pressed further, the messenger recounted that the Queen had said she missed my company, as did the Prince, asking if His Grace would not relent and have me back. The King seemed doubtful of my good behaviour, but the Queen assured him that I would behave exemplary and never more offend him.

'And what said my father to that?' I cried. The lad reported that the King had looked pleased and announced that he would write to me touching my return. 'Said he so? Have you a letter for me from him?' said I, all eager.

'I have, my Lady,' he said, fumbling in his pouch, 'and others. One from the Queen, one from the Prince — here, take them, I pray you.'

I snatched the letters, impatiently unfolding that from my father.

★ ★ ★

A few more letters raced to and fro over the London-Hertford road, and then I was upon it, journeying southern wards with my household and baggage, vowing that I would be a pattern princess, quiet, meek and learned, if that was what my father wished of me. I succeeded too, for there were no more complaints. Indeed, I was ready to deny my whole nature if need be, to make the King smile upon me and give me words of praise. Many there were who said how I had changed. Some remarked that I had improved, some that I had matured, some that I had grown very womanly. In truth, all they meant was that I was quiet, repressed and showed nothing of my real self.

One day, one sweet day, I swore, I will show you all what I am truly like. You will stand back before me and consider my every whim. My words will be my own, and others will guard their tongues for fear of offending me. I shall do as I wish, speak as I wish, and all will be as I wish one day! I spoke these thoughts to Robert Dudley upon a summer evening.

'H'm,' said he, 'I thought you had grown strangely mumchance and silent. It must be difficult to have a King for a father.'

'Ay, it is,' I agreed, 'but something marvellous too. If I am as good a Queen — '

'Ho, treason!' he laughed. 'Would you wish your father dead?'

'Oh nay, Robert, never. I was but dreaming.'

'Of Queenship, eh? You have small chance of it Bess. There would have to be several deaths without issue would there not? It would seem a very long chance to me.'

'And to me,' I murmured. 'Too long to be possible. Yet it sticks in my mind, Rob, like a burr in new wool.'

'Forget it,' he advised. But I could not.

★ ★ ★

81

Never grow careworn with ruined looks, did I say? Facing me now is my mirrored self, an old hag of sixty-nine years. Oh, ruined indeed. Like a witch, whispers my secret self. The long curved nose, the long curved chin, the sunken mouth and eyes, the sagging jaw, the wrinkles, the look of weary watchfulness. Like a witch, whispers my inner heart. Well, since I am being fully honest with myself, I must admit that never was I truly beautiful. Nay, rather 'twas mine own inward certainty of it that illumined me, and bewitched others into thinking me so; that and youth, and that alone when youth began to fade. Even now, when I am in good spirits, I can give the illusion of a certain handsomeness. When I am dressed, painted and bejewelled, radiating the splendour of Queenship and sovereignty, I see a look of awe upon the faces of those who behold me. And I am no painted puppet, I. They all know it who see me. I rule, I am the Queen, and the reins are in my hands alone.

I had a book in my hands in my first portrait, and I wore a much-favoured gown with a headdress to match. Such arguments as this caused, God save me.

'The colour will not match with that of your hair,' protested Kat. 'Such a bright tawny-pink — it will not do, sweeting.'

'But it will do, for I like it and will wear it. I shall stand demure with my books, as befits a meek and learned lady, serious and mild, but my gown shall say; 'Not so! She is not truly so!' I will wear it, Kat.'

So I wore it. The portrait was made and turned out as I predicted, except for one small thing. Demure, serious and learned I looked, but meek not at all. Nor was this due entirely to the gown. It was some expression in my face; a glancing look of wariness and inner knowledge that the artist caught, despite my efforts at nullity. My father approved it when it was done.

'Ay, it is well, it is very well,' he said, viewing it from all angles. 'I like it. It will give a good impression of her learning and elegance. Who told her to wear that gown?'

There was silence as all wondered if he was pleased with the choice. I broke it. 'No one told me, Sire. I chose it myself.'

'Excellent!' he pronounced. 'It gives a brilliance that pleases me greatly. I like it with the hair. It is unusual. You have chosen well, daughter. I will have it hung at Nonsuch.'

I could not repress a triumphant glance in Kat's direction at such vindication of my personal choice. After that, I was allowed full freedom to choose my own wardrobe. Even so, I restrained myself for I knew it would not be politic to burst out in untrammelled radiance. There could be only one sun. My time was not yet and I realised it. So I kept mum under the guise of a modest princess who had eyes for nothing but her books, and a tongue schooled to give only answers that could please. Although I was happy at Court with my dear ones, I was constantly treading the tightrope between my own nature and the behaviour expected of me. Perfection is a hard goal for which to strive and

I was set upon the path full early, with consequent violence to my inner spirit. Aye me, so long ago . . . Still my father was pleased with and called me a model daughter; all that a young female should be, he said. For this approval from him I would have forsworn myself for ever had it been possible to do so.

He was growing old, the sun in my sky. His hair and beard were almost white, his eyes twinkling in beds of fat, his jowls heavy in a purplish face. His girth, too, had greatly increased, his weight causing pain in his ulcerous leg whenever he stood upon it, which was now seldom enough. The leg itself was nauseous and hugely swollen beneath its bandages. He wore heavy robes to hide it, and they hid his size too, giving him a flowing majesty which suited him. His temper was irascible for his nerves were fretted by constant pain and fear for his health. And this with good reason, for the stench that arose when the bandages were removed was unspeakable, like rotting meat and worse. He would let no one but Ma Mie near it, and the dear Lord knows how she managed it without spewing her guts up before his eyes. She never showed distaste or anything but a wish to tend it, and all were mighty thankful that it should be so. Even the physicians were glad to retire when the bandages were off. How could any man, even one of such magnificent constitution as that of my father, fail to weaken under such a disability? For sure, his leg made him think of death and the grave.

He had a carrying chair made for use indoors, to save him too much exertion; yet outside he still made shift to ride until the pain grew too bad. From looking younger than his age, he now looked older, with a heaviness and sadness which I now understand but too well. To embark upon an uncharted course is difficult and fearsome in life, but it is part of life. To embark upon something like death, however strong one's hope of Heaven, is lonely and terrible indeed. For a sovereign, there is the added burden of leaving one's greatest charge to another who may not bear the charge so well.

Did he feel as I do now, my father? Did he feel as I do, that no matter how many fur-lined mantles are huddled round me, no matter how close I creep to the fire, no matter how many warming possets I drink, that my veins are filled with ice and my once lively heart beats unwilling and slow? He died in the drear cold of winter, he who loved the warmth and colour of summer with its green trees and birdsong. My tired eyes ache to behold another sweet summer, but this I shall never do. I do not ail, I am not sick, apart from this plaguey rheum; yet ere summer visits my England I shall have left her. Great God, I shall fight! Death shall have no easy victory over me. Ah, but in spite of all, I shall be the loser. I would it were not so, for the knowledge weighs me down like a rock round a drowning dog's neck, stifling my will away . . .

★ ★ ★

At this period in my young life I met the great scholar, Roger Ascham. He was a goodly man, with

85

a head of dark curls and a round, merry face full of sweetness and good humour. He advised my tutor Grindal, and he praised my dear Kat for her diligent overseeing of my studies. She was no mean scholar herself and well able to converse with Ascham. He told her to favour my intelligence in a process like pouring water into a goblet. Too much learning at once would dash out, but slowly it might be filled to the brim.

As well as my mastery of European languages, I had acquired a speaking knowledge of the Welsh tongue from good Blanche Parry. I have ever had the trick of tongues and it has been a boon to me in such a life as mine has been.

I spent the November of 1546 with my dear little Ned at Hatfield. My father's health was so poor and his temper so easily fretted that it was judged better that we, being young, should be away for a while. Always loving, we drew closer still at this time, for Ned, despite his coolness, was never cool to me, and when we were alone together, revealed much of his true self. Poor lamb, I longed to protect him and guard him from the loneliness of his life. I loved him very dearly. But our companionship was rudely broken. Orders arrived from the Council to send Edward to Hertford and me to Enfield Chase, and there, summarily we were sent. Children as we were, it was not for us to question such matters. At once I wrote to my little brother, bidding him to be of good cheer, for although we could be no longer together, an exchange of letters would be the next best thing. He answered me in Latin, well writ and constructed, on the fifth of December, and a wistful little letter it was, in which he hoped to be allowed to visit me soon.

That visit was made, and sooner than either of us had expected. An iron-cold day it was, grey, icy, with a wind like a sword-blade that seemed to cut its way through the heaviest hangings, the thickest robe. I had been out riding and my horse had slipped several times upon frozen puddles, but the exercise had warmed my blood and exhilarated me to singing as I rode. Upon my return I went to my studies, and while I was at my books I heard a bustle in the forecourt. Almost before I realised it, I heard the names of my brother Edward and his elder uncle Lord Hertford being announced, being followed by that of Sir Anthony Denny, Gentleman of the Bedchamber to the King. I leaped to my feet as they entered and Ned ran into my arms, babbling with delight.

I stared over his head into the pale blue eyes of the man I could never like. He looked white and haggard with the cold, his face drawn into an expression of intense melancholy, but with an excited sparkle in those blue eyes, a sparkle strangely at variance with the look of misery. Before I could say more than a word of welcome he had stepped forward and laid a hand upon Edward's head and one upon mine. I twisted my head abruptly and his hand fell away, coming to rest upon my shoulder, which I liked no better. I jerked my shoulder impatiently, but he had begun to speak.

'My dear children,' he intoned in a voice heavy with woe, 'it grieves me to hinder your merriment in being once more together, but I have news of the gravest and most dire to impart to you.'

Edward turned, caught by his uncle's unusual manner. 'Why, what is it uncle? Can it not wait until my sister and I have finished our greetings?'

'Nay nephew, I fear not. You must hear it now, whilst your sister may support you and you her. My heart bleeds for you upon this day.'

'In Christ's Name, what is it?' I snapped, irritated by his show of melancholy. 'You sound like a strolling player in some cheap tragedy. Drag it no further my lord, but tell us now.'

Thus roughly checked, he spoke more naturally and therefor with greater effect. 'Then hear this. I must inform you both that your royal father, King Henry, passed away at the Palace of Westminster upon the morning of the twenty-eighth of January.'

Gasping, Ned and I clutched one another in anguish, half choked with shock. To add to our horror and confusion, Lord Hertford knelt before Edward seizing his hand and carrying it to his lips whilst crying aloud: 'Long live His Royal Grace, King Edward the Sixth of England!' My brother and I stared at one another. Little Ned was King. Our great father was dead. For a moment it seemed like the end of the world.

'Alas!' I wailed, high and shrill. 'England's wall is broke, her rock is crumbled. God help us all!'

Edward's chin trembled, his face crumpled as he strove to contain himself. Suddenly he burst into loud sobs, burying his head upon my shoulder. Appalled, with the feeling of a cut stalk in my bosom, I followed suit. We wept for hours and none could stop us. We were given soothing draughts, we were cossetted and cuddled, put to bed in darkened rooms and still we wept. All agreed afterwards that they had seen nothing like it. They said that they would never have believed that two such quiet children could reveal such depth of feeling. They said that Royal children were more sensitive than others, for the Lady Mary, too, was utterly prostrated. At last we slept, only to wake to more tears.

'Oh sister, I am sore afraid,' wept Ned. 'Now that it has come, I shall not know what to do. I cannot be like my father. Mayhap none will take heed of me. Mayhap I shall do foolish things. Mayhap I shall be parted from those I love!'

I comforted him as well as I could, and with such success that he was able to leave with Lord Hertford for London the next day, cheered into charity with himself by the size of his retinue and the servile behaviour of his uncle, who bowed and scraped unceasingly before him, charging others to do the same.

So the little King rode off and I was left behind at Enfield, alone with my grief. I could not believe that I should never see my father again, never hear his deep voice, his great laugh, his glorious singing. Never again could I thrill with pride as I thought: This is my father, the greatest King in the world. He was gone for ever, my nearest and dearest, the fount of all my pleasure, the source of all my pain.

I fretted and moped, but I wrote to Ned continually. Was he not at once a King and my small brother? I thought of him often and worried about him far away in London, trying to behave as a King; he so young and little among his sixteen guardians, each appointed by my father. I was third in the Succession at that time, made so in my father's will, and treated therefore with great respect, although none dreamed in those days, that I should ever rule. Living as I did, away from the Court, I had to depend for my news upon that brought by messenger, the contents of letters and upon hearsay. I heard a great deal, for my ear was always attuned to the pulse of the moment.

'The King's uncle puffs himself up,' I remarked to Blanche one day while we were at our Welsh.

'Indeed he does!' said Blanche excitedly in English. 'Why, some say that he is grown more important than the King.'

'Well, he has prevailed upon my brother to make him Duke of Somerset and has brought Parliament to his heel as well, it seems.' At Blanche's look of query, I went on: 'Why, I heard that he has become Lord Protector of the realm, with powers to act as he wishes without Council's advice. This was not what my father desired. He wished none to have more power than the rest. This Somerset thinks only of his own advancement and uses my brother's youth to gain it.'

'People say that he is very high-minded and seeks to do good,' said Blanche. 'He wishes to teach folk how to turn to God and fine life everlasting.'

I gave a hoot of derisive laughter. 'Ho, it is but a cover, I'll wager! It is this life that concerns Somerset, not the next. He is too canting and mealy-mouthed to admit it, though, and prefers to hide his self-seeking under a cloak of holiness. I know his kind, Blanche. I can smell them like a close-stool that is concealed under velvet and carving, yet still stinks in spite of all.'

'He is a well-looking man,' murmured Blanche.

'So they say,' I answered briskly. 'I admire him not. I believe him to be a clever fool, and as such, he is no man for the place he covets.'

'Eh, but you are your father's daughter,' said Blanche smiling. 'At times you speak in his own words. What a King you would make!'

'Yes,' I agreed quietly. 'Or a Queen.'

We sat silent for a space, then Blanche shifted in her chair. 'The Duke would be bound to seek further power my Lady, for he is blood-uncle to the King. He would feel like no ordinary Council member, and would have much influence by reason of the relationship. No doubt the Council finds it politic to bend to the prevailing wind while it blows from Somerset.'

'I fear so, Blanche. This man means to be King in fact, if not in name.'

Blanche nodded. 'The Duke's brother gains advancement also, look you,' she said.

I raised my brows. 'Does he so? Why, is he become a Duke too?'

'Nay, but he is given a post of power. He is made Lord High Admiral and Lord Seymour of Sudeley.'

'Ah, they move fast, these Seymours. Is the new Lord Admiral well thought of? It seems to be yea and nay from what I hear. For myself, I always thought him gay and kind. Do people regard him askance?'

Blanche looked dubious. 'The ladies speak well of him, the gentlemen not so well.'

'Aha!' I laughed. 'He is handsome, sitha.'

'Oh, very handsome and with such courtly and winning ways. But — I would not trust him, sweeting, not I, and I cannot tell for why neither. 'Tis a feeling within me.'

'The Queen trusted him, did she not, before she married my father? Mayhap he will ask for her again.'

'Lord, I know not. 'Tis too soon to think of such. Best put these matters out of your head, lovey. These are strange times.'

I said no more upon the subject then, but spoke of it to Kat upon another day, while we were practising dance steps in the Long Gallery. We had two musicians sitting in the bay of the oriel window, and the piping and tapping they made covered the sound of our talk. 'Kat,' I said as we processed along, hand in hand in a Pavana, 'what of the new Lord Seymour of Sudeley? Will he now marry Ma Mie? They were promised before.'

'I am not certain,' answered Kat, pointing the toe and circling with great deliberation before dropping to a curtsey. When she rose, she said slowly and thoughtfully: 'Well, you had better know. He wants you.'

'Me!' I shrieked, drowning the music which faded to a clatter and a wail. 'Me!' I cried, dropping Kat's hands. 'I'll not believe it! Oh, get you gone!' I called to the musicians. 'Get out of here, and quickly!'

I yelled, as they seemed disposed to linger ears a-cock, and tongues ready to babble as soon as the doors closed behind them. When they had gone, I rushed at Kat and shook her by the shoulders. 'What mean you? What in God's name mean you Kat?'

'Now, now my Lady, quietly I do beg you. Come, sit upon this settle with me and I will tell you the little I know. The Admiral has asked his brother for your hand, and has been refused.'

I stared. 'What! Has this — Protector, as he calls himself, grown the full powers of a King that he can dispose of me as he wishes?'

Kat shrugged. 'King or not, he has the power now, you see. The Sovereign himself is but a child.'

'I do see. He means to keep Ned under his thumb for as long as he can, lining his pockets the while. And was I to hear naught of this offer for me?'

Then Kat told me that the Admiral had already written to her upon the subject and that she had answered him saying that such matters were out of her province and that she did not know my feelings in the business. Then he had replied that he would write to me himself.

'Good God!' I expostulated when I had regained my breath. 'The man's a fool! How can I marry anyone so soon after my father's death and against the Protector's wishes, seeing that he holds the Government and the King in his hands? 'Twill turn all folk against me. And besides — ' here I faltered as a thought struck through my fine

93

indignation, 'what of Ma Mie? Does she not still love him?'

'She had said naught,' answered Kat, 'but remains quietly in mourning, as befits her state, at Chelsea New Manor.'

'Jesu, what a coil! What shall I say to the Admiral's letter? I shall have to refuse him Kat.' Kat looked at once regretful and dubious. 'Well, but Kat!' I protested. 'You must see it.'

'He is a very proper man,' sighed Kat. 'There is not a lady I know who would not wish to bed with him. When I see him, my legs go weak, I swear. He would make a marvellous vital husband. You would have a baby every year, I'll warrant.'

'I do not want a baby every year! And anyway — ' I began to giggle, 'my courses have not started yet. I am but a green apple still.'

'Not for long,' said Kat knowingly. 'See, have not your breasts grown lately? Your bosom is becoming truly elegant, and this means that your courses will start at any time. Have you not had any aches in the back or the belly, or a tiredness in the legs?'

'A little. I thought I was overly weary or sickening for a rheum.'

She nodded wisely. 'Aha. Depend upon it, they will begin at any time. You are ripe for marriage.'

'I shall refuse him Kat. It is too weighty a matter and too dangerous. Marriage is a troublous thing, it seems to me.'

When the messenger came, there were two letters for me. One asked for my hand, which I refused; the other asked for my company at Chelsea New

Manor, and this I accepted with delight, full of longing to see dear Ma Mie again and comfort her in her loneliness.

While preparations for my departure were going apace, I thought oft of my Lord Admiral, of his bedding with me and what it would have meant. I imagined his kisses and my blood shook within me with desire. I had not seen him often, but he was not easy to forget, so tall, comely-limbed and handsome, with a warm beguiling manner that cozened the senses. If Ma Mie and he did decide to wed after all, she was to be envied. Yet I could marry no one without permission of the Council, by my father's law. Then perhaps as a lover? Nay not before marriage — that would lead to death and disaster, for royal-born ladies must be virgin before they marry. Besides, I was feared to wed. These thoughts and new-awakened longings lost me many a night's sleep at this time. And Kat had been right. Before I left for Chelsea, my woman's courses began. I was glad because they proved me a woman grown, but the pain and discomfort I suffered pleased me not at all, for I had to take to my bed with wine possets to ease the cramps in my belly, a hot brick at my feet and the bed curtains drawn to soothe the ache in my head. I was happy enough when it was over.

It was marvellous good to see Ma Mie again; to run into her arms and be held close. We both wept for present joy and past sadness and had much to say. Chelsea New Manor had lain empty since the execution of Sir Thomas More of gentle memory. Now, under my father's will, it belonged to Ma

Mie, the Queen Dowager. She looked amazing well, my dear stepmother; almost girlish, and disposed to dance and giggle in a way that I had never seen in her. I had always supposed her to be dignified, level-headed, with a calm outlook on life as if she knew all its secrets. Now here was one who seemed as youthful and hot-blooded as I. I wondered at the change, but as the days went by I discovered the root of the mystery. She was being courted by her former betrothed, Thomas Seymour of Sudeley.

At first I felt piqued and gave myself some little torment about it, then I realised that as I had refused him and had meant it from the heart, there was no reason in the world why he should not return to his former lady. This comforted me, and I held it in the forefront of my mind to stifle my confusion. Yet, despite all my efforts, I did feel at once jealous and triumphant. Jealous that sweet Ma Mie should be delighting in the embraces I could have enjoyed, and triumphant that he had preferred me. But why had he? Why, for my superior youth and beauty, I answered myself readily. But in truth why? persisted my deeper consciousness. Was it for wealth? He had that already. Was it for position? Well, but he had that too, being uncle to the King and raised to Lord High Admiral. Then — power? Ah, power. His brother was virtual ruler of the land, with almost supreme power, and Lord Thomas was reputed to have been jealous of his brother since childhood.

I propped my chin on my hands as I sat at my reading table, gazing through the long, small-paned windows at the river wandering lazily past the reeds and sedges under a milky blue sky, at the trees breaking into leaf on the Surrey bank, at the boats bobbing merrily at the landing stage of the manor. I let my mind probe deep; my book, the prospect, my surroundings all forgotten. Power, that was it. I was next heir to the throne after my sister Mary. Ma Mie was a popular Queen who had very lately been wife to a reigning King. Was he using us? Women were but pawns in the game of statecraft and the amassing of power, mere creatures to be bought and sold as stepping-stones to higher things. Was his gay charm but a cover for tireless ambition and cold greed? *Ay*, said my inner heart. *Nay*, cried wishful thinking, for to believe so would reduce my desirability in mine own eyes and make a fool of dear Ma Mie. So I allowed wishful thinking to have sway, and who could blame me at not quite fourteen years of age?

Lord Thomas paid many visits to Chelsea Manor, and I was sworn to secrecy, for 'twould not have done for it to be known abroad that the Queen was entertaining a lover so soon after the death of her husband the King. I was heated beyond reason by the excitement between the lovers and the undertones of jealousy and desire in my own heart, for Lord Thomas flashed me many a hot glance and pressed my hands and even my waist when others were too busy to observe. Later, his attentions to me grew more marked, but were disguised under the assumption of the affectionate but casual behaviour of an uncle. There was no doubt that self-seeking, ruthless and unscrupulous though he might have been, he found me intensely desirable and could scarce hide it. As for me, I was on fire at the sound of his voice. Ma Mie, alight with the love and happiness she had longed for all her life, saw none of this. The eyes of her awareness were closed and she saw her lover only as perfection.

They married in April, those two, and when it was discovered, a blaze of scandal burst in Court circles. All professed to be shocked at such unbridled behaviour upon the part of the Queen Dowager who could not contain her lust, but must wed another, and a known ladies man at that, before four months were out.

'Disgusting!' tattled the censorious tongues. 'Why, King Henry's blessed body is scarce cold before her hot blood sends her to bed with another. At her age too! It is disgusting!'

The new-made Duchess of Somerset joined in, giggling spitefully. 'Well, she has lost rank and precedence by her folly. She is below me now, and I will take no note of the fine airs of a one-time Queen, I promise you. She will find it hard to be humble after having lead of us all, ha? She must learn her place now, say I!'

But no one spoke so at Chelsea Manor. All there were devoted to Ma Mie and wished her only well in her late-found joy. My joy, however, was not unadulterated, for, to my annoyance, little Jane Grey was brought to stay at Chelsea also. At first I feared that she might usurp my place in the affections of Ma Mie and her husband. Yet Lord Thomas treated her only as a child and my jealousy subsided, although I found her presence a great irritation. Oft I was sent to walk with her and amuse her. Certes, she did not amuse me with her constant questions and her aura of righteousness.

'Doth the Lord Admiral love you dearly, Bess?' she asked one day as we sat on a bench watching the river. 'He takes your hand often and strokes your arms. His eyes are always upon you. Does he love you more than the dear Lady Queen?'

'Of course not,' I snapped. 'He is fond of me for her sake.'

'Then he must be very fond of her,' pronounced Jane, 'for it seems to me as if he is oft wishful to kiss you.'

'Oh, what in Heaven's name do you know of what lies between men and women, wedded or not, Jane Grey! Why should he not wish to kiss any child of whom he is fond? He has kissed you, has he not?'

'Yes, and I misliked it.'

'You would!' I retorted. 'You prate of what you do not understand.'

'Ay, but he does not look at you as if you were a child,' persisted Jane. 'And you are not, are you, Bess? You are near fourteen and marriageable.'

'You should keep your eyes upon your books and not upon what does not concern you, Mistress Nosey-Parker. I suppose you have been listening to your nurse's tales.'

She blushed. 'I have, Bess. I am sorry indeed, but I did not know it was wrong. I would not wish to be thought as interfering as Dr. Matthew Parker. Truly, I have but little knowledge of worldly ways.'

'More fool you then,' I said. 'Well, I will add to your knowledge. If you listen to any more of this talk, or repeat a word of it yourself, I shall get you sent from here.'

'Oh nay!' she cried. 'I am happy here. I would not be sent away.'

'One word from me to Lord Thomas,' I boasted, 'and out you go. You had best keep your poking nose and prying eyes out of affairs which are not your business.'

Poor child, she fixed those large hazel eyes on mine beseechingly and promised her discretion. Upon what, we scarcely knew, yet the feeling of unease and awareness of undercurrents was within us both.

None of that unease was felt by Ma Mie. Not then. She was so happy that all laughed with her, and the gay summer days flew by. She, Thomas and I oft played together, and right foolish we were. They would chase me, shrieking and giggling, about the garden, and no matter how I ran about, dodging and evading, I was always captured breathless and wildly laughing at the end. My captor was usually his Lordship, he being able to out-run and out-tire Ma Mie. Then he would tickle and squeeze me, giving me a playful kiss on the cheek the while. It seemed innocent enough, but it was not.

My room, both at Chelsea and at Seymour Place in London, was directly above that shared by my stepmother and her husband, and he took to visiting me in my bed before I rose in the mornings. He would slap and tickle me, and growing wilder, would pull off the covers.

'It is no more than a father would do!' he blustered, when challenged in concern by Kat Ashley.

Mayhap not, if I had indeed been his daughter and but a babe at that. I was not a babe. My woman's body was growing in beauty by the day, and I was not his daughter. In common with all, I slept naked. When he whipped back my bed-coverings he could be sure of seeing part if not all of my nakedness, curl up and try to hide as I might. So I took to wearing a shift a-bed, and irksome I found it, but it served to protect me in some small wise.

Yet I encouraged him by my giggles and excited protests, though all unwittingly. Scared, breathless, guilty though I felt, under all this I enjoyed it. He dizzied me with his maleness, his beauty, his vitality. He was a resplendent creature, and I was too young and unknowing of men to see the crabbed smallness that lay beneath. My maids were no support to me, for though scandalised, they laughed and shrieked as loud as I, sensing the passion behind our antics. John Ashley saw and understood all, but spoke not of it to me, wishing not to make me too aware and so perchance fall into real disgrace. To his wife he did speak, fretting much upon the matter. I knew none of this until much later when the gaiety was done and the laughter stilled.

'Wife, take heed,' he had said gravely to Kat. 'Take heed, for I do fear that the Lady Elizabeth does bear some affection to the Lord Admiral.'

At once Kat protested my youth and innocence

and as yet untried heart. Was she not there to guard me? Had she not already warned his Lordship? John was glad to hear it, he said, but whereas the Lord Admiral was a grown man wise in amorous pursuits, knowing when to advance and retreat, the Lady Elizabeth knew naught of any such tricks. John thought that the Lady Elizabeth possessed a passionate heart and hot blood. Did not Kat realise that these attributes, combined with great affection, could prove the downfall of innocence with dread results for a Royal princess? 'Already she desires him, though she knows it not,' he warned, 'so his aim, whatever it may be, will be that much easier to attain.'

This put Kat in such a pucker that she took his Lordship well to task. He had slipped into my room earlier than his usual time and there had ensued a wild chase ending in horseplay that was more like love-play. Before his arrival, Kat had gone to the house of easement to relieve a pain in her belly through overeating of dried plums the night before. Hearing the racket, she came running.

'My Lord, my Lord, you exceed yourself!' she cried forcefully, rushing across the room and pushing him from me. 'It is not meet that you use my Lady so. It is causing talk in this household that is detrimental to my Lady and unkind to your wife. My Lady is a King's daughter and second in succession to the Throne. She is my charge and responsibility. This being so, I must speak. You must not come in here alone!'

'Oh you women, how you prate!' he grumbled pettishly. 'God's precious soul, you see ill where no ill is meant! I thought nothing of it. She is a child still. I but take her father's place.'

'Nay,' said Kat, 'she is no child sir, and well you know it. The Lady Jane Grey, who dwells here also, is truly a child, yet you leave her untroubled by your wish to be a father, do you not?'

He flushed up angrily and flung out of the room, muttering under his breath, leaving my maids standing all agape and Kat pink and anxious, her blue brocade bedgown huddled round her, one hand grasping my gold satin bedcurtains, the other clutching her robe.

Thomas was out of temper all that day, treating me with irritated circumspection that upset me not a little. The next morning, when he visited my bedchamber, he brought Ma Mie with him and they both teased and frolicked with me. I was at once relieved and disappointed, scarce understanding my own feelings, being just past my fourteenth birthday and having known no man. And so it went on, through the shortening days of autumn and into winter.

In December Ma Mie fell pregnant and all must share her joy. She had given up all thought of such and it seemed like a miracle to her. The babe would be born in August and she hoped for a boy. So all was merry, but still Thomas pursued me and my peace of mind grew ever the less. Oft I caught little Jane's eyes fixed upon me in a mixture of censure and admiration as I gave my Lord answer for answer, and that right saucily. I knew that Thomas wished to fix Jane in my brother's affections, was being paid handsomely by her father to do so, and hoped to gain more power and glory thereby. I also knew that if this came to pass, there would be children and I would lose my place in the Succession. This gave me no fears, only regret, for all believed then that my brother was bound to wed and that children would follow. It was in the nature of things.

One February day brought with it the sweet promise of spring and we ventured into the garden at Hanworth Manor. 'See!' I cried, pointing. 'In spite of the sun, ice still lies in the shadows.'

'Ay, and the wind is keen,' shivered Ma Mie cuddling her cloak round her more securely.

'Let us run then!' I shouted. 'Come, quick, down to the field-gate! I will be first, for I have the start of both of you!' So we ran, and reaching the field-gate, I dodged away along the alleys, across the lawn, until Ma Mie cried for mercy, leaving Thomas to continue the chase. Feeling him close upon me, I ran to Ma Mie. 'Save me!' I shrieked, laughing hysterically, and she flung her arms protectively round me whilst Thomas lunged at us.

'Gr-r-r! You shall not balk me of my prey! Deliver her to me at once, I say! At once, or I will cut her into collops and feed her to the birds! Gr-r-r!' He drew his dagger, and with mock ferocity advanced upon us. We squealed with uncontrolled excitement as he came nearer, his savage growls broken by spurts of laughter. Suddenly he seized the skirt of my black velvet mourning gown and cut it into jags and ribbons as if possessed by a demon. Our shrieks died to a shocked silence, while

Thomas stepped back, startled into his senses by what he had done.

'Husband!' gasped Ma Mie. 'What has come to you? You have cut Bess's gown and petticoats clear to the waist!'

We stood as if turned to stone, so amazed were we. I felt no cold, though the wind blew through the rags of my skirts until my legs showed to the knee. Suddenly Thomas dragged off his cloak.

'Take this!' he burst out. 'Take this and cover yourself. Go inside — get you gone into the house!'

Flinging me the cloak, he turned on his heel and walked rapidly away. I stared at Ma Mie, bewildered, and she at me no less so. Wordless, she put her arm about me and we hurried into the house, where she sent me to Kat, who, horrified, found me a fresh gown. From that day Ma Mie changed, growing ever more quiet and unsmiling. As the babe in her belly grew, so her nature seemed to shrink. She began to question Thomas as to his whereabouts, his company, his thoughts, she once so generous and trusting. Me, she treated ever more coolly. I missed her embraces deeply, and the sweetness of her surrounding love, but excitement rose in me, for Thomas was hotter for me than ever, but in secret now. Feeling direly guilty because of Ma Mie, I tried to restrain my feelings, but young and untried as I was, I could not. I did not seek him out, for he was always seeking me.

Three more months passed in this wise. The weather grew mild, the skies sunny, and sweet Maytime and Whitsun were upon us. I was as if on the rack. Ready to weep at Ma Mie's sad, wondering eyes upon me and at the thought of causing her pain, I was also near crazy with frustrated physical desire which burned in me like a hot coal, losing me my sleep and my temper. Heavy with guilt and misery, heated with excitement, my wits then were as close to being addled as ever in my life, until now. Now it is because the blood runs slow and thin along my cold, old veins; then it was nearer to bursting through them. God save me, it was sweeter then, if such agonies could be called sweet, for I was young and all my life lay before me. Now there is little time left, and at the end of it lies the end of my earthly crown.

One evening, Thomas caught me alone in the garden behind the boxwood hedge. There was none to see his kisses on my mouth, my neck, my breasts, my legs even, when he knelt in the grass at my feet. He had never kissed me so before, and after the first moment of startled surprise, my mouth opened eagerly under his and I clung to him, my heart pounding, murmuring small nonsenses for him alone. He bore me to the ground, all unresisting.

'Oh, my darling, my beautiful one, I have longed for this, burned and agonised for this. We are safe here, none spies or guesses. Let me have you Elizabeth, let me make you mine. I will be careful, gentle, I swear to you. Come to me. It will be as if you are my bride.'

The manifest falsity of this last statement acted upon me as a douse of cold water. I jerked in his arms, wary as a cat. 'But I am not your bride!' I hissed. 'Nor ever shall, nor can be. Let me go. We are mad. I cannot. I must not.' I strove with him, using all my strength. 'Let me go, I say, or I shall scream!'

I meant it and he knew it. Scrambling to my feet, I ran wildly through the darkening garden, into the house and up to my room, where I straightened my disordered gown and hair. At supper I was very gay and Thomas very grim, his eyes hot and lustful. I was afeared, for I knew that we could not play this game for ever. Something would have to come of it.

Something did. Two days later, on the day of Whitsun, Thomas entered my room where I was alone. Sweet he was, and my heart failed me. I went into his arms and was lost in his kisses and rapturous caresses. I cared not for sense nor safety, for my wits were clean gone and his too. Suddenly the door clapped open and I lazily turned my head. There, in the doorway, stood Ma Mie. At my cry, Thomas turned also. Stock still he stood, uttering never a word.

'Oh God!' whispered poor Ma Mie. ' 'Tis true then. And I would not believe it. Not my little Elizabeth, I said. Not my own dear husband. And they were right, they were right after all!' Her voice rose on a wail of agony and she blundered away, sobbing and moaning.

'Christ Jesus!' Thomas, restored to action, shoved me aside and sped after her, crying: 'Kate, Kate! Listen to me! Wait! It was not as you suppose. Kate, listen to me! Wait!'

I remained transfixed by the wall until Kat came

hastening to me aghast. She got me to my bed, where I lay stupefied at the misfortune I had helped to precipitate.

The next day I left for Sir Anthony Denny's house at Cheshunt in Essex. Ma Mie sent me away. She was quiet and kind and looked a full ten years older.

'My Bess,' she said, 'you must go. I do not blame you, for you knew not what you were about. But he knew — full well. He swears you are still virgin. Is it true? You would not lie to me? Nay, I know you would not, poor deluded child. I fear he is a bad man Bess; heartless and self-seeking, under a warm and comely exterior. Rather I should send him from me, not you, but I cannot, for I dared much to wed him, and now I am to bear his child. For your own sake you must go. And for all our sakes we will say naught of this, but make it seem as if you but take a holiday.' I wept most bitterly, feeling my heart almost broken with sorrow and shame, and she took me in her arms. 'Nay, my dearest, weep not,' she said. 'You must show a high head and dry eyes to the world, come what may. You are a King's daughter, never forget that. Good-bye my child, and remember that I love you, though the parting may be long.'

★ ★ ★

At Cheshunt I was among friends. Sir Anthony I knew well, while his lady, Joanne, was elder sister to my own Kat, so it was not as if going to strangers. This was fortunate, for I fell ill soon after my arrival, and remained so for many weeks. Poor Kat was my nurse, and was put to it hard, for I wanted her all the time, weeping if she were out of my sight for more than a minute. I could not work at my books, even though Roger Ascham did his best to woo me thereto. Ascham had succeeded Will Grindal as my tutor when poor Grindal had died of the plague the previous winter. Ascham was now of my household and had come with us to Cheshunt. We dealt well together, for he had a lively wit and much gentleness added to a true understanding of young minds.

Ascham was very friendly with Kat and her husband John. Indeed, I had striven with Ma Mie for him as a tutor. She had favoured a Mr. Goldsmith, but I wanted Ascham, and won my way in this as I did in most things when I set my mind to it. He called me 'his most brightest star,' and was near to turning my head with the praise he lavished upon me and my attainments. John Ashley and Roger wished to shake me free from my melancholy by archery and riding, at which they were experts. Ascham had written a book of archery called '*Toxophilus*,' used throughout the land by those who wished to better themselves at the sport, and this had earned him a life pension from my father. John was also at his pen, compiling a book on the art of riding. Both of these pursuits I loved when in health, but at Cheshunt, at this miserable time, I could do naught with body or mind. Sleep and appetite forsook me and I grew thin and white as a ghost, fretting and sorrowful, my thoughts flickering away from those I had left, yet ever and oft returning, causing me to flinch anew.

The memory of Ma Mie's tragic face haunted me night and day. It rises before me still. Often I wrote to her, asking how she did and assuring her of my love. She always answered, writing that she was well, and returning my love with her own in sweet words. Ah, I would rather she had hated and spurned me. 'Twould have eased the anguish of remorse I bore. To Thomas I wrote also, but only in answer to what he had writ me of various small doings, daring to do no more. In my letter to him I told him that I was a friend not won with trifles, nor lost with them and he could make what he liked of that.

Sir Anthony and his lady did their very best to cheer me and make me feel welcome, but still I pined, feeling them put to trouble because of my presence and my sickliness. While I languished, Thomas was busy, ostensibly with his naval duties, but secretly intriguing to overthrow his brother. These doings kept him much from Ma Mie who lay at Sudeley Castle in Gloucestershire to await the birth of the babe. Ah me! The child was a girl and her mother died in delirium and pain, accusing Thomas of neglect and lack of love.

The news came to me that at the last he did all he could to atone for every fault, but this tenderness came too late and she would have none of it. I could not believe that she could be dead but nineteen months after my father's passing. Methought that if she had not married, she would have been with us still, for children come with men and marriage, and childbed fever with children, and with childbed fever comes Death. Marriage and death, it is all one in the end.

'Did your Ladyship's keen ear hear that Lady Jane Grey was chief mourner at Queen Catherine's funeral?' asked Kat as I sat idly with my lute in Sir Anthony's little summer parlour. Thunder was brewing and my head ached. The pale blue hangings were still as if carved in coloured marble, the sky was grey as lead and no birds sang. I picked listlessly at the lute strings and felt as heavy as the leaden sky.

'Yea,' I sighed, 'I had heard of it. I heard too that her parents wish her home again and Thomas will not let her go. He still hopes to wed her to my brother and to earn himself power and fat profits thereby. But what of it? It is not new.'

'The Lord Admiral frets full sore for the loss of his sweet lady,' said Kat. 'Mayhap it would be seemly in you to write him a letter condoling with him in his sorrow.'

I turned my head and stared at her straight. 'Well, I will not, for he needs it not.'

Soon after this came my fifteenth birthday and I spent it abed with a migraine and misery for company.

During the late autumn I removed to Hatfield, my health still unimproved, although I was able to study more, which gave Ascham and me some pleasure. I sadly wished to see my brother, but could not for I had no London house in which to lodge myself and my retinue. When I thought of this lack, I grew mad enough to bite, and 'twould have been the so-saintly Protector I would have bitten had he been near enough, for he had stolen my house without a query or question.

Durham House in the Strand had been left to me in my father's will, but the whey-faced Edward Seymour had used his self-appointed powers and had appropriated it, turning it into a mint wherefrom he could issue his debased form of coinage. Being a Princess of the Blood, with an entourage of over an hundred persons, I needed a roomy town house, and this my father had provided. But it was ever Somerset's wish to keep me down, and Mary with me, for we would follow after the King, and where would his Dukeship be then, should his young master die of a sudden? He would get no favour from Mary or me, and that he knew full well. I fumed and fretted about the loss of my house so greatly that near everyone knew of my need. I sent Thomas Parry my treasurer, a fool, but an honest fool, to see what accommodation he could find me. When he returned in December, he was big with news, so I spoke with him at once.

I was in the solar, off the Great Hall at Hatfield, when he came to me. I liked this room, for it caught what sunshine there was, being built for the purpose some hundreds of years agone. The fire crackled as I sat at my desk, the bright flames reflecting in the polished wood. As Parry entered, pushing aside the tawny velvet curtain, I laid down my pen and turned to face him. 'Pull up by the fire, Tom,' I bade him. 'You look blue with the cold, man. What news?'

Drawing a stool to the fire and stretching his

hands to the flames, he answered me eagerly. 'Well madam,' he said, 'someone has offered you a house; a handsome one, with all its staff complete, for as long as you care to use it.'

'Why, this is wonderous great!' I cried. 'Who is this generous someone, and what is this handsome house?'

'The owner is the Lord High Admiral and the house is Seymour Place, my Lady. How say you to that?'

I drew a deep breath, my heart jumped and the colour flew red to my cheeks. Parry laughed. 'You like it?'

'Very much,' said I. 'It is a fine house indeed and his lordship is most thoughtful of my comfort.'

'What, no more than that, my Lady?'

'What more should there be?'

'Madam, the Lord Admiral is deep enamoured of yourself.'

'He told you this?'

'Ay, he did. He can talk of none but you and your wit and beauty. It is plain he holds you very dear and that his heart is smitten.'

'Not for the first time, nor, I dare say, the last,' I answered drily. 'His heart is swift to recover from all blows, it seems.'

'Well, but my Lady, he cannot wear the willow all his life. He is a lusty man, thou knowest, and hot blood will have its way.'

'So out with it Parry! Do not sit there prating of smitten hearts and hot blood. What is it you truly wish to say?'

'This, Madam. If the Council should approve,

would you be willing to wed the Lord Admiral?'

I sat silent while my heart and mind strove one against the other for mastery. I struggled for compromise, as my heart cried 'Yes!' and my mind warned 'No!' I wished not to commit myself either way, for each course seemed troublous to me. At last I said: 'When the time comes, I will do as God puts in my mind.' 'Twas the best I could think of and I hoped it would satisfy Parry. It seemed to do so, for he nodded wisely. 'What else said my Lord?' I continued with what was a fair assumption of easy interest.

I learned that Thomas had suggested that my lands should be exchanged for others that lay beside his own, in the West. 'And he would not say such,' said Parry earnestly, 'unless he go about to have you also.'

'What is his plan for such an exchange? Did he say how it should be done?'

Parry leaned forward in the firelight, his elbows on his knees, and told me what Thomas had suggested. My Lord had thought it meet that I should sue for friendship with the Duchess of Somerset to gain the exchange. I detested the woman as much as I disliked her husband, and well Thomas knew it. She had insulted Ma Mie, withholding her own property from her, had interfered in the running of her household and had forced her to give precedence. Moreover, this Duchess had caused an almighty stir once, when Kat had allowed me to go on a river-boat party at night, crying that Kat was not fit to have governance of me, for she was too free in her ideas. I would have none of the lady, and said so, roundly.

'Make suit to *her*!' I screeched. 'I would rather bow to an ape!'

'But my Lady!' stammered Parry, 'she is sister-in-law to the Lord Admiral and has great influence in many matters. If you could bring yourself to conquer your aversion, you might prevail.'

'Well,' cried I, 'I will *not* do so, and so tell him!'

'What is to be done then, madam?' asked poor Parry, all confusion at my anger.

'Nothing at all,' I answered. 'I will have none of it. Parry, you must tell Mrs. Ashley all you have said to me and all that the Lord Admiral told you. I will know nothing but she know it too. This seems to be to be a devious secret matter, and I must not keep silent, for fear some should say I made a plot with my Lord and wished none to know of it.'

I misliked the whole affair. It seemed to smack of connivance to a greater end, with myself as the bait. Indeed, my Lord might say he loved me, but he meant to use me also. Wed to me, his position would be higher than it had ever been as husband to the Queen Dowager, yea, equal to that of his brother, the Protector. Full of mistrust, yet my blood ran fast at the thought of him, of his arms, his mouth . . . I was a green fool, doubtless, in matters of the heart. In those of the head I knew I held my own with any who confronted me; therefore I judged it best to speak out upon the matter lest I be accused of treason in time to come. Troubled, and with tears in my eyes, I turned to Parry who was watching me with concern.

'Go now, and tell Mrs. Ashley what has been said,' I commanded, my lips trembling with emotion and anxiety. Parry leaped to his feet, eager to soothe my disorder by rushing to do my bidding, tripping over the stool as he did so. 'Oh, get you gone!' I cried, exasperated. 'Find Kat and leave me to my thoughts. Pah! That I, my father's daughter, should sue to the Somerset bitch! My Lord knows me not if he think I would do so!' Left alone, I flung my pen to the floor, following it with the sand-castor. Finding that this did naught to relieve me, I jumped to my feet and ranged about the room, kicking the fallen stool each time I passed it, mouthing words that even Kat might have stood amazed to hear.

So the web grew, the net enlarged and the lurking shadows darkened. I could do naught but wait. For sure, I was used to that.

★ ★ ★

All this was full fifty years ago and still it pains me. My memories are clear enough even across half a century. Had I but known it, I was entering upon ten years of almost unceasing nervous strain and inward terror. Those years left their mark upon me in irritability of temper and an inability to give things away with easy generosity. Indeed, I had never been renowned for easy generosity before these troubles overtook me, but I was immeasurably worse afterward. I have thought in my musings that I hold fast to my possessions as a symbol of the security I have never had, for even as Queen, my realm and my person have been threatened. Now that I am old, these possessions behoove me nothing, yet unto them still I cling. What of my three hundred gowns in their oaken presses, my gloves, my slippers, my hats, my wigs? I shall not need them for much longer, but part with any one of them I cannot. My personal monies and jewels, my small boxes and gew-gaws, I would keep them about me still, all and entire. What will become of them after I am gone? Will they be worn by another, or cast aside as outmoded and useless? Who will finger my beloved objects and count my coins? Nay, best not think of that, for these are things my eyes will never see, my eyes which once saw all . . . I had a gown, years agone, with eyes and lips embroidered all over it. I see all and say nothing, said I, and it was truth. I was famous for't.

But in the winter of 1548 I saw but little, and that treacherous. I made no suit to the Protector's lady and perforce remained at Hatfield. It was a hard, cold winter and I felt cold in mind as well as in body, no matter how we strove to drive dull care away.

I mind one of those days that we sat about the fire in the winter parlour playing dice and cards. The trees in the park were bent near double with the wind, an icy rain fretted the window panes, and although the chamber was panelled, the tapestries stirred and shivered as if concealing a careless assassin. I wore a fur cape about my shoulders and my ladies were huddled in shawls and wrappers, for although the fire scorched our faces, a mighty draught froze our backs, despite a painted leather screen placed betwixt us and the door. Later, when I had dismissed my ladies, Kat and I sat on by the fire, drinking spiced wine and eating sweet cakes and comfits.

'Now he is free again, you may have him if you will,' observed Kat, her mouth full of marchpane.

'He?' I queried. 'Who is 'He' '?'

'Oh save me, such disdain!' tittered Kat, licking her fingers. 'The Lord Admiral, thou knowest.'

'Nay, I think not,' said I, eyes downcast.

'Ha, you would not deny it and say nay if the Lord Protector and the Council were pleased therein!' she rallied me. 'Parry told me of my Lord's doings touching yourself and his wish to wed you.'

'I instructed Parry so,' I answered. 'For see you, Kat, you should know of these weighty matters as well as I, you being my governess, then none can talk of plots and subterfuges.'

'Indeed so, my love. Even Parry knew not the true reason why we left Chelsea Manor so sudden.'

'Does he know now Kat? Did you tell him?'

She hesitated, looking confused. 'Well — I did. I am sorry, chuck, I could not stop my tongue. Fret not, Parry will keep close.'

'The fewer to know, the less to tell,' I said. 'Is that not the lesson you were always at pains to impress on me? Now, this business is like to touch me nearly. I would you had said naught to Parry about Chelsea. It could be used by persons to blacken me.'

'Oh, my darling, surely not! Why, 'twas all my Lord Thomas's doing, and he was but hot-blooded and foolish.'

'Ma Mie did not think so.'

'Well, but did he ever love her, dearest? Sure, she was a sweet lady and lovesome, but his heart must have misgave him when he saw you stand beside her, making her look old and tired.'

'Ah, Kat, do not remind me. My heart aches with guilt.'

'But do you not feel for him, love? He is such a proper man, and I long to see you happily wed.'

'I know, dear Kat,' I said, patting her hand. 'My body feels for him, indeed, but my mind does not follow. My mind sees naught but darkness and trouble surrounding him. Nor do I trust him. I do not wish to be dragged into aught that could besmirch me in the eyes of others. Chelsea was bad enough, God knows; so say no more of that to any other, and you love me.'

'Certes, sweetheart, I will not. I am full sorry believe me. I am turning into a loose-tongued chatterer in spite of all my fine ideas.' She shook her head as if puzzled. 'Though I cannot understand what you fear. What danger can there be?'

'Nothing is ever as it seems, Kat. There are those who seek to use the high-born for their own ends. Plots can be made in our names of which we know nothing, yet we are held as guilty when the plots are uncovered. So I must keep myself apart from any such. My name and character must be as unsullied as possible, although I fear it may be difficult now.'

119

Kat stared at me a moment. Then she took my hand. 'Sweeting, you speak as if you see ahead, as if you know more than any of us what is to come. Do you in truth know more?'

'I cannot tell,' I answered sighing. 'It is something deep within me that speaks, for when I turn my mind to't I have no more foreknowledge than any other. Less in fact, for I am kept close here at Hatfield, away from the stir of state affairs and politics. I know that I must never lose the love of the people, for if I do I shall lose all.'

'All what, my love?'

'All my future, Kat. I am serving apprenticeship for it now.'

* * *

While I abode at Hatfield through the dark winter, half sick, often abed, Thomas was about his concerns. He plotted high and dangerously, although I knew naught of it then. He drew the King into the net of his affections, which he was well able to do, being of a spirit most beguiling to the young. Yet I already was wary and my brother to become so before long.

I longed to see my dear Ned. I had heard he was kept short of ready money and far too hard at his books, that he suffered from lack of fresh air, exercise, and the gaiety of young companions. I knew, too, that he suffered these omissions not through cruelty or unkindness, but from lack of understanding only. The Lord Protector was a high-minded man who believed that all others surveyed the world through his eyes, and so made his every mistake. Thomas was like him in this fault and made his errors likewise. Both misjudged my brother, to their great cost. They believed he loved them. He did not. They believed that being a child, he would forgive and forget. He did not. Edward loved but three beings; his old nurse Mother Jack, Ma Mie and me. I knew this from his letters in which he oft wrote something of his heart, using our private cipher. His life as King was grand, cold and empty, poor sweet one, with one uncle kind, yet remote as the evening star, and the other who eagerly sought to buy his affection with gifts of money. Edward, chilled by the coolness of one, alarmed by the warmth of the other, was truly attracted by neither.

★ ★ ★

Our Christmas celebrations that year were dull enough. I had little heart for merriment, and still less some three weeks later when the first thunderings of ill fate were heard at the great gate of Hatfield early on a frozen grey morning. It was Sir Anthony Denny rid up from London with his company, upon the Lord Protector's business.

'Duke Somerset has business with me?' I asked Parry, who came in haste to me, his face white as milk. 'What is it man? You shake as if struck with the ague.'

'Oh my Lady, quavered Parry, 'have a care what you say, I implore you. It is ill business and I would

121

ye were well out of it. I would I had never been born.'

I said that I would see Sir Anthony and bade Parry take command of himself before sending him off. As he hurried away, I bethought me that Sir Anthony's arrival might have something to do with the Lord Admiral and his desires concerning me. I had done naught, yet felt a shiver of nervousness which I quelled swiftly, composing my face to calm unawareness as Sir Anthony entered my chamber.

'Lady Elizabeth, I would speak with you alone,' he said briskly. 'The matter is of grave import, I fear me.'

'Indeed?' I queried. 'And how can aught of grave import concern me, living quiet here at Hatfield?'

'Certes, I hope it may concern you but little Madam,' said Denny. 'Will you pray send your ladies away that we might be private?'

Judging it best to agree, I bade my ladies leave me then waved Sir Anthony to a chair which he drew up to the table, resting his elbows thereon, staring at me searchingly. 'Know you,' he began, 'of the Lord Admiral's arrest?'

My heart almost stopped, but I kept my face bland and smiling as a mask. 'Nay,' I said coolly. 'How should I know? What is it to do with me?'

'Naught, I hope,' he answered, looking at me straight. 'Would you tell me of your dealings with his Lordship?'

I affected to consider, looking thoughtful yet not much interested. 'He offers me his own house, Seymour Place in London, seeing that the Lord Protector filched mine own from me, but I took

122

it not and no more was said of the matter.'

'Is this all my Lady?'

'What else should there be, Sir Anthony? What do you wish me to say?' My mind raced like a mouse in a cage. Why had no one told me of my Lord's arrest? Were they afeared? Had Kat and Parry spoken too much together and had others heard? That must be it, for why would Sir Anthony be sent to me for information unless there was held to be somewhat betwixt me and the Admiral? I caught my panicking thoughts and strove to be calm, for in truth, there had been nothing between Lord Thomas and myself, although enemies could make it so. This was my fear.

'My dear Lady Elizabeth,' said Denny, 'I have known you since you were a nursling and I have much regard for you and great concern. The Lord Admiral be arrested for treason.'

I drew a deep breath to hide my gasp of horror and bit my lips to still their tremble. 'Treason? But he loves the King, Sir Anthony. He spoke of it oft at Chelsea. Besides, he is blood uncle and was fond since my brother was but a babe. I cannot believe what you say.'

'You would do well to, Lady. The Admiral had somehow possessed himself of keys to the King's sleeping chamber, creeping in at dead of night to do what villainy God knows. His Majesty's little dog barked and the Admiral shot it dead. The noise of the shot brought the guard who challenged my Lord. He could give no satisfactory answer, so was arrested, and at daybreak, brought to the Tower.'

'My God,' I whispered. 'What a fool.'

'Knew you aught of this plan, my Lady?' asked Denny instantly.

'Nay!' I countered hotly. ' 'Twas a fool's action whatever his plans may have been. His head must be turned by his sorrows, methinks!'

'I think this will do more than turn his head, Lady Elizabeth. It bodes fair to bring it clean off his shoulders.' To this I gave no answer, and Sir Anthony leaned forward impressively, his handsome gaunt face distressed and kind. 'Remember, my child,' he said, 'pitch sticketh. It soils whomever toucheth it, whether by chance or no. I will leave you now, for I have more business to do and orders to follow. I have your permission to retire?'

'Ay,' I said wearily, 'and I pray you send Kat Ashley to me.'

He hesitated as if he would have said more, then bowed and left me to my thoughts which were neither serene nor pleasant. It had been a warning, that much was plain. So wrapped up was I in my musings that I knew not how much time had passed before I became aware that Kat had not answered my summons. Rising, I seized my little golden handbell and went to the door, ringing it loudly and shouting impatiently for Kat.

Blanche Parry came running, her face white, her eyes wild, her words bursting forth in sobs and lamentations. What she told me turned me as deathly pale as herself. Sir Anthony had arrested Kat Ashley and Thomas Parry and taken them to London as his prisoners. 'Twas as if all the breath were knocked from my body in that minute. The windows dipped and swayed before my eyes, the walls advanced and receded, the floor shook beneath my feet as my jaw dropped and I struggled for air. I gripped the edge of the table like a spent swimmer grasps a lone rock as he is swept past in the tide. Blanche ran toward me, casting her arms about me, wailing like a lost soul. This brought me to my senses quicker than aught else. Pulling myself upright, I seized her hands in mine.

'Sweet Jesu, Blanche! Have done with that infernal caterwauling. 'Tis help I need, not howling. Do not give way now, or all my household will be in hysterics and of what use to me then? I think that I might be in grave danger. Do not deny me your support, dear Blanche!' As I had hoped, her tears ceased and she grew more sensible being able to help me to bed and send for warming pans and hot bricks to still my shivering. 'Hearken well to what I say,' I told her when all was done. 'Hide your fears, Blanche, weep not, and keep a close tongue if you love me. Say I have the migraine — nothing more. There have been too many loose tongues tattling round me. Now if you do not wish me to follow Kat and Parry, keep your's still. Swear it.'

'But, my love, what is it all about?'

'Swear it, I say!'

Blanche swore herself to silence and kept her oath well. There was alarm and curiosity, but no terror and no weeping. Best of all, my ladies, thinking I suffered a migraine, troubled me not and I had time for thought. I had done no wrong in any way, but there were those who sought to destroy Thomas and who would stop at nothing to do so, using anyone and anything to achieve their ends. If they could

125

reach him through me they would do so, even if I were to be destroyed in my turn. Sure I was a princess, but not a reigning one, and so of little account. 'Twas not the King these men wished to gain, but power over him and thus over the realm. His dear person mattered not. And there was more; I could see it plain as I pondered it. The King must have shown some little partiality for Thomas, and this might give Thomas ascendancy over him. All knew Thomas's wish for power and the jealousy he had for his brother. One Seymour is enough, let us destroy the weaker. I forced my thoughts to their painful conclusion. So then, if one Seymour were brought down, the other would not show as invincible. If the Protector's own brother could be killed, why not the Protector himself, in order to leave room for — Who? Who?

Who was so coldly self-seeking, so able to manipulate his fellows? I must watch and listen as never before; for although I could not alter the course of events from my youth and relatively helpless position, once I had learnt the identity of this man, I could suit my actions to his prevailing mood. I could keep out of his way.

It was clear to me now. Through Kat and Parry to me, through me to Thomas, through Thomas to the Protector, through the Protector to the King, through the King to the realm, through the realm to the world! Therefore I would have to disrupt that progression. Whatever poor Kat and Parry said or were tricked into saying, mine enemies would get naught from me. Not that there was much to get, but enemies had ways of twisting words and misrepresenting innocence until the whitest angel could be made to seem a very devil of iniquity. I knew well how the guiltless could be proven guilty to suit the desires of others. Had not mine own mother been one such? Well, her daughter would not be so served. Not now or ever. As God was my judge I swore it!

Little sleep I got that night, for I felt as though I were strung on wires and jointed with ratchets. I had no Kat to soothe me through the long dark hours, no loving hand to reassure me, no warm sweet voice to lift my heavy troubles. Hard I prayed, for I felt my case was bad.

Worse was to follow, for Sir Robert Tyrrwhit arrived at Hatfield forthwith. He was Commissioner to the Council and had come to question me so that my words should prove the downfall of Thomas Seymour. I was standing by the window in the winter-parlour when he was announced. I clutched the maize-coloured curtain in my hand, wishing him dead and myself afar off. Yet I flashed round upon him like a wildcat when he came in.

'Where are Mrs. Ashley and Thomas Parry?' I cried, glaring at him.

'In prison, Madam,' he answered smoothly, 'and there like to remain until we are satisfied in this matter.'

'Are they well housed?'

'Nay, why so? They are under lock and key, as any common criminal!'

Suddenly, I beheld a vision of my Kat, cold and hungry, in a dark cell, mayhap chained, mayhap tortured. My command deserted me, and flinging myself into a chair, I wept aloud. Sir Robert called my ladies to calm me, then left us, saying that he would return when I was in my senses once more. I recovered soon enough and declared myself ready to face the man and his odious questionings.

We sat across from one another at the long table with the carven legs that were beginning to take the place of trestles. Grim he looked, and humourless, his blue velvet cap pulled low over his eyes, his dark beard outthrust.

'Madam,' said he, 'I must remind you that you are but a subject and therefore to be prevailed upon to answer whatever questions I put to you.'

'Ha, and by what right?' said I, determined to show a bold front after my tears.

'By right of the Council and my position therein. Now, Madam, we know that you are but young and without a man to guide you. Therefore, if you will confess all, the Council will acquit you and lay the blame where it deserves to be laid; on the shoulders of your elders!'

'And who are they, pray, who must suffer for me, and unjustly too, since I have done no wrong?'

'Your governess and your treasurer, Madam,' answered he with a fine show of patience, as if to a want-wit.

'A shameful suggestion!' I cried. 'I have nothing to say. I am no ferret, no weasel, to harm those who love me, and so remember!'

He tried all he knew, poor wight. He used soft words and cunning phrases, seeking to entrap me; he used threats in order to terrorise me, he raged and shouted, hoping to cow me. All to no avail.

'I have been looking at your accounts,' he blustered at last. 'The man Parry knows not his work. The accounts are so indiscreetly made that it is plain to see that he has little understanding of his office. Every total is wrong and the monies are tangled beyond setting right. If you cannot trust him to keep your accounts, sure you can trust him in naught else.'

'Nonsense!' I shouted. 'Fool he may be, knave he is not. I have no knaves about me willingly, Sir Robert Tyrrwhit.'

Exasperated, he left me and sought his chamber. My household had seen to it that it was an uncomfortable one, and feigned sudden deafness to his demands for service. He had little pleasure at Hatfield that winter. The windows would not close and the chimney smoked. His bed was old and shaky, with a mattress taken from a servant's bed. 'Full of lumps and little visitors,' giggled one of my ladies who had superintended the operation. The rushes remained unchanged upon the floor and no one answered his hand-bell, jangle it how he would, until he had given up the effort. Then someone would dawdle along, all slow and stupid. His slops went unemptied until he bribed a serving man to perform the office.

Some days later, Lady Browne arrived to visit me. I was not best pleased to see her, being so troubled in my mind, but I tried to make her welcome. Her company was soothing in a way, and insensibly I relaxed, letting the lilt of her pretty Irish voice lap over me as little ripples lap over a stone. She showed me much sympathy, and after a while I found myself sorely tempted to babble out my wrongs. Swiftly I checked myself, becoming alert on the instant.

'Lady Browne,' I said suddenly, cutting across her chatter, 'do you come here to cozen me into speech that you may carry reports to Sir Robert Tyrrwhit or the Protector?'

She checked like a horse that stumbles in full gallop. 'Carry reports, my Lady? Sure and didn't I come here just to cheer you and gossip with you in your troubles?'

'Oh ay,' I replied, 'and to hope that you could loosen my tongue. You and I have never been close, and I see no reason for your visit other than to use beguiling words to worm secrets from me. Well, I have no secrets and your words beguile me not. You may tell that to your masters.' So saying, I rose and left her. If I had not been so beset, I would have laughed to see the foolish expression of surprise on her face. Beautiful she might be, subtle she was not, for as I turned at the door, I saw that she looked as guilty as a serving boy caught skimming the cream.

'You make a mighty poor spy, Lady Browne,' I observed. 'Your thoughts are mirrored on your face for all to read.'

What she did after that I know not, except that she left soon after. Then came a letter from Protector Somerset himself. Kind, it seemed, filled with protestations of his regard, queries for my health and concern for my welfare, yet cunningly mixed with suggestions as to how I could improve the latter. Snorting angrily, I threw the letter from me and took to my bed in gloom and hopelessness.

Before the week was out, Sir Robert Tyrrwhit revealed the current gossip told about me. He was sitting on a stool by my fire, eagerly stretching blue fingers out to the blaze and sniffing dolefully, looking frozen cold, as well he might. I met his watering eyes with a haughty flash from mine own.

'Have you an ague?' I asked. 'You shiver like a wet cat.'

'I have caught a rheum,' he said. 'My chamber is draughty.'

'The weather is cold,' I replied with studied carelessness. 'We must expect to suffer chills at this time of the year. What is it you want of me now?'

He eyed me up and down in a way that was slyly insolent and I felt the red rage begin within me. 'Know you, Madam, what is being said of you in London and round about?'

'Nay, and I care not.'

He smiled and I could have cut the smirk from his lips. 'They say that you are in the Tower.'

'Well, you and I know that I am not.'

The smile deepened. 'They say you are pregnant by the Lord Admiral.'

I stared him full in the eye. 'Then 'They' lie. I am no more pregnant than you, Sir Robert. Virgin I am and virgin will remain. My belly will not swell, wait ye never so long. I am not betrothed to the Lord Admiral, nor am I pregnant by him. Call a doctor, Sir Robert!' I shouted, jumping to my feet.

'Call your own doctor and let him examine me. I promise you that his diagnosis will agree with mine. These are shameful slanders and I will have none of them!'

Sir Robert's face changed. Hitherto, his expression had been polite but bullying. Now, by some subtle alchemy, it became almost respectful. A small frown appeared between his round brown eyes, whose hard stare had altered to thoughtfulness. He drew a breath.

'If you can name your slanderers, sure, the Council will punish them,' said he. 'I shall have to inform my Lord Protector of your words to me,' he added, somewhat lamely.

'Have no fear, I shall inform him myself!' I countered swiftly, with the boldness of truth and innocence. 'I mean to do so now and will leave you to your spying.'

So saying, I marched from the parlour to the solar, where my writing desk lay, and at once penned a letter to the Protector. I knew with all my soul that Somerset would not wish me in London, proved slandered and innocent. Myself, an unprotected girl, falsely accused, deliberately besmirched to serve the ends of ambitious, scheming men would not advance his own popularity one whit. Besides, was I not the daughter of my great sire and much loved by the people? They would rally to me, whether I wanted or no, and make me the figurehead of their disaffection, threatening his own position. He would not wish such a confrontation, not he.

'*My Lord*,' I wrote, '*these are shameful slanders for which, beside the great desire I have to see the*

King's Majesty, I shall most heartily desire your Lordship that I may come to the Court that I may show myself there as I am . . . ' and more to the same tune. I had it sent by special messenger the very same day.

Yet my boldness took a deal of effort, for there was no one to whom I could turn for love and support. Without Kat my heart was bereft, and oft I shook with terror. Blanche was kind and loving, but my Kat had my heart. She loved me as her own and knew me as no other could. So another week dragged by, I ever growing more tense in expectation of some dreadful fate that was soon to burst upon me. I could not eat, for the muscles of my stomach refused to unknot themselves; nor could I sleep, for my eyelids flickered and would not close. My fingers fretted my lips and my teeth gnawed at my nails. I could settle to nothing, pacing up and down like a very guardsman when indoors, or riding like the devil when out. They were cruel days and I bear the scars of them still.

In the first week of February Sir Robert came to me with some papers in his hand. I was lying on my daybed in the gallery by the fire, half-covered by a fur rug, for the cold tormented me at this time and I trembled from morn 'til night, despite warm furs and hot possets, for my chill was within. Sir Robert still suffered a heavy rheum and was sneezing mightily.

'Have a thought, I beg you,' I protested fretfully. 'Would you pass your affliction on to me? I feel unwell enough already.'

'If your treasurer had kept better accounts,

mayhap my chamber would have been more comfortable and I should not now be sneezing fit to burst my eyes from their sockets!' he retorted smartly.

'If you have aught to say, say it!' I snapped impatiently, for I felt that he was heavy with news of some sort, and to judge by recent events, it could only be bad.

For answer, he laid the papers in my lap, and at the foot of the topmost, I saw Kat's signature. I stared at it in a panic, and when I had read the depositions I knew not what to say or do, while the breath half choked in my throat. I ruffled the pages, noting first Kat's signing, then Parry's, my eyes catching words and sentences here and there. It was all down; how Thomas had cut my gown at Hanworth, how Thomas had visited me abed, to the dismay of my women; how he had singled me out, how Kat's husband John had warned her as to my seeming partiality for Thomas. There, too, was written of Ma Mie's sadness and puzzlement growing to suspicion, of her discovery of our embrace and my expulsion to Cheshunt.

Parry, in his turn, had told of his words with me upon the subject of Thomas's plans to marry me and how he spoke of it to Kat afterwards. Kat had then said that Lord Thomas could bring the marriage to pass well enough by the Council's hands, adding the reason of our removal to Cheshunt, which Parry swore he had not known of before. So mean and small it looked, so tawdry and yet, for my part, nothing criminal in it. For all that, my heart pounded and my hands shook as I read, for I felt stripped naked to be jeered at. In my mind, I could hear the giggles: *'Like mother, like daughter.'* *'Did they not call her dam the Great Whore?'* *'See how the base blood will out,'* and the like and more of the like.

My lips trembled and I could not speak, so I read on. Sure, they must have been in mortal fear to betray me so, poor souls. Thank God that things had gone no further 'twixt Thomas and me. So near had he been to being my lover; why, at the last, 'twas only lack of opportunity prevented, for my blood was as hot as his. Now my blood was turned to ice and my proud head bowed in humiliation. Sir Robert watched me closely, hoping for chance words of self-betrayal, so I read on. When I came to the end, my heart near failed me, for here was my Kat, ill and cold, begging the Protector for another prison. 'For by my troth, it is so evil that I cannot sleep in it, and so dark,' she had said to those who had writ down her words. As I read further, I learned that the cold was so great that she had been forced to stop the empty windows with straw. I lifted my head and stared full into Sir Robert's eager eyes.

'So,' I said boldly, 'they have said no more than what is true, despite all the troubles they have been put to.'

'Well then,' answered Sir Robert, 'I would not trust them, for they made a promise to themselves and to their examiners not to confess until death, and here, after so short a discomfort, have tumbled out all; if it is all.'

I shrugged my shoulders as if uncaring. 'Ay, it

were a great matter to make such a promise and then to break it,' I said coolly.

'Have you no more to say, Lady?' he cried.

'No more,' I replied, 'for they have said it.'

'Is there nothing else you can add?' he persuaded. 'They might fare better if so. Mayhap you would be less loyal to the traitor Seymour, had you known that he had asked your sister to wife as well as you,' he went on spitefully, his eyes gleaming with malice.

This was a shock, but I had to smile in spite of it. 'What?' I cried. 'Lord Thomas asked Mary? I did not know that. I'll wager she refused him! He is impudent in his dealings indeed. But as to information, you have already told me more than I can tell you.'

He charged me to search my mind in the interests of Kat and Parry and I did so with all my might. I bethought me of any small happening that Kat might have forgot and could call to mind but few. Yet I set them down in fair writing, saying therewith that I had not wittingly concealed these things, but being so trivial, I had forgot them. Two days later, I called Sir Robert to me and handed him the papers, which he almost snatched from me in his eagerness to read the damaging disclosures I had written.

'Why,' said he, chapfallen, when he had done, 'there is no more here than trifles.'

'Nay,' I repeated, 'for there be no more.'

'But, Madam, will you not confess that Ashley or Parry, or both, willed you to practise with the Lord Admiral? Were there no messages or writings? Only confess and sure, you can save your servants.'

I slammed my hand upon the table. 'Sir Robert!' I shouted. 'Will you have done? You can get no more of me; there is no more to get. Are Parry and Kat in danger of death, that I must save them? So then, I have done all I can, except you would have them and me to lie, and confess what is not true! Try not your Council tricks on me! Get you gone with your tales and your papers, and make what you can of it, Sir Muck-scraper!'

Glaring at me as if wishful to hit me, he stamped from the room, leaving me to weep with rage and despair . . . I had more to weep at a few days after this, when Sir Robert's wife arrived at Hatfield. I refused to see or receive her, and was only persuaded thereto by Blanche who told me that the lady had come with baggage and two women, as if to stay. Bouncing to my feet, I rushed into the Great Hall, shouting for my servants to send Lady Tyrrwhit at once to me.

'What do you here, madam?' I screeched, before she was fairly through the screen door. 'Why are you here with your baggage? By whose permission do you dare enter here without my let?'

Curtseying, she attempted to answer, but I refused to listen, ordering her out box and barrel, yelling for my people to remove her.

'Nay, my love,' protested Blanche in a flutter, 'you cannot send Lady Tyrrwhit away — see, it is snowing — and besides, she is here by order of the Council.'

'What!' I screamed. 'Another creeping spy, another Council mammet to poke and pry, is that it?'

'Oh nay, nay, my Lady!' cried Lady Tyrrwhit. 'It is not of my wish, and indeed I am most unwilling to be your new mistress.'

At these words I was so enraged that I seized a pewter tankard and flung it to the floor, following it with all the moveable articles that I could hurl. My pincushion hit Lady Tyrrwhit and some reels of silk too. Jesus, I was in a passion, shrieking that only Kat was my mistress, and that I had not so demeaned myself that the puking, crawling Council needed to appoint another. At last, I ran to my bedchamber where I wept all that night.

The next day I sat by the fire in my solar, speaking to no one and eating nothing. I felt like enough to die. Indeed, I wished I had never been born, for my birth had brought naught but trouble. I felt as uncared-for, forlorn and harried as the veriest little bastard maid in the Kingdom, for all my royal blood. Nor was I all royal, but half only and therefore not worthy. Yet my brother, the King was but half royal also and he was eminently worthy. Then how dared they treat me so! I was the King's own sister, was I not? And second in the Succession was I not? Ay, I had been slandered, and this must not be, for the people might believe the slanders and think ill of me. My mind began to stir, to compose a letter to the Protector, and immediately my spirits lifted and grew calm.

I rose in the morning in better heart, taking some food and playing awhile on my clavichord while I arranged the phrases of the letter in my mind. When I went to my desk, the words flowed easily and I wrote that I objected to

Lady Tyrrwhit's governance over me, for I thought that slander might say that Mrs. Ashley was taken from me because of my light behaviour. I thanked the Council for offering to punish my slanderers, but declined to name them, for I did not wish to seem vengeful in the eyes of the people. I also enclosed a draft for a proclamation forbidding rumourous slander of the King's sisters. Surprisingly, the proclamation was made and my draft for it used.

The days crawled by. I could scarce be civil to Lady Tyrrwhit, for she was not Kat. Besides, she was Ma Mie's step-daughter by old Lord Brough and mistrusted me. I wished her far off and myself in Cathay.

At last the news came. Thomas was condemned to death. There was naught I could do for him, but I must think of Kat and Parry in danger and misery. So again I wrote to the Protector, interceding for them and begging his mercy for Kat, because she had taught me learning and honesty. I implied that the Protector would feel that if the King's best loved sister be ill thought of, it might sound badly on the King himself. All knew the King loved me dear and would not let me be treated ill. Moreover, I was exceeding popular, and any unkindness to me might cause disturbance in the land. The Protector knew this as well as I, and although he wrote back, somewhat sharply, telling me that I seemed to be too well assured of myself, Kat was released. She was forbidden to return to me, but I was not done yet, not by no means.

During the next few weeks it was as if all fell

still to await the Lord Admiral's death. I was strung tighter than a taut bowstring and twanged like one if any spoke ill of him, though I strove hard not to say overmuch and so give rise to evil suspicion. My nerves were bad and my temper was worse in those days. Lady Tyrrwhit's task was a heavy one, for I argued and quarrelled with all she said and saw hatefulness in her, whether or not. Now I realise that she was not unkind nor wishful to be, merely stiff-necked and humourless, with no understanding of such as I.

I could not truly believe that Edward would allow his own uncle to die. A blood bond surely was strong, or I felt so, and Thomas had always been good to him, showing a certain knowledge of the youthful mind. Thomas had done many foolish, even wicked things, but not enough for a nephew to consent to his death — oh, surely not. I was wrong. His nephew lifted no finger to save him, merely signing the warrant with a steady hand. On the twentieth of March 1549, Thomas Seymour, beautiful, virile, much hated and much loved, paid the penalty for his follies, losing his head to the executioner's axe.

That evening, they told me. A messenger had arrived for speech with Sir Robert Tyrrwhit. I showed little curiosity, being afeared to learn the news, but when Sir Robert entered the Long Gallery where the candles had just been lit, it was written in his compressed lips and knowing eyes. He came up to where I sat, picking at the keys of my clavichord and making a sorry twangling of it. He paused by his wife, sitting stitching by the fire, and I saw the lift of her eyebrows, followed by his nod. So it was done. My brain raced, trying to find a suitable phrase for my lips to utter that would conceal my anguish. He came over to me and I allowed my hands to fall as if carelessly from the keyboard and my eyes to look guilelessly up into his face, which showed a curious mixture of triumph, excitement and apprehension.

'Well, Sir Robert?' I said quietly. 'You wish to speak with me?'

'Ay, Madam,' he answered heavily. 'The Lord Admiral is sped. He met his death by execution this morning.'

My face felt frozen and expressionless, but the ready words rose to my lips, which mouthed them almost outside my own will.

'Is it so indeed?' I remarked. 'Then this day there died a man of much wit and little judgment,' and I turned back to my clavichord; but not before I had seen their looks of amazement. The memory of that look does me good still, by God it does! They stared at one another and back to me, as if I had turned black before their eyes. They got nothing out of me, witch's daughter that they plainly thought me. No young girl could have such unnatural command over herself unless she had recourse to spells and charms, so felt they.

My heart was not theirs for the handling. Nay, not anyone's. I am the daughter of Great Harry himself, and I bow down to none, nor ever will. They had forgot that, those Councillors, those Tyrrwhits. I have iron and steel in my blood and my father's kingly spirit in my heart. He and I gave way to no man. Nor do I now, nor will I, although my sun is setting.

★ ★ ★

This mirror into which I stare so long and deep, is framed in white enamel set with posies of jewels to simulate flowers. 'Twas give me long ago by dear, handsome Kit Hatton who loved me. Outside the casement, the wind is wild and rain spatters upon the glass. I stare at my wrinkled reflection and see it shake its head as if in amazement at its ancient ugliness, when once it was like a white blade crowned with fire. Well, I am still crowned with fire, but it is a false one, being a wig. Underneath it my hair is white, streaked with grey and rusty strands. When first I discerned grey in my hair, I had several wigs made in different colours and affected an increasing fancy for these. Thus, I made wigs the fashion so that even young women wore them. Who was then to say that the Queen was showing her mortality and turning grey like most elderly folk do, fight they never so hard against it?

Heigh-ho, I am tired of White Hall and would fain move off. First I will consult Dr. Dee, and if he agrees, I shall remove to Richmond. 'Tis a pretty place and far from the noise and stinks of London. I shall stay there for the spring, methinks, and watch the young leaves burgeon, if I am spared, although like poor Thomas, I may be cut down before mine eyes have glimpsed their beauty.

3

OUT, BRIEF CANDLE

1549 – 1553

Well, time passes and we with it. The darkness in my life lasted long enough to make me fear it would never end; but end it did, as all things do, praise be to Him who watcheth from on high. Sure, I thought His face was turned from me then, yet never did I wholly despair; my spirit would not let me, although at times I was hard enough put to it. Time and again I rose above mine enemies until I reached my appointed place, which was given to me by God and the people to hold until my stewardship runs out. Pray Jesu I relinquish it with ease and grace.

After Thomas's death I began to notice a lack of energy in myself. I seemed to tire quickly and oft I wept. My touchy appetite nigh forsook me altogether, my head ached constantly and my thoughts held naught but black hopelessness. Lady Tyrrwhit, though shy and reserved, tried to soothe me and raise my spirits. I would catch her eyes upon me, full of kindness and concern, and though I found her pedantry and primness irritating, I recognised and was grateful for her sympathy.

Soon I could not leave my bed, my heart was so low. Lady Tyrrwhit strove to cheer me, and one day showed me her collection of mottoes which were commonplace enough, but for one which I fancied. It was 'Be Always One.' I thought of it much and murmured the words to myself in Latin: '*Semper Eadem.*' I thought I would take it for mine own, and spoke of it to Lady Tyrrwhit, who was pleased to give it me. So I never forgot her, because, when I rose to my glory it became mine own device, used by myself alone.

Dear Roger Ascham came every day to my bedside, but I could not work. I had lost all desire, for my brain would hold nothing but my troubles and he was unable to rouse me. When the bright summer sun of that year shone down, I cared no more to live, nay, not even when the Lord Protector wrote to me that I was no longer under suspicion. He added his regrets for the news of my illness and that he was sending Dr. Bill to recover me. I cared not, for I had no voice of love to raise me, no dear familiar presence to comfort me, no one who knew my whole soul and loved me for what I was. I had drawn forth all I had in me and, without support, I could sustain my heart no longer. Lady Tyrrwhit did her best, but 'twas Kat Ashley I needed. Without her, I thought I would die.

One July morning when the sun's rays streamed through my chamber windows, lighting up the panelling, gilding the folds of my blue bed-curtains, Lady Tyrrwhit came rustling over the rushes, followed by a gentleman in the square cap, black robe and bands of a doctor. I gazed at them both, too dejected to lift my head from the pillow.

'Here is Dr. Bill, Lady Elizabeth,' said Lady Tyrrwhit encouragingly. 'Mayhap he can cheer you and cure you.'

His face was rosy and kind, smiling over a bright brown beard, his eyes brown and twinkling. 'Nay, my Lady,' he said in a fine, deep, resonant voice, 'it is a shame to see you abed this merry summer morning, and you so famous for your high step and high heart.'

I invited him to sit and he pulled a stool to my bedside, desiring to be alone with me. 'Your Ladyship mislikes that lady?' he asked, a twinkle in his eye, as Lady Tyrrwhit left us. I shrugged, offering no answer, staring languidly at the hangings. 'She is, perhaps, not sympathetic to your Ladyship?' he persisted.

'Oh, she is well enough. What matters it?'

'Well, you have no fever, no infection appearing in spots or pustules, so Lady Tyrrwhit tells me. Merely the headaches to which you are constitutionally subject, together with loss of appetite and great lassitude.'

'It is more than that,' I retorted, stung to protest. 'I cannot sleep, my limbs are feeble, and my headaches that you brush aside have worsened so severely that there is scarce a day when I am not retching and vomiting in agony. What difference does my liking or misliking Lady Tyrrwhit make in all this?'

'Is there another you would prefer?'

'Oh, tease me not, Dr. Bill. It does but increase my sorrow.'

'So my Lady Elizabeth does have another in

145

mind. Who is it, I wonder? I ask, because it seems to me as if a change of companion might wreak an improvement if not a cure. Ah, you look hopeful, your dull eyes brighten a little. Mayhap old Dr. Bill is on the right track, ha?'

'Well,' I said sadly, 'I had sworn not to think such thoughts, for I began to despair, longing so much for what I could not have.'

'It is as I thought,' he smiled, snapping his fingers. 'Your malady is of the spirit and the heart, and frets your brain with consequent effects upon your body. Now, for this, I prescribe plenty of fruit, wine and red meat gravy, also good fresh vegetables if you can eat them. That prescription is for your body. For your mind, I recommend a change of companion, preferably one known and loved by you, and who loves you well in return. I know of someone admirable who will fill the gap in your Ladyship's heart.'

Upset and agitated, I half rose in my bed. 'Nay!' I cried. 'Nay, good doctor, I want none of your choosing. There is but one for me, but one — ' and I fell to sobbing.

'Tell me,' he urged, 'that I may advise the Lord Protector, for he is feared for your life after hearing the Tyrrwhits' reports.' Leaning forward, he took my hand in his. 'My Lady Elizabeth,' he went on, soft and kind, 'is the one for whom you pine called Katherine Ashley?'

'Oh, Kat, Kat!' I wailed. 'Come back to me, or I die!'

'So!' announced Dr. Bill with the air of one who solves a deep and desperate problem. 'Then

Kat you shall have, or I am no true doctor. See thou, dear my lady, it may not be wrought all in a moment. It may take a se'ennight or two, but you shall have your Kat Ashley, I give you my word. We cannot have the King's lovely sister dying of a melancholy. What would England say? Nay, what would our foreign enemies say?'

At this I gave a feeble laugh and he fell into a fit of delight that I should do so, causing me to laugh again at him as he affected to dance a jig for pleasure. I promised to drink the wine and red gravy that he had ordered, and when he left, the sun's beams had a new light and warmth for me.

I have ever loved deep and strong, it is my way. Once my heart is gained it is never lost, no matter how buffeted, so long as the holder of it truly loves me in return. I give my love not lightly, nor to those who would not cherish it, but I give it for ever. I know not whom I resemble in this. Not my poor sister Mary, for she, though loving and faithful, chose to love those she could not trust and so reaped a harvest of gall more bitter than any she had known in all her sad life. Eh, it is strange how our patterns are writ for us to follow; how those, seemingly born with all, die cold and empty, and how those turning to life with the hand of Fate held against them, end their lives full of riches and respect. 'Tis a strange puzzle and one that I daresay will never be solved.

★ ★ ★

My Kat was returned to me by the end of the month and I took heart from then on, my health improving apace. At this time, there was a poor family suing for my help. I had been able to do but little for them by reason of my illness, but with the return of my strength I began once more to take an interest in those outside my gates. I wished to aid the poor woman, mother of many children, whose man was taken by the State and now lying a prisoner. I thought mayhap he could be exchanged for a Scot that I knew to be prisoned at Colchester, but where would I find one to assist me in this attempt? I asked Kat, still thin and pale from her detention in the Tower.

'Ay,' said she lazily, face upturned to the blue summer sky, for we were lying on cushions behind a box hedge, 'there is one who might give an ear to your suit. He holds the Protector's confidence and is not unsympathetic to a certain red-haired princess.'

'Ho,' I laughed, 'an unknown admirer, is it? What is his name and how do you know of him, Puss-Cat?'

'He is the Protector's own secretary, a young lawyer,' whispered Kat conspiratorially. 'It was he that good Dr. Bill came to for my release, saying that my darling would die if I did not return to her. He was deep distressed, going with Dr. Bill to the Protector and adding his words to those of the doctor.' Here the tears filled Kat's eyes and she snatched my hand in hers. 'Oh my love, how can I ever live with myself after I betrayed you? Sure, they tricked me, saying that Parry had confessed all when he had said naught, but I had promised to stand true until death. I am but a weakling and knew it not until I was tested. Oh, I am most bitter ashamed!'

I flung my arms around her. 'Kat, my dearest dear, cease your tears. We are all weak in our different ways and God loves and forgives us. So you must forgive yourself. Why we have near drowned in tears, the two of us, during these first days of your return. Let us now forget, and thank God for our deliverances. Please, Kat, for if you weep, I shall weep too.' I kissed her. 'Now tell me more of this young lawyer, for I have need of good friends.'

'His name is Master William Cecil, and he is most sober and earnest, with a grave, quiet demeanour, which hides, I believe, the most subtle brain and supple mind.'

'He is for me, you say?'

'Ay, he says he is for the right, no matter in what guise it appears.'

'A useful fellow,' I murmured, chewing a grass blade. 'I would know more of him.' Pausing, I flashed Kat an impish grin. 'Is he well-looking?'

'Incorrigible thou art!' she cried. 'Well, he is not, being short and thin, with the worried look all lawyers seem to acquire. His hair is brown, his skin sallow, but he has beautiful eyes — large, brown and very bright. They are full of soul, Madam.'

'And you think this soulful lawyer would help me?'

'It is worth trying, love.'

'Well then, Kat, do you write the letter, for I

am weary.' In truth I was, for it took but little to tire me. I was content to lie in the sun, breathing in the scent of the box hedges and the rose garden they enclosed, pillowed on my blue and rose cushions, wearing a loose robe of maize-coloured tissue bound with gold, dabbling my fingers in the cool grass. 'Do you write it,' I repeated, 'and I will add a word or two at the end.'

So Kat wrote a graceful letter, that evening, to Mr. Secretary Cecil. 'Ha!' she said suddenly, quill upraised, 'I had forgot. Cecil is related to poor Parry. I meant to tell you. I daresay he will see to it that Parry is restored to us before long. Now my pet, the letter is done. Here is the pen.'

Taking it, I wrote: 'I pray you further this poor man's suit. Your friend, Elizabeth.'

And what I asked was done.

In the next month, near to my birthday, Parry returned. 'Twas as good as a gift, indeed, and I had Master Cecil to thank for it. Yet, ever after, I examined the accounts myself and signed my name at the bottom of each page, for I had learned a lifelong lesson in care and supervision.

As my vitality asserted itself, I was able to spend more time with Roger Ascham at my books. We did much translation, and held converse in French, Italian, Spanish, Latin and Greek, for I was fluent in all. Of all my studies I loved History the best, and would spend hours a day at it. Ascham was pleased with me in all I did. He even praised my dress, for at this time I judged it best to eschew all show and appear as plain as possible. My hair, too, I did plain, combing it straight to fall down my back, sometimes catching it into a knot when I went riding.

Although my general health improved, my headaches grew no better, and oft I could not work for days at a time, unable even to dictate a letter to my dear brother. When I could, I wrote to him in Latin with my own hand, to reassure him that I loved him ever, even though at times I might be too unwell to write, reminding him that I had been his fondest sister since he was a babe.

Edward wished much to see me, and resented my being kept from him, for this is how it was. His Uncle Protector feared my popularity and influence with the people and my brother. Edward felt that his uncle understood him not at all, caring for his kingship only, and disregarding his personal feelings.

Times were not easy, moreover, for there was unrest all over the country, even in London itself. My messengers brought this news to me. I heard that men in Devon and Cornwall had risen against Cranmer's new English prayer book, which offended their feelings. Those in East Anglia and Kent rioted against enclosures which took away their common grazing land; while in London there was great dissatisfaction against the Protector himself. He had caused St. Margaret's Church in the City to be demolished, and worse than this, had taken the North Cloister of St. Paul's for the building of his new mansion along the Strand. Somerset House was this palace to be called, and the stones for it had come, not only from St. Paul's and St. Margaret's but from the old Priory Church at Clerkenwell Village and St. Mary-le-Strand also. The Londoners were enraged at this despoliation, and loud was the grumbling and groaning.

Meanwhile, John Dudley, now Earl of Warwick, father to my good friends Mary and Robert Dudley, had newly returned from a successful campaign against the rebels in Scotland and was much thought of as a leader of men. He was thus sent off to put down the Norfolk rebellion, which was led by the brothers Will and Robert Ket. This he had done most severely, hanging both brothers after all was over. Robert swung from the walls of Norwich Castle and Will from the spire of Wymondham Church. Then Dudley rode back in triumph, for after his Scottish victories he had become a popular hero. In London, most folk cared little about miseries in country parts, land enclosures having small interest for those dwelling in a great city. Dudley's star seemed to be rising and I wondered what would come of it, for there could not be two risen stars upon the same Council.

I was not to wonder long, for in the November of that year, Edward Seymour, Duke of Somerset, Lord Protector of the Realm, was sent to the Tower. His place was taken by the Earl of Warwick, said my messenger giving me the news.

'What!' I exclaimed. 'Is John Dudley now the Protector?'

'Nay, Madam, not he,' answered the lad, on one knee. 'He says he is too modest to take such a title to himself.'

'He modest?' I cried. 'The heavens would fall rather! How has this happened, Jack? Sure, you must know, 'tis your business. Come, get up off your knees and tell me.'

So bidden, Jack rose to his feet, his fair face still grey with the cold ride from London, his yellow hair blown from the wind. 'Well, my lady, 'tis thus. After Warwick's victory of Pinkiecleugh in Scotland, he picked out some two hundred men to whom he promised double wages for bravery in the field. The Protector refused to pay the double wages.'

'Why so? 'Twas presumptuous in Warwick to promise this without permission, but only a fool would have refused to grant such a request.'

'Just so, Madam. The Protector said that the men's self sacrifice could not be rewarded with filthy lucre. He said that prayers of thanksgiving would be more in keeping and better for the soul.'

'He would!' I cried. 'And this, of course, is held against him.'

'Ay, Madam. Against him with the people, who cry out at such ingratitude to the brave soldiers, and against him with Warwick who was made to look a fool.'

'And who whipped up popular feeling, no doubt,' I murmured.

'Indeed so, my Lady. The Protector, feeling his position threatened by Warwick, determined to raise an army to show his own strength. He had bills posted about the country, calling for men to rise to the defence of the King and the Lord Protector.

But Warwick had been before him all the way, and but a handful of men came to Duke Somerset's call. Then the Duke decided to ride with the King by night to Windsor where the defences were stronger than at Hampton Court.'

'By night? In November? What of my brother's health?'

'He had caught a cold before the ride, my Lady. Now he is abed with a fever.'

'Oh, the poor lamb, it is too bad! Come now, what next?'

'Lord Warwick used the fact of the King's fever to show that the Protector had not sufficient regard of the King's person. Moreover, all the Lords of the Council were dissatisfied with the Protector and were ready to believe Warwick's promises,' continued Jack. 'The Duke of Norfolk had resented the Protector's position, calling him a Johnny-Jump-Up, he being not of the old nobility.'

'And yet Norfolk would follow Warwick, a lawyer's son? Jesu, what times are these! Such doings almost make me favour the Protector, 'faith they do. What of my brother now, Jack?'

'His health is not good, Madam, and for this the Protector is blamed. The King has little love for Windsor, so to please him, Lord Warwick took him back to Hampton Court, where he is petted and indulged and told nothing.'

I sent Jack off to the kitchens for a warming wine posset, for now I wished to think. Pacing up and down the Long Gallery, as much for warmth as to keep time with my hurrying thoughts, kicking the rushes out of the way as I walked and hearing them

154

rustle under the hem of my gown, I knew now for whom Thomas had been done to death and Edward Seymour put away. And I knew too that this same one would not hesitate to destroy me if I made any false move. At last I ceased my restless pacing, pausing at one of the tall windows. Sinking down on the window-seat, I gazed through the panes to the world outside, grey and leafless in the darkling afternoon. What of my friends, Mary and Robert Dudley? It would be long before I saw them again, perhaps never. Would I be held from my brother? I could not tell. England's enemy, thus mine too, stood revealed. I had known and distrusted him all my life. John Dudley Earl of Warwick, loving father, doting husband, cold, calculating, heartless towards his fellow men and power-mad. He was the one to fear. I knew it now.

I sat on and on in the window-seat, thinking of my great father and how he would have crushed the upstart as none in these times knew how. My father had understood men as Edward Seymour would never do in all his now undoubtedly numbered days. Young as I was, I too understood men, and so I feared did John Dudley, or how else could he have climbed so high? I resolved to lie quiet as never before, for I meant to live, not to meet my Maker by way of an axe.

Kat and the candles came in together. She cried out at seeing me sitting so still on my cushions, asking why and wherefore?

'Matters of state,' I answered with a glimmering smile.

'Ah, you must not bother you pretty head with

155

such weighty affairs,' she cried rallyingly.

'I must,' said I, 'for I wish to keep it.'

* * *

Christmas and Twelfth Night came and went, winter merged into late-come spring. In April we heard that the one-time Lord Protector was released from his prison and re-admitted to a place on the Council. We were packing up to remove to Ashridge when the messages came.

'Ho!' said Blanche, struggling with a jewel casket. 'So his Lordship is out again. Back on the Council too! Curse this casket, it will not shut!'

'You have overfilled it, stupid. Give it here,' said I taking it from her and sorting over the contents whilst my women swirled about me, running here and there with rolled up bedding and hangings, chattering like magpies. 'See, Blanche,' I went on, 'it is these two big clasps. You must take them out and put them in another box. And be careful or you will dislodge the pearls from their setting in this one and then they will be as difficult to replace as the Duke into the Council.'

'Sure he will have but a lowly position thereon,' chirruped one of my ladies. 'Does your Ladyship wish this yellow gown put with the grey one and the rose?'

'Ay Anna, lay them all together. You are right about the Duke. Methinks he will not last long in any place.'

Ashridge was pleasant that spring and early summer. Not as dear as Hatfield, but most

156

charming. It was necessary to leave Hatfield to be sweetened, for I had been living there for some months, and it is not good to dwell too long in any one palace, no matter how well run, for after a month or two it grows noisome and stinking.

'Twas from Ashridge I sent my latest portrait to my brother as soon as it was finished. I was not overly enamoured of it, but it was like enough in its way. Methought I looked too grim and glum, but mayhap that was all for the best, for I did not wish to present an impression of frivolity. The hair turned out well, and the hands, so I sent it, putting with it a note saying that I wished it were truly myself and not a poor canvas copy that was sharing his company. This I meant verily, for I longed to see little Ned again to mark how he had grown in body and mind. Yet I did not press to visit him, for I judged the time to be not ripe. He expressed the wish to see me in every letter he wrote, but I felt there were those about him who held not my interest at heart. I thought it better to wait for a suitable opportunity than to race hot-foot and unpolitic to Court. I wished not to do my cause harm with my brother, nor with the world. There were still many who would be all too ready to point the finger at me for a lightsome jade, rather than respect me for the modest figure of rectitude and learning that I wished to show, so I would wait as I knew so well how to do.

That summer of 1550, John Dudley had himself created Duke of Northumberland, as befitted the virtual ruler of England. He had climbed higher on other men's shoulders and his eventual downfall, when it came, was steep and swift as so often happens with self-elevated men. But now, while his star was high, he took for his secretary William Cecil, who silently allowed himself to be filched from his post with Duke Somerset. Kat was put out at this.

'Such disloyalty!' she protested when she heard the news. 'How can one trust such a spine-bender who changes his coat to the colour of whomever is in power?'

'Well,' I said, 'it may seem so, I grant you. But did you not tell me Kat, that he was for the right, no matter what shape it took?'

'So you think that the Duke of Northumberland is right?' Kat dropped a lapful of gilt buttons in her start of agitation, and we had to scrabble for them.

'Nay, he is not right,' I laughed, as we bumped heads beneath a chair, 'but do you not see that if Cecil is his secretary, right may yet be done?' Kat looked puzzled and I sat back on my heels, the better to explain. 'Who knows what secret wickednesses may be wrought by one such as Dudley? And who will be in a position to know, eh, Kat? And who will, I am sure, send messages, also secretly, to those concerned, if the right of the Succession be threatened?'

Kat scrambled to her feet, her dear face thoughtful. 'Think you it may come to that then?'

'I do,' I answered. 'For see, Northumberland, as he is now to be called, can keep his place only while my brother is subject to him or married to one of his creatures. Failing an heir from Ned, Northumberland would get but short shrift from Mary or me. He knows that well, so he may try to alter the Succession. It could be done, believe me. Secrecy and trickery may accomplish what honesty and truth cannot, as Cecil himself knows.'

'Marry!' exclaimed Kat. 'What times we live in!'

'Ay, 'tis a tortuous web, and woven tight about the King, I fear. Come now Kat, put away those buttons and come riding with me. The packing will be done as well without us. Let us forget politics and enjoy the sweet air while we may.'

* * *

Soon after this I was to learn the usefulness of having a friend such as Cecil at Court, for £3,106 a year came to me to maintain my state as a princess. With this came also the title deeds of various manors, Ashridge and mine own Durham House, which pleased me greatly.

With the ending of the summer I moved back to Hatfield, and there it was that Roger Ascham came to me, asking to be released from service, for he had secured an appointment as Secretary to the Ambassador at the Court of my sister's cousin, the Emperor Charles V in Germany. I let him go with my dear and affectionate blessing.

He kissed my hands, murmuring as he always did about 'his brightest star,' which warmed my heart as all praise and acclaim did, and still does for that matter. My taste for it has never lessened, even though in these days I am praised more for my age and ability to survive. Better that, say I, than naught. It is more than vanity; it is a deep and fearful need. Nowadays it takes the place of love, for those I loved are gone; it takes the place of friendship, for those I called my friends are gone; it takes the place of beauty, for that is crumbled away. All that is left is flattery and acclaim. I know it for what it is, but when I hear the shouts of the folk who have come out to see me pass, I know that I am still alive and not yet but an ancient shell.

In my birth month of September I fell ill with a high fever and had to take to my bed. I sadly wished to see my brother, and wept as much to Kat, who spent all her days and most of her nights at my bedside. When I recovered somewhat, I bethought me of William Cecil and determined to request a visit to the King through him.

'I shall write myself,' I said weakly but firmly to Kat, who was clucking over me and shaking her head. 'I will so, Kat. Bring me pen and paper now, and I will write to Duke Dudley, shaky though my hand may be. Let him see that I am ill — why not?'

I sent for Thomas Parry and gave him my instructions. 'Tom,' I said, when he came bowing to my bedside, 'listen to what I have to say to you.' I shook my letter in his face. 'Here is a letter from me to His Grace of Northumberland. I wish it to be sent to Cecil in a letter of your own. I want you to write to Cecil yourself and tell him that I am well assured that he doth not forget me. Parry write indeed that I *assure* myself thereof. Remember this, for I wish him to know that I trust him and that he has a true friend in me. That is my own message to him, but I would rather it were writ in your hand. 'Tis safer and he will understand my meaning. Repeat the message man, for I would you make no mistakes.'

So the letters and the message went, and during the following months they wrought to such good effect that I was invited to Court on the seventeenth of March in 1551. That winter passed happily, full of preparation for the coming visit. I charged Kat to keep my gowns plain, unbejewelled and with little ornament, for I wished to look the antithesis of anything that could be called lightsome or whorish. Yet I wished the colours to be those that suited me best and showed off my colouring. In this way I knew I could stand out in any throng, jewels or no.

We left Hatfield on a brilliant spring morning, having several days in which to get to London, for I meant to travel in state with a large retinue, as befitted the King's sister, so my pace would be something slow, although I meant to stop only one night each at Mimms, Barnet and Highgate.

At Highgate I rested at the Bishop's Park, Bishop Bonner's fine palace, now without a master to welcome me. He was at that time in the Marshalsea Prison for refusing to accept the King, a minor, as Head of the Church, stiff-necked old cleric that he was!

Upon the morning after my night's rest at the Park, I stared long at my reflection in the polished steel mirrors held up by six of my ladies and was satisfied. So that the people could see me easily I had chosen a gown of creamy satin with silver beads. No broidery, no jewels upon it. I wore my hair in a smooth coil over each ear, and upon it a small flat cap called a pipkin, made from the satin of my gown. I perched it on the top of my head, slanted a little over my left eye, where it looked at once dashing and demure.

Then the time for departure coming, we hustled outside, and I mounted my pretty white mare, holding her steady as my people grouped around me. I saw their faces upturned and heard a concerted sigh of admiration like the wind through a cornfield. I was to hear that sigh often enough in later life, but this was the first time. I knew then that I had inherited that quality of attraction from my father; a born-in splendour that drew all eyes in approval. Certes, I knew how to set it off to best advantage, but all would have been useless had I not possessed this appeal to begin with. Poor Mary never had it, nor did my little brother, sweet young King that he was. Mary wished to and could not, Edward did not wish to and could not, I cared not and did. Fate willed it so.

Brisk and fresh that morn was I, after a good night spent in Bishop Bonner's own bed in his goodly house on the top of Highgate Hill. The hooves of my mare struck sparks from the cobbles as she pranced and fidgeted, eager to be off. We passed through the gate and out on to the road. While Parry paid the toll-keeper at the Gatehouse, I reined in my mare to view the panorama of London spread before me in the valley below.

There it lay, gilded by the early morning sun. I could discern, in tiny clarity, the Tower white-gleaming, huddled by the silver ribbon of the Thames; the slender wooden spire of St. Paul's reaching to the heavens from Ludgate Hill, the dark cross-stroke that was London Bridge, the tree-crowned hills of Surrey, the chequered fields of Kent and the river-girdled curve of green beyond which was Greenwich and my birthplace, the palace of Placentia. My London — nay, not mine, not yet — maybe never mine, but there it lay, circled by its wall, guarded by its nine gates, waiting now for me.

'On!' I cried. 'Forward — to London!'

Down the hill we trotted, laughing, calling and chattering. Still I gazed about me, for I could never look enough upon this sight. To the west I could just see the peaked roofs of Westminister Hall and the Abbey and a pale blur that I knew was Archbishop Cranmer's palace at Lambeth. This was in my direction for I was bound for St. James's, that 'house in the fields,' built by my father for my mother long ago. I lifted up my voice and sang for joy.

'*Sing we now merrily, our purses are empty,*' I carolled, '*Hey Ho!*' And my people joined me in singing the catch all a-down West Hill to Kennistoune. Then we took the right fork and rode down the lane, leaving Totten Court and St. Giles on our left, with the trees in bud and the sun glancing from thatch to hedgerow as we reached the fence of the park, wherein lay the palace of St. James and my darling brother. Swinging away

163

to the right we made for the park gate, and my heart beat high as I thought of the meeting and of all who would be there, ready, I doubted not, to point the finger, to titter behind the hand. Well, they should see; and when they had done so they would gossip no more, for gossip cannot live if rumour be proved false. Once through the gate, I saw that the way had been strewn with fine sand. Sure, all was being done to mark my arrival and in spite of my nervousness, I grinned to myself to notice the number of stately persons mustered to greet me with ceremony at the Court Gate, all bowing with wondrous civility.

Pausing in my chamber only long enough to make tidy, I went in state, hearing my name and rank called before me as I made my way up the Hall. Whispers I heard, pointing fingers and nudges I saw, but of mocking smiles there were none. The lords and ladies all swept down to make obeisance, rising again after my passing like the billows of the sea. I, too, swept down to curtsey the full three times as directed by protocol, as I moved towards the Throne and my brother. Swiftly did we clasp and embrace and swift did the tears slip down our cheeks, no matter who saw, for we cared not. He had grown, my little Ned; near as tall as I was he, and he but thirteen.

'So tall!' I exclaimed, between tears and smiles. 'So tall that I would not have known you, my love.'

'Nay, sweetest Bess, I am still the same. Come, sit ye here beside me. Let us share our joy. You look more bright and beautiful even than I remembered. You put all the ladies to shame, I swear!'

He promised to be a long lad and his voice had lost its shrillness, being now low and husky, cracking every so oft, for he was approaching manhood. As we chatted, I appraised him and liked not what I saw, for delicate he looked, frail and sickly, as if there were no strength in him. Ah, little Ned, you are gone and my turn to go comes soon. Perhaps we shall meet again in Heaven.

On this bright day we sat knee to knee, his hand 'twixt both of mine. His hand was hot. I remarked upon it.

'Oh sister, you sound like dear old Mother Jack!' he laughed. 'She is forever prating of 'too hot' and 'too cold,' and right weary I grow of it. 'Twas but a chill I had and it hangs about me still, a little. It is naught, let us forget it and talk of you and me, or of you rather, for you are far lovelier than the likeness you sent me. You stand out here like a bright goddess, for all you are dressed so plain and your hair combed so smooth. Bess, I am so very glad to see you. Are you recovered from your grievous sickness? It was truly your illness that kept you from me, was it not?' I assured him of this, and he leaned towards me and whispered in my ear, the feathers in his cap tangling with my hair. 'They said,' he muttered, his breath warm on my cheek, 'they said you were lightsome and no fit company for me, I being young and a King. They said you were pregnant by mine Uncle Thomas. They said you cared only for frivolity.'

'They said much, did they not?' I remarked drily.

165

'What else did they say?'

'They said no man could be safe with you. They said you were a witch and poisoned ladies' hearts by spells and magic.'

Smiling, I turned my head and kissed his cheek. 'And did you believe these stories?'

Ever truthful, he paused to consider his answer. 'I was sorely puzzled,' he said at last, fixing his blue eyes on mine. Sad and haunting was their stare and my heart twisted in my breast with love and compassion. 'Oft I asked to see you, nay, demanded it, but it seems that even Kings can be too young to be obeyed when it suits not those around them. Yet I could not believe it, not of you my dearest sister; and now I see you so proud, so pure, so much as ever you were, my heart is calmed.'

'I am glad,' said I, 'for I did no wrong.'

He lifted his head, his eyes burning. 'Marriage is holy!' he exclaimed violently. 'The Scriptures tell us so. Lust is evil; it is a deadly sin! Sister, you have been but an innocent brand snatched from the burning and I rejoice that you are saved untouched and unsullied.' His expression softened to tender boyishness. 'Indeed, I fear I would have pined and died if it had not been so.'

'Let us forget it,' I reassured him. 'Despite all rumour, I am virgin still, and here we are together at last, brother. Hey, we should make merry for happiness so long withheld!'

His pale face flushed with excitement as he began to recount his plans for my daily enjoyment. I was a little alarmed at his religious fervour, but

166

relieved that he could still take pleasure in some frivolities. 'Did'st enjoy Mary's visit?' I asked after a moment.

'She left the day before you came, Bess. Well, she is old and so misguided in her religion. 'Twas sad, but we could agree upon nothing. I did not enjoy her company at all. Northumberland's men, nay, Cranmer himself, could not move her when they examined her and talked with her on holy matters. And Bess, what thinkest thou? She pities me because she says I have the wrong religion and will go to Purgatory when I die. As if a King could go to Purgatory! Besides, it is *her* religion which is wrong and I told her so. But I could not move her, not one whit! Some say,' he lowered his voice to a whisper, putting his mouth close to my ear, 'that I should cut off her head!' He leaned back to observe the effect of his words upon my face and I must have shown some concern, for he nodded solemnly. 'I knew you would be shocked,' he said. 'But I cannot do it, for until I marry and sire an heir, she is after me in the Succession, and she is my sister, though very old. I fear, Bess, what would result if I should die of a sudden and Mary became Queen. She will never change her wicked beliefs and England would be forced back into Catholicism and evil, with certain promise of hell-fire and the pit for all. I do worry greatly Bess. I must not let this happen.'

'Oh Ned,' I cried, 'you are but thirteen! Why, you will wed and have many fine sons. Sure, poor Mary will die long before you. She is thirty-four already and in weak health.' Yet in my heart I feared too, for he looked to me not of the sort to make old bones.

'Nay,' he said seriously, 'death is with us always. We should keep ourselves holy for fear he whisks us away all unknowing; and I should be mindful of such matter, for I am betrothed. Did'st know that, my Bess?'

'Yea, I knew, for the news had reached me,' I confessed, smiling. 'My messengers keep me well supplied with information about you, my dearest. You are seldom from my thoughts.'

He kissed my hands and went on to tell me that his betrothed was the Princess Elisabeth of France, rich, and therefore preferable as a bride to his cousin Jane, daughter of Duke Somerset. At my look of surprise, he informed me that the idea had come to naught because it had been said that Protector Somerset had wished for the marriage to Jane in order to gain control of Edward and the Throne.

'You know, Bess,' he continued, 'I do grow so weary of Uncle Edward's prosing. I feel I am never my own master when I am with him.'

'And do you now?' I queried.

'Much more so,' he answered with enthusiasm. 'My Lord Northumberland sees to it that I am no longer treated as a child. He says the French marriage is fitter for one of my rank.'

Here was Northumberland's influence yet again. It seemed to me that Ned's uncle had truly a grievous enemy, bent on his downfall. I resolved to cross no swords with Northumberland if I valued my life and future. Looking out across the assembly, the sounds of laughter and chatter fairly drowning those of the musicians in their gallery, I caught sight of the Duke himself. A full head above the others he stood, his black eyes fixed upon me. They held no warmth, no friendship, yet neither did they express menace or warning. It was a look of thoughtful assessment. For a second I stiffened, then graciously bowed my head. He bowed his own, a flickering half-smile playing for a moment round his wide mouth. I understood the message of that meaning smile only too well. My enemy had declared himself. For the time being, I would retreat. I turned back to my brother who sat, unconscious of this byplay, in his carved chair of state.

'And how will you like this marriage, think you?' I said smoothly as if I had felt no shock of knowledge in my breast.

Ned wrinkled his nose. 'To tell truth, Bess, I like not the idea at all. 'Tis not the lady,' he amended hurriedly, ' 'tis the state, you understand.' I raised my brows enquiringly and Edward gestured to the company to step back from us. 'We have matters to discuss with our sister that is for our heart and hers alone. Back, we say,' he ordered.

Obediently they moved back, meaning looks exchanged as they did so. And as the Court talked, called and laughed about us, Edward confided to me his fear of the married state and his wish to remain unspotted before God. I endeavoured to soothe and reassure him, but he shook his head frowning, as he pursued his subject.

'Yea, but I think I should marry and get sons to

keep the realm safe from Mary and her false beliefs. I fear to marry, but I fear not to. So sometimes I wonder,' he hurried on, 'if 'twere better to alter the Succession. I could use my kingly powers to have it done, for I am the monarch after all, and at the last, my word is the final one.'

Northumberland had wasted no time. Inwardly I shivered, imagining the turmoil such an action would precipitate. There would be a great rebellion, I was sure, for Catholic or not, my sister had the right as the only surviving child of my father's first wife. Our people do not like injustice, and even little Ned might suffer at their hands for empowering an injustice of this magnitude. So I advised him to use great caution on this serious matter and not allow himself to be rushed in any way. Because the words were mine, they calmed him and he let the dangerous subject go to my great relief, bringing his mind to merrier things, for suddenly he turned in his chair, beckoning and eager.

'Oh see, sister, there is my dear Henry Sidney. Come hither, Harry, I would present you to the Princess Elizabeth.'

I beheld a pleasant, square-faced gentleman with a smile so infectious that I returned it instantly. Edward told me that he was of Penshurst Place in Kent and was to be married in a few days to Mary Dudley, friend of my childhood. 'Their marriage is to be soon and private, for they are mad in love, but they will have a public one later and then we shall have rare junketings, eh, Harry, my friend?'

I was afire with eagerness to see Mary and

soon Sir Henry brought her to me. Forbearing all ceremony, I rose, kissed her and asked her fondly how she did. Lovely did she look then, my dearest Mary, blushing with joy to be with her Harry and with excitement at seeing me. A steadfast friend was she to prove in the years to come, and this to her sorrow and mine, for in nursing me of the smallpox, she was to take it from me and lose her looks for ever. So hideous did it render her that she wore a veil over her face for the rest of her days. But this lay all in the future; we guessed naught of such evil mischance at this merry time in our lives. Viewing her now, I saw that she had grown tall and like her dark, handsome father — a beautiful girl indeed. She said that I was expected to be present at her wedding at Esher on the twenty-ninth of March.

Later, when I had begged Ned's reluctant permission to retire to my chamber, I sent Kat to fetch Mary Dudley. She came in all haste and delight and we embraced joyfully.

'You look wonderful, Princess — Madam — Bess!' she exclaimed. 'I knew you would grow in beauty.'

At that we fell a-laughing. 'All princesses are beautiful!' we shouted in chorus and laughed again.

'Nay but it is true!' protested Mary. 'Hey, I wonder what our Rob would say to you now.'

'He saw me last June,' I said coolly. 'I was at his wedding. He had no eyes for me then, why should he have now?'

Mary smiled. 'Ay, but that was last year. A year

can change much, and it has changed you from a mouse to an eaglet.'

'Mayhap you are right,' I shrugged. 'But I have hardened in the changing, Mary.'

'One must survive,' she said.

'Is Robert so soon tired of his marriage that he would already have eyes for any other than his plump, snub-nosed wife?' I asked.

'Indeed he is,' answered my friend, 'for she is so stupid — a real country cabbage. Her father has some means, but little above the ordinary. She was no catch.'

'Not wealthy? Then why did he marry her?'

'Oh, it was for love, Bess, as he always promised.'

'Mighty short-lived then,' said I. 'Are you sure it was a love-match? Mayhap she was pregnant?'

'No fear of that, she is virtue itself. Sure, he desired her and could get her no other way save through marriage, and she was as hot as he. And, you know, Bess, that our father can never bear to refuse any of us, he is such a fond parent, so he let Rob have her.'

'And love was naught but swift-cooling passion. Unlucky Rob. What is her name? I have forgot. Amye or Emele or some such?'

'Amye Robsart, she was. Unlucky Rob indeed, for having satisfied himself upon her body, he has found that she has nothing in her head, and so grows bored and restless. Now he moans of naught but disappointment and disillusion as if they were new discoveries, poor Rob. You will see him at my wedding, Bess. Do you like my Harry? Is he not adorable? Oh, I cannot wait for the day. If I am

172

not careful I shall play at naught with him and be pregnant when I marry. But truly, I would go to it virgin, and so I must fight with myself and him!'

* * *

My meeting with Rob I remember well. It was near a year since I had seen him, and through the days that passed until Mary's wedding I amused myself at odd times with wondering about him. I own that I felt excitement for the day of the marriage, and not for Mary's sake alone, although I kept these thoughts to myself.

The twenty-ninth dawned fine and brilliant and I was full of anticipation. Would Robert Dudley think me as beautiful as he had once promised I should be? Would his feelings be as easy and friendly to me as they had been when we were children? Sure, I had seen him at his own marriage when he had had no eyes for me, but only for his new wife. He had stirred me greatly then, for I had found him right desirable, wishing that I could have been in the place of his bride, yet afeared at the thought. But the thought had recurred often during the past year, and now I was to see him again. Oh Rob, my dear love, when our eyes met on that day, I scarce knew where I was or what I said. All is a jumble save the part you and I played, and that was short enough.

Tall, long-legged and broad shouldered, you came forward with that easy, swinging step you never lost, most elegant in murrey and silver. Black hair, black eyes, dark aquiline face, there stood my

173

fate, my beautiful Rob. I put out my hand, feeling proud of its tapering whiteness.

'Give you good day, Lord Robert,' I said airily. 'Well met indeed after so long.'

He took my hand and kissed it, his eyes never leaving mine. 'Even as I foretold,' he murmured, low. 'You have grown to be beautiful and more than beautiful. I knew it when we were young.'

'Is your wife with you, Lord Robert?' I asked loud and clear. 'I should be pleased to have her presented.'

He released my hand and stood upright, laughter twinkling in his eyes. 'Nay, Madam, she is not with me,' he said as loud and as clear. 'She is shy and feared of crowds and grand occasions.'

'You have left her in the country?'

'Ay, she is happier there. But me, I could not miss my sweet sister's marriage day. Now it is brighter still because of you.'

'Well, you may escort me awhile,' I replied, mighty calm and cool. 'I wish to walk about, and it will be pleasant to talk over old times with you.'

And that was all we did. I dared not admit how deep was his attraction for me, nor acknowledge mine for him, for the shadow of Thomas over my life was too near and too black for me to do aught or even think aught that might lead me from the path I had chosen at this time. I saw Rob again at the public ceremony at Ely Place, Holborn, at Whitsuntide. We talked polite prattle only in spite of his eyes and hot glances and my fluttering heart. That was the last I saw of him for many a long day and I trained my thoughts to dwell not upon him.

I stayed at Court for several months. It was good to be popular, my looks and style admired, my words respected. I succeeded in keeping my thoughts under a strict cover of smiling blandness, having spent my life doing so. Duke Northumberland watched me closely as I was amply aware. It was as if he waited to pounce at one careless word or false move. When I thought back to my childhood and recalled the merry hours with his children, yea and with him too, I wondered at the ways of ambition. Handsome he still was, though old, being over fifty years, yet none would have guessed it. He was a very proper man and fit for any lady's bed, for all he had eyes only for his wife. She must have enjoyed him, lucky jade.

His son was as proper a man, God rest his dear soul. My sweet Rob, how I wish that our ways might have been different, for of all men, you were he whom I would have wed had I not been what I am. Yet for all that, I would not truly have wished to be any other, dream as I might. Rob and I, we had our happy times and our loving times when the world and its cares were forgot. Oh ay, we did, although none would believe, to look at me now, that I had lain full oft in the arms of the handsomest man in the land. Well, I loved him and he knew it. And he loved me. 'Twas known by all and I cared not a straw for their head-waggings and moanings. I treated him hardly, I know, but I could not do otherwise, being how and what I was. Alas, he has died and left me near fifteen years agone and I have missed him every moment of each day since his passing, my darling Rob.

Sweet Jesu, so appealing as he was; the total of such manly beauty as ever I saw. Why, I could scarce keep my hands from him, or forbear kissing him for all to see! We lit a flame between us that would not die, for although he is gone, my ancient heart beats high still at his memory and the leaden tears of old age slip down my cheeks to the ruin of the white paint laid upon them.

His father, though hot for his wife, was cold in all else as my Rob could never be. His father watched and planned and moved men and women about like pawns on a chess-board. Well, he would not so move me, I swore it . . .

Spring wore into summer and merry was the time my brother and I spent. It was warming to me to see little Ned shed his serious ways and laugh and romp as any boy should. During this time, upon one brilliant day when all were out a-riding or playing games, Ned lay abed with the headache. I had stayed indoors to be near him, to comfort him and also to bathe the styes upon his eyes to which he was subject. Having performed this task, I was on my way through an empty ante-chamber, when I saw the King's uncle, the onetime Lord Protector, approaching me. As we came abreast I gave him good-day and made to pass on, but he stayed me, desiring to speak with me. I stared at him coldly, wishing not to stop.

' 'Tis of the King and my brother Thomas,' he pleaded. 'I must speak, for I fear my time here runs out apace.'

'What, are you ill?' I asked.

'Nay,' he replied sighing. 'Mine enemies would see me sped, I mean. Will you hear me, Lady Elizabeth?'

'Very well,' said I. 'We can talk here, 'tis all deserted, none is by to eavesdrop and gossip.'

We sat ourselves upon the padded crimson velvet window seats, the casements themselves standing open to admit the sunshine and sweet air. Then he spoke of his brother, saying that there were those who had wanted Thomas dead and himself dishonoured to serve their own ends. He said that Thomas had been kept from him and the little King's signature put to the death warrant before ever he, Somerset, realised what plots were being hatched under his unseeing eyes. He told me that Ned had been turned against him by unscrupulous men who were eyeing him askance now that the King was looking more kindly upon him. He said that he was divulging these things so that I might beware for Ned and myself. The tears ran down his cheeks as he spoke, and I swear that at that moment I was nearer to liking Edward Seymour than ever before in my life.

'Oh my Lord,' I said kindly, 'now that you have spoken to me, I bear you no ill will, for I see how it was. I will not grow too high to listen to the misfortunate, nor will I hearken only to mine advisers at the expense of my heart.'

'I am glad to have had speech with you, Princess,' he replied. 'I would not be at outs with you who love the King. I would set all straight, but my time is short.' Upon this we parted, he kissing my hand

177

and I laying my other hand upon his shoulder, for indeed we were both joined by our kinship and love for our Sovereign.

Following hard upon this meeting with the Duke of Somerset came the seventh of September and my eighteenth birthday with merry feastings and junketings. I had meant to speak to my brother about his uncle, but was too much caught up in gaieties and forgot it for a while. In October, the news that he had been sent to the Tower jogged my memory uncomfortably, and I spoke of the matter to Ned. He listened to me as he always did, seriously and with interest.

'Well sister, I know not what to do,' he said at last, 'for Northumberland will have it so. He says that Uncle Somerset is a centre of disaffection and wishes to seize the Throne for himself.'

'Oh Ned!' I cried reproachfully. 'How can that be? Why, although I was never his friend, it was always clear that he revered you and your position most highly.'

'Feathering his nest the while!' put in Edward sharply.

'But Ned, he was as nothing compared to Northumberland, who, not content with feathering his nest, truly wishes to grasp the Throne and to make every man his puppet.' I said this in a whisper for fear of being heard, although we were alone.

'Are you verily certain Bess?' Ned's voice was as quiet as mine. 'Have you real proof? These are grave matters, dearest sister.'

I was forced to disclaim any proof, to my great annoyance. I had also broken one of mine own rules in mentioning Northumberland's name in any but a non-committal way. What had prompted me to such a perilous course was not stark fact but a deep, inescapable feeling, and as such, impossible to prove without definite evidence. Yet my feelings about those who work for or against me have never been wrong and were not wrong then. The man was a rogue. He held the King and country in his hand and still was not satisfied. He was utterly ruthless and would stop at nothing to gain his purposes. I knew too, as did everyone else, that Somerset's days were numbered unless the King held out for him, and this, I feared, would not come about.

Edward became fourteen years of age this same month and great were the rejoicings, so that it seemed Duke Somerset was entirely forgot by his nephew. However, one afternoon when we had rid over to Hampton Court from Nonsuch, my brother seized the bridle of my mare and drew me on ahead of the retinue, commanding the company to leave us alone. The hooves of our mounts rustled through the leaves already fallen, the sky was blue and clear, the air brisk and fresh about our ears; the trees of Bushey turning gold on our left, the river lively on our right. We spurred forward together and Edward told me his mind.

'Sister, I wish to speak to you of mine uncle. I minded what you said of him and Uncle Thomas. I wish to see him and reason with him, but Northumberland will not have it. He says his way is right and Uncle Somerset is wrong, knowing not how to rule men. He says that Uncle Somerset would lose my kingdom for me

179

and that while he lives there will always be plots to make me unpopular. And Bess, though I often try, Northumberland is most hard to gainsay. He listens to me, but oft I think he takes his own way.'

'Well, but do you like him, Ned? Are you fond of him?'

'Fond of him?' repeated Edward, looking surprised. 'Nay. But I do not hate him, for he treateth me as a man and does not criticise me. He sees that I have money as befits my rank and defers to me as he should. Nor does he keep me forever at my books, for he knows I love them enough without that. He gives me good conceit of myself, whereas Uncle Somerset gave me none and never ceased his prosing.'

'Have you no spark of feeling for your uncle, Ned? He is your blood-relation, dearest.'

'Well, there is no law that says we must love our blood-relatives, Bess, for all you seem to think so. Sometimes I feel that I could, then he begins his lecturing as if I were a little schoolboy of low degree and not a monarch. I like it not at all. Besides, my uncle should have discovered for himself about Uncle Thomas. His eyes were ever in the clouds, whereas Northumberland knows what is going on about us.'

'Does Northumberland tell you all he knows?'

'Oh ay, and we make great plans together. He says you are marvellous clever and witty. Too clever for a mere woman, he said,' declared Edward. 'But I told him that your brain is the best in the land, that you are all woman, that all men love you, and that any who are against you are against me.'

I smiled fondly at him, but felt that after this I should not be suffered to remain at Court much longer. The Duke, it seemed, was growing concerned at Edward's fondness for me, at my popularity and spirit. I made a wager then, with myself, that Ned and his Court would be crying me God-speed before the year was out.

In that October came Mary of Guise, the Regent Queen of Scotland, to be entertained by my brother on her way to Scotland from France. There were splendid festivities to welcome her. It was a merry time, and all the ladies went mad for French fashions, tumbling over themselves to copy the Frenchwomen and outdo one another. I did not join in this contest, for I cared not to be one of the herd, preferring mine own way and mine own style in dress, as in all things. I could lead, but I would not follow. So I kept to my usual habits and changed not with the others. Also, I did not wish to appear frivolous and easily swayed. John Aylmer, who was then tutor to Jane Grey, was delighted at my seeming modesty.

'The Princess Elizabeth has altered nothing,' he remarked to my brother, 'but has kept her old, maiden shamefastness. I am happy indeed to see this. Though her wit be sharp, her ways are godly.'

I agreed with him as to my wit, but my ways were mine own. If they marched with God's, why then, so much the better for me.

★ ★ ★

Mary of Guise was a tall, dark, pretty Frenchwoman who had wedded my cousin, James V of Scotland, now dead. He had been the son of my father's elder sister Margaret, who had married James IV of Scotland. My father had never favoured this sister of his and did not overly bestir himself in her troubles. Nor did he in those of her son, who suffered much from low spirits and melancholy, for his had been a life of turbulence and disappointments of a kind that make a romantic tale, exciting to the hearer, full of hopes and heart-break, but misery to he who experiences it.

I had heard oft of my cousin James, of his short-lived marriage to Princess Madeleine of France against all advice. I had heard how he wed her and carried her away to Scotland. She was but sixteen and it was Maytime. Two short months later she was dead of a consumption, killed, it was said, by the Scottish mountains. Then came his marriage to Mary of Guise, followed by the loss, in death, of all his baby sons by her. Finally she bore him one daughter who survived, and who even now lived in France, a Queen in her own right.

I had seen a portrait of James, and by my faith, 'twas a haunted melancholy visage limned there, staring from the canvas as if gazing upon misfortune, which was true enough. He drew trouble to him like a lover, and his daughter was the same. Now, from far ahead, I can see the resemblance between those two. The unlucky, star-crossed Queen of Scots was her father's mirror in almost every way. He passed his ill-omen on to her as a black legacy indeed, to all our cost.

My father had forecast that her birth would bring naught but trouble to the world, and a sage prophet he proved to be.

'Twas told me, in my young days, that James had foreseen his own end after the battle against the English at Solway Moss, fought when I was but nine years old. I would beg with ghoulish insistence for Kat to tell and retell this tale.

'But he was my cousin,' I had cried, 'and my father was his uncle. How could they make war together? 'Tis horrible!'

' 'Tis politics,' was Kat's answer. 'They reck not of any blood tie, as you will learn.'

'But tell me, Kat,' I would urge, 'tell me of his death and his prophecy.'

'Oh, I have told you a mort of times!' poor Kat would protest. 'You know every word — 'tis a waste of breath.'

'Nay, nay! I would hear it again. Nay, Kat, I will sit upon your knee. Make room for your Bess, put your arm around me so, and I will lay my head upon your shoulder. Now, begin at the part where Kirkcaldy's wife says: '*Come, your Grace, my King, be of good cheer —* ' '

' '*Be of good cheer and take the work of God in good part*',' Kat would continue in a resigned voice. 'And the King answered: '*Nay, my portion of the world is short and I will be dead in fifteen days*'.'

'Go on, Kat,' I would urge. 'When his servant asked him where they would be for Christmas he said — Go on, Kat, do!'

'Well then, as I have told you so oft, he said:

183

'*I cannot tell; choose ye the place. But this I can tell you. On Yule Day* — ' '

' '*You will be masterless and the realm without a King!*' ' I finished triumphantly. 'Now tell me of his death. Come, Kat, tell!'

'Oh me, you are the veriest gadfly! Well, he went to Falkland whilst the Queen lay at Linlithgow to be confined, and when he was at Falkland he took to his bed, sometimes crying out in despair at his defeat, sometimes in a silent melancholy. Then he heard of the capture of Oliver Sinclair, his favourite.'

'Oh ay! That was when he screamed out: '*Oh fled Oliver! Is Oliver ta'en? Oh fled Oliver!*' Go on, Kat.'

'Then came a messenger from Linlithgow to say that the child was a girl and he sighed aloud, saying: '*Adieu, farewell, it came with a lass, it will pass with a lass.*' Six days later he was dead at the age of thirty.'

'On the fourteenth of December!' I had cried. 'Before Yule, even as he had said. Is it not wild and romantic, Kat?'

'Not for him,' said Kat. ' 'Twas the death of him. Myself, I prefer life. Now come, 'tis time for your hot posset and bed.' And off I had gone, protesting.

I thought of this as I sat in my chamber, wrapped in a loose robe of rose-coloured velvet, waiting for Kat to come and dress me for the evening's banquet. A brazier had been lit, for it was chilly that autumn, and I stretched out my hands to the warmth, wondering at this daughter who had been

184

the death of her father — or so folk said. She was reputed to be of ineffable sweetness and charm, so that all competed for a smile from her. She was also said to possess great beauty, having a pure white skin, red-gold hair and amber eyes. A perfect child, the French ladies rhapsodised. 'And too good to be true, I say,' I remarked aloud, as Kat bustled in.

'Who is too good to be true? Come, sweeting, up on your feet. I have brought the grey satin for tonight.'

'Why the daughter of Mary of Guise,' I answered, drawing myself lazily up from my chair. 'Oh Kat, I grow weary of this Perfect Child, her virtue and her beauty. Has she no flaw at all? I have heard enough of her to last me for life!'

'Why, the little Queen sounds lovely, my pet.'

'All Queens are lovely!' I said laughing. 'Did you not know that, Puss-Cat? She may be as plain as a pie in sober truth. Now pull those lacings tight. I may not follow the French fashions, but none shall say that my figure is anything but good. 'Tis said that females follow their father in looks, so she may have Cousin James' hooded eyes and great long nose, for all we know. Then again, she may be as tall as a maypole like her mother.'

'Jesu, sweeting!' cried Kat, tugging at the strings with a will, while I grasped the bedpost to keep from falling. 'You make a monster of the poor child. Tall as a maypole, with hooded eyes and a great long nose — what a vision of beauty she must be! No wonder all rave about her, and she not quite eight years old!'

I laughed. 'Oh Kat, what a vision indeed! Well,

let us forget her. I daresay she is but a stupid little puppet when all's said and done. Petted children often are.'

'You are severe, my love. Would you not like to see her?'

'Ay, I would,' I confessed. 'One cannot help feeling curious, and she is kin of mine after all.'

'They pet her so that she will not miss her mother,' said Kat, 'for they are very close at heart and now must live apart.'

'Ah, I had forgot. Yet she is lucky to have a mother and remember such love, Kat, so I do not pity her. And she is a Queen.'

'That does not make for happiness as you know full well, my pretty,' answered Kat, smoothing the sleeves of my gown.

'It would make me happy,' I said.

★ ★ ★

Before that year of 1551 was over, I was wending my way out of London. True enough, I had won the wager I had made with myself in the autumn during my conversation with Ned upon the works of Black John of Northumberland. That gentleman had at last decided that I was too disquieting a companion for the King. I was too prone to shed light in dark places and far too good a judge of character for His Grace to breathe easy near me. So back to Hatfield I had to go. Sad I was, although I had expected it. My little brother wept sore before our final parting, showering me with kisses and gifts, the greatest being the Palace of Hatfield

186

for mine own. This gave me much delight, and once I was fairly on the open road, thoughts of its redecoration filled my mind.

Trotting past the grey stone wall of St. Bartholomew's Priory, I halted my mare and turned in the saddle, looking back. It was a soft, grey day and the air was mild and clear. Behind me rose London Wall, heavy and dark, seeming to touch the sky. I could just see the battered portal of old, ruinous Aldersgate, under which we had come, left open as was the rule, until sunset. Beyond that portal lay my sweet brother, and I felt a pang at the thought. But before me lay the road to Hatfield and hope of the future. I looked up to the twin hills of Highgate and Hampstead, the two windmills upon Hampstead heights etched sharp against the pale sky, and pointed with my whip.

'On to Highgate!' I cried. 'I would reach the Bishop's Palace by noon!'

It was an easy journey back, and my messengers sent ahead to warn those at Hatfield to make ready for my return had got through apace despite muddy tracks, so all was bright and fettled to greet me. I spent many happy hours walking with Kat and Blanche Parry through the rooms, ordering, suggesting, changing here and there.

It was a happy winter during which I received many messages and letters from Ned which I answered quickly for I wished him to know that he was ever in my heart. Indeed, I spent much time at my desk writing letters. In one I asked Cecil to be my surveyor, but he begged for his deputy to do it, pleading pressure of work. At first I was annoyed at this, seeing it as a rebuff, but on consideration I decided that 'twas wisdom on his part, for how could he aid me openly, being Northumberland's man and close to his secrets? So I said naught, for I knew Cecil to be true to me and mine.

1552 came in, chilly but bright, and my sister Mary and I exchanged gifts. Sometimes I travelled to Hunsdon, sometimes she to Hatfield. In early March when I visited her, she looked ill and older than ever in a bright yellow gown which did not suit her. She had been thirty-six years old in February and her face showed every day of it and more. Poor soul, she suffered from countless ills besides the migraine, and for that I had much sympathy. Her fingers were becoming knotted with rheumatism, and she told me that her ears ached so oft and so badly that sometimes she felt she could run mad and howling through the park. And she fell in agony with her monthly courses, in pain and sickness, she said sighing.

'I see very few myself,' I replied. 'Kat says I am but a green apple still, but it is less than other damsels of my age, and I am over eighteen, thou knowest.'

'Well, I envy you, Elizabeth,' said Mary. 'As ever, you are fortunate. Your lack may not be right, but sure, it is more comfortable than my frequency. Mayhap childbearing would cure us both.'

My face must have shown my feelings, for she gave a sardonic laugh. 'So,' she said, 'you think I am too old for childbearing, do you? Mayhap you think I am too old for marriage also?'

'Nay Mary!' I protested. 'I said naught, and after

all, Nature is a wonderful thing. I know too that happiness can work miracles in looks and health.'

'So I shall be ugly and ill for ever, then,' grumbled Mary, 'for it is set that I shall never marry or live a natural life like other women.'

'What if you should become Queen?' I said softly, daring.

'You are bold, Bess! It is fortunate that we are alone.' Leaning forward, Mary whispered: 'I tell you, if that came about it *would* be a miracle and a sure sign from God that my faith is right and that my birth was for good reason. I should surely marry then. Let us leave it be now, for too much thinking on't troubles my heart.'

During the next week I left for Hatfield in the wild winds of March. While those winds were blowing towards April and spring, the news came to me that Edward Seymour, Duke of Somerset, uncle to His Majesty the King, had been executed and gone to his Maker. The way was now clear for Northumberland.

* * *

In that very April of 1552 my brother fell ill with the smallpox, that dread disease we know so well and for which there is no cure. A few, and I was one, may recover unmarked, but this is a near miracle, rare as miracles are. Some poor souls who do survive often wish they had not when they see what their mirrors reveal.

I know not whether my brother was marked or not, for I never saw him again. No sooner had the

189

pox passed than he caught the measles with such severity that his eyesight and hearing were sadly impaired. When he was able, he wrote and told me of this, yet full of hope, poor sweet soul. Near unto Christmas he wrote that the cough which had never left him since the measles was now worse. My messenger told me that to his mind, my brother was mortal ill. I determined to go to London, but despite my pleadings, Northumberland would have none of me. He kept me from my sweet brother in his hour of need, he worked to destroy the love and trust that Ned had reposed in me, for Ned knew naught of the Black Duke's antipathy to me and all I stood for. All others knew, but 'twould not have suited Northumberland for his young sovereign to discover how his chief statesman hated me.

So I dwelt away from Court and nagging worry was my close companion. I feared for my brother's health and for the Succession, which seemed, from reports I received, to stand in danger. Ned had become obsessed by two ideas, which, as life and vitality receded occupied his brain to the exclusion of all else, fostered in their growth by the Duke of Northumberland. One of these ideas was to prevent Catholicism at any cost; the other was his role as an absolute monarch answerable to none but God; one who could not make mistakes, his mind being God-inspired.

This put my sister Mary in a position of great peril, she being as mad for Catholicism as Ned was not. It seemed to me that Northumberland would do all in his power to prevent her from taking up her rightful Queenship when the time came. I wondered how he would accomplish this. When the news reached me that the Duke's youngest and only unmarried son, Lord Guildford Dudley, had been wedded to Jane Grey, I began to see the shape of a plan, for plan it had to be, since the marriage was a forced one. Parry, who had been to London to see to the running of Durham House, told me of it. He came to my summer parlour, big with the tidings.

'Come Tom,' I said, 'let us walk in the park. You can talk freely there, with no chance ear to listen.' So we strolled through the garden where the lavender and roses blew, and into the Great Park with its huge quiet trees, their leaves lightly fluttering under a cloudless sky. 'No hedges here to conceal an eavesdropper,' I remarked. 'We can see who comes and quickly turn our talk to common matters. Now, tell me of Jane Grey and this marriage.'

'Her parents beat her, for she wanted him not and struggled against her fate, but to no avail,' he told me. 'Never was there such a miserable bride, nor such a glum groom. I saw the procession. Poor little Lady Jane, I felt much pity for her.'

'What is she in age? Fifteen?'

He nodded. 'She is mighty learned, Madam. She can speak Hebrew as if 'twere her native tongue, they say.'

'Much good that will do her, a-bed with Guildford Dudley!' I snorted. 'Back you go to Durham House, Parry, and find what more you can discover of this strange union. There is more in't that seems, I'll wager. Get Cecil's ear if you can, but use great secrecy I do command you.'

Parry soon returned, and with alarming news. The King had altered the Succession, naming Lady Jane to follow him, and her heirs male, or the heirs male of her sisters.

'Jesu, so that is it!' I cried. 'That is Northumberland's doing! Is my brother seriously ill? He must be to have acted so.'

'Ay, he is ill right enough,' murmured Parry, his voice low, even though we were again in the park. 'He has the consumption, Madam. I have it on good authority. He cannot live long.'

I ceased my walking and leaned against a tree. I had half expected it, yet to know it for truth was worse. Tears trickled down my cheeks as I grasped Tom Parry's hand.

'Oh my poor little Ned,' I choked out. 'Ill in mind and body and shut away from those who love him. Did you see him, Tom? No? Did you then hear how he looked? Speak man!' Parry blinked, staring at me dumbly. 'You did hear something,' I cried, catching his sleeve and shaking his arm. 'Tell me at once. I will know, so out with it!'

And oh God, what he told me turned me sick and shaking with horror and pity. E'en now I know not if 'twas full truth or all gossip, but more than a grain of substance must have been in't to have brought so ghastly a tale. Every lip in London was muttering of it, he told me. It was said openly that Northumberland was poisoning the King; that it must be so, else why had he not been seen since that day in May when he was held up at one of the windows of Placentia to watch the ships pass down the river on a voyage of discovery? They had sailed past the palace, their guns roaring in salute, the crowds roaring to match the guns. And now it was near July and no one had seen their King since that day, when his looks had terrified them.

'Terrified? How?' I queried, almost feared to ask.

'All London throbs with it, Madam. It must be more than a consumption, for I heard that his hair has fallen out so that he is bald, that his face is sunken like an ancient's and corpse-white withal. 'Twas said that he is as bony as a corpse too, and unable to stand alone for the constant trembling that shakes him like an ague. I heard that he cannot speak for coughing, and spits blood; that his finger nails are fallen off, and his whole toes too. I heard — '

'Oh say me no more!' I gasped, clapping my hands to my ears. 'I cannot bear it. Quick, we must haste to London with all speed. Quick, Tom, get ye and see to it!'

At dawn of the next day I was on my way to London with a very small company in order to make all haste possible. I knew that villainy was at work, for if a Protestant were needed to succeed my brother, the choice should fall on me as my father's own child and named by him in the Statute of Succession. Jane Grey was but his great-niece and of the line of his younger sister only. It was obvious to me that she was destined to be Northumberland's creature if aught should befall my poor brother.

We had gone almost halfway upon our journey

when we were stopped by one of the Duke's men leading a small force. The fellow had brought a message from the King, he said. I was to return to Hatfield; my brother had commanded it. For a moment I was fain to give him the lie, but he and his men were armed, whilst I and mine were not. Also, had the message been true, I could have been in grave trouble for disobeying a royal command. So we returned apace, in much anxiety.

Scurrying to my chamber I pulled out my writing desk and began to scribble Ned a note, telling him of my urgent fears for his health and my great desire to see him. I told him of my abortive journey, and added that nothing but his message would have stayed me from finishing that journey. Methinks my letter was never allowed to reach him, else he must have answered me.

I spent the next few days in such agony of mind that I could not keep still, but paced about, calling upon God to aid my brother and me. I could not sleep, my appetite forsook me, my temper was like a crackling flame, flashing in a frenzy of nervous irritation at all who tried to calm me. At last, on the sixth of July 1553, I awoke with a pounding head and a sickness in the belly. All that day I writhed and wailed like a mad thing. Kat said it was the thunderstorm that threatened, for the summer afternoon had turned black as Pluto's Underworld. Within the hour, a fearful tempest was upon us, the wind howling wild as a lost soul, the thunder roaring like the mouth of Hell itself. At six in the evening, my migraine grew bad enough to render me unconscious. When I came to myself in the early hours of the next morning, my pain and terror had drained away. I turned my head on the pillow and saw my faithful Kat watching by my bed.

'Kat, my brother is dead,' I said, quite calm and quiet. 'He went in the storm, when my senses left me. God rest his sweet soul.' Then I slept through what was left of the night and through most of the next day.

When I awoke that evening I was told that a messenger had just arrived, having rid post-haste from London. I had him sent straight to me as I lay in my bed. He was young, travel-stained and weary, his breast still heaving as he knelt. 'Princess,' he panted, 'this news is most secret. You must breathe it to no one, or your life will be forfeit, and your sister's too.'

'Tell me,' I breathed.

On his knees, he moved nearer, his voice as he spoke, dropping to a whisper that I had to bend my head to hear. 'The King is dead, but 'tis to be kept close whilst plans are made. You must not stir from here, no matter what tidings come to force you to London. If you go, you will be arrested.'

'What are these plans? Do you know?' I whispered, quiet as he.

'Jane Dudley, who was Jane Grey, is to be proclaimed Queen, while you and your sister are to be imprisoned, mayhap killed. A messenger to you is following and should arrive tomorrow. Heed him not, and say naught of me, as we value England.'

'Who sends you?' I sighed, scarcely moving my lips.

The answer came, the faintest hiss. '*Cecil.*'

I nodded, for now I knew whom I could trust above all others in a world turned upside down. I knew at last, and the knowledge was good. 'Does any know of you?' I queried after a moment.

'None,' he said. 'My master takes no risk of that.'

'Yet he takes great risk for me.'

'For the Princess Mary too, Madam. He says that the present situation holds the greatest risk of all, for in it, right would be overset. He says that the people of England will not stomach such a thing. Now I must go. My horse should be fed and watered by this time.'

'Where go you now?' I asked tensely.

'On to your sister, Madam, for she is the rightful Sovereign.'

So Mary was Queen. Queen in right, but not yet in name. The next few days would settle all. I wondered if the messenger would reach her or be prevented in some way. In any case, I was ready, up and dressed, for Northumberland's man when he came.

'What!' I cried, with every appearance of surprise and concern. 'My dear brother sends you to bid me to London, for he hath need of me? Why then, I must go!' And away I hurried, calling to my women until all was a-bustle. Then I retired to my bed, giving out that the excitement had brought on a migraine and I was too ill to travel. I stayed there all the next day, and the next, and the next. 'Twas safer so.

Even Kat was fooled at first, but as I remained

abed, blooming with health, I could tell that she was wondering what game was afoot. During these days, Ned's death was announced publicly, cousin Jane was proclaimed Queen, and still I stayed abed. No news reached me, so I had no way of knowing that Mary had indeed set out for London upon hearing of Ned's supposed last request for her company in his great need. Nor did I know then that she had suddenly commanded her train to turn about upon the road to Enfield, making off across country to Framlingham Castle in Suffolk. I would I could have known, for I fretted myself wretched over her safety.

I received no further commands to go to London, so I surmised that Northumberland was too busy saving his own skin to bother about me and mine. I wondered about cousin Jane and Queenship. Certainly none would impose upon her if she felt it her duty to refuse a request. Indeed, she was not unlike Mary in nature, but of the two, Jane was far less persuadable and far less human in feeling. I could see no place in the world for her. She would have made an excellent nun of the fanatical sort, but she was fiercely Protestant. Nor could I imagine her in the marriage-bed, unless 'twere as a martyr. Guildford Dudley would get but little joy from her, poor fellow. Methought she would not last long as Queen. I felt that the people of England would rally to Mary's side, despite all plots to the contrary.

And I was right. Ten days settled all. The people of England declared for Mary. She was able to raise an army, and had written to the Duke from

Kenninghall in Norfolk that if he and the Council showed repentance for their disloyal behaviour and would conduct themselves like true and patriotic gentlemen, she as Queen, would understand and pardon all.

Northumberland scorned this and went out to fight, taking all his sons but Guildford with him. But his men melted away to join Mary, and few would listen to his words when he sought to persuade them to his side. At Cambridge he gave in, for most of his followers deserted without ever a fight, so he cried out at the Market Cross for Mary. It behoved him little, for he came back to London to the howls and groans of the populace, overwhelmed, dishonoured and covered with muck and filth that the folk had flung at him as he passed by on a broken-down, spavined nag which was all that was given to him to ride. His sons, John, Ambrose and Henry were with him, but not Robert. He had commanded an army himself and had proclaimed Jane as Queen at King's Lynn, where he was captured. For this, he was put in the Tower for a while to cool his hot blood, but he suffered no harder punishment. I knew naught of all this until later, for when a messenger arrived for me, he told me not of Dudley's downfall, but that I was bidden to join Mary.

As soon as the door closed behind him, I leaped from my day-bed where I had been lying, still aping the invalid. 'Hey, Kat!' I shrieked. 'Kat, quick! I am to join Mary at Wanstead and we are to ride to London together! How say you to that? The

198

messenger was from her. She is Queen indeed, and right glad am I!'

'God grant you may remain so,' muttered Kat sourly. 'She will bring us to a pretty pass with her priests and her candles, you mark my words.'

'Oh peste! What a croaker you are! Well, so she may — she has no common-sense, God knows, but for the moment she is content to have me with her on this great day, and for the moment I too am content. So let us look through my gowns. I would not wish to shame her by appearing shabby.'

'Nor must you outshine her, my lamb. Remember that.'

'Oh lord, yes! Ne'er mind, there will come a day when I shall please myself, and then I promise you that all eyes will pop and all mouths gape at my magnificence. Wait you and see Kat, wait you and see!' And, laughing excitedly, we scuttled about to make ready for the journey to London and Wanstead.

★ ★ ★

Heigh-ho, so long ago as it all was! Well, I mind as if it were yesterday that meeting with Mary at Wanstead on the thirtieth of July. The aged, raddled face that eyes me from my hateful mirror smiles at it still. I see the hooded orbs dart and twinkle, the carmined, sunken lips twitch and stretch, sending the whitened cheeks into a score of wrinkles. Ugh, a grinning death-mask! Ay, and mine own too, save that mine own true death-mask will not smile, but stare blindly forth from closed lids. Right glad am I that my funeral effigy was modelled from me when I was younger and still handsome. Maximilian Colte made it, and 'fore God, it is so lifelike I swear it would answer if questioned. 'Tis of wood and coloured in true shades, unlike the figure in stone which he has made for my tomb. That looks like a corpse, i'faith, so cold and rigid, and they who see it will wonder how any could have called me 'siren' and 'spell-binder.' But 'tis done now and there is no time to make another, so it will have to suffice.

Still in the mirror the mask of age smiles. As it smiles, I see in my mind fair Wanstead, brilliant in the sun, its grey stone and old wood thrown into bright light and sharp shadow. I see the vivid pink roses hanging in swags and garlands between tall posts, themselves rose-twined. I see the dun-coloured flagstones of the courtyard quivering in the heat. Behind me ranged my company of nobles, my horsemen in Tudor green-and-white, with the pink Tudor rose upon their breasts, and behind them the glimmering, dark forest through which we had come. I see all this through the eye of my mind, where the memory lies like a prisoned jewel.

Within the house waited my sister Mary the Queen. She was seated in a carved chair upon a dais in the Hall. Impulsively she rose as I came through the screen door, standing with hands outstretched in welcome. We kissed and cried over one another, but Mary's sharp eyes were upon me and her tongue was swift to speak her mind.

'Why so plainly dressed sister? Do you wear

funeral weeds, or a nun's habit in my triumphal procession?'

'Nay, dear Mary,' I answered warmly, glancing down at my sober yet elegant robe of grey and white satin. 'I would be but a foil to you. 'Tis your day, and you must shine brighter than the sun.'

Indeed she near did, so ablaze with jewels was she; wearing a most unbecoming gown of brilliant purple, with the kirtle a very goldsmith's shop of glitter. Yet the sun, glancing through the high windows, gilded her greying hair to a youthful foxy red and warmed her lined face into smiling rosiness, its habitual tenseness relieved by triumph, for she had shown both spirit and bravery in this, her hour. She looked almost pretty as she smiled, her eyes bright.

'Well, I feel happy enough to do so,' she replied. 'God has answered my prayers in full measure, has He not?'

I bowed my head, feeling that mayhap the English people had taken a greater share in this turn of events than had God, but forebore to say so. I did not wish to provoke a theological argument on that day.

We rode into London that afternoon, leaving Leyton High Stone upon our right and clattering down the lane to leafy Stratford-atte-Bow where we splashed through the stream. How the folk ran out to cheer us as we passed! Then, over the River Lea at Bow Bridge with its cluster of thatched cottages and tall elms, and on to the pretty farms of Mile End, where the first of the multitudes from London and round about stood cheering. After that, our progress was slow and slower yet as people ran into the road and pressed about us. The sun shone full in our eyes, and I was glad of the clustering trees upon either side of the way and the shade they afforded. As we came to Whitechapel Bars, I could see London Wall rising before us, bold against the vivid sky, for we were less than a mile away. The great portal of Aldgate stood wide and all the bells were ringing a deafening clangour. It was seven o'clock of the evening as we went through the gate, and I rode second only to the Queen in a roar of yells, bells and gunfire. I saw Mary going before me, bowing stiffly from side to side, occasionally lifting a jewelled hand to wave or to wipe the tears from her cheeks as the people of London shouted her name. They shouted mine too.

Every house had its decoration of bright carpets and cloths hanging from the windows, every window was jammed with cheering heads; there were bonfires leaping and crackling at every corner, while flowers flew in the air like so many coloured snowflakes. The people loved us, they wanted us, we were theirs, they were ours.

We left our armed escorts at Aldgate and proceeded slowly to the Tower, surrounded by excited throngs, and here, as the sun went down, Mary pardoned some of the captives enclosed there. She smiled upon the Duchess of Somerset, widow of the late Protector; Stephen Gardiner, Catholic Bishop of Winchester, she dubbed her Chancellor, at which I thought, 'ware Bess for squalls! She restored Framlingham Castle to the old Duke of Norfolk, and kissed the cheek of young Edward

Courtenay, son of the beheaded Marquis of Exeter, whose eager blue gaze was only for me, troublesome fool that he was. Rob I saw not, nor his father. Nor did we visit Jane Grey who was lodged in Mr. Partridge's house against the Tower Walls, and there treated with respect in accordance with Mary's orders. Ascham, who had returned to my service, wished to visit her, but I judged it better not for policy's sake.

I saw much of my sister, who, by her merciful behaviour, was making herself very well-liked. Of her attitude to me I felt uncertain. She was bringing strong pressure upon me to hear Mass, and this was only the beginning, for she intended all England to hear Mass in time.

In August the Duke of Northumberland publicly recanted, going over to the Church of Rome in order to save his skin. 'Twas no manner of use, for his life had been forfeit from the moment that the country had declared for Mary. I pitied him, but was not sorry to see him go, and go he did by way of the axe, that same month.

It was at about this time that Mary and I removed to White Hall, the palace my father had made so much his own. It had been York Place when he had it from Cardinal Wolsey, enlarging and beautifying it until it was indeed fit for a King. The Great Hall he had caused to be painted white all over outside, which had given it the popular name of White Hall; nowadays this is used in place of any other. The White Hall itself stood out clear against the red brick and timber buildings of the rest of the palace.

While we were at White Hall my sister's behaviour towards me began to harden. That cursed Simon Renard played upon her weaknesses until her religious fanaticism was whipped to a ferment and her equivocal feelings towards me fanned to a flame. He wished me dead, for he and his had much to lose should I inherit. Renard was Ambassador from the Emperor Charles V, Mary's hideous Spanish cousin, and wished to ally England with Catholic Spain. In his eyes I was heretic, dangerous because loved by the people, and therefore enemy to him and his royal master. To Mary, everything Spanish was sacrosanct, so he had her ear from the beginning. He did not understand the English and scorned to try, so it was much of his doing that she lost all her popularity and died in lonely misery. The moment that I caught the malevolence of his glowing dark eyes, I knew that here stood an enemy far greater than any I had yet encountered. There was to be no respite for me, my struggle was not ended, and how 'twould end I could not then say. I knew only that it would be to the death.

'That Renard!' I exclaimed to Kat in my candlelit chamber as I prepared for bed upon a night not long after my twentieth birthday. 'He will see me dead if he can.'

'Sure, for you stand in his way for an alliance with Spain.'

'There's my clever Kat! The French are disposed to befriend me. Ambassador De Noailles has already made overtures in my direction.'

'He only wants your friendship in order to grab England for France through the little Scottish

Queen,' said Kat shrewdly. 'She is betrothed to the Dauphin and will be Queen of France as well as Scotland. She is an heiress of the Blood Royal to the Crown of England through her grandmother.'

'Why did my father's sister ever have to marry that wretched Scottish James!' I exclaimed irritably. 'It has caused naught but trouble and still seems like doing so.' I paced about, kicking the rushes. 'Foh! These rushes stink like a midden! Of course, if sister Mary were removed, the King of France would have the chance to control England, or so he thinks. What would he do with me, I wonder? Try to marry me off? Kill me?'

Kat, busy turning down sheets, stood upright. 'Oh save us, 'tis like a spider's web twining all about us.'

'Yea, and growing tighter by the day,' I answered. 'Yet I will retain De Noailles' friendship, for while he is my friend, he could be of help to me when I need it. Be not feared that I shall say too much, Kat. I shall let him do the talking and feed him what morsels I think fit.'

'On my oath,' sighed Kat, pulling the shutters clattering across the windows, 'it seems that you are in more danger now than ever before.'

'Of a surety; for I am closer to the Throne than ever before,' I said. ''Tis all upon Fortune's wheel, Kat. One moment up, the next down. We cannot escape it and I do not mean to try. I will live my life to the end, whatever it may be. It is God's will.'

4

IN DARKNESS AND
THE SHADOW OF DEATH

1553 – 1555

When I look back to the days of my sister's reign, if I had fully known what Fate had in store for me, my nerve must have cracked, for my life hung like a bauble on a chain swinging this way and that. For five years did she wear the Crown of England, and five dark, dangerous and terrible years they were, not only for me but for all.

I would not go to Mass. Force me as she tried to do, I managed to evade it. To have heard Mass would have been as bad for my spirit as it would have been for Mary's had she been made to change to the New Religion. She was pressed hard enough to do so as a girl and suffered much misery by remaining steadfast, yet she chose to forget her own experiences and harden her heart against me. I had more cogent reasons for holding to my own religion, moreover, for what figure would I have cut before the people of the realm if I had given way? I felt it was necessary that they should know that I, the present heir, was neither fanatical Catholic nor grim Protestant, but moderate and governed by reason rather than the emotions.

'Hah!' snorted Kat. 'Governed by reason, eh?

'Tis a good thing that your precious people cannot see and hear their White Hope when she is yelling and stamping in a rage at having her princely will crossed, when there is a spot on her gown, or the meat is not to her liking!' I gave her a shove in the back, causing her to drop a jug of flowers she was carrying from window to table, breaking the jug and upsetting its contents on the floor. 'There now!' she scolded. 'Water everywhere and the jug smashed. So much for calm reason!'

'Then you should not provoke me, hateful creature!' I giggled. 'Kat, you know what I mean. Leave the stupid jug and listen to me. Get one of the women to clear it up. Ring the bell and attend to me! I must keep the people's love and respect,' said I. 'They must have someone they can trust, although I hope Mary and I do not come to open strife. I am afraid of plots, you see.'

'Plots against you, do you mean, sweeting?'

'Nay, foolish one! Plots against Mary in my name is what I mean. Why, if I were to seem to lead an uprising, or be at the head of a plot, 'twould be the end of me. The Spaniards would see to that.'

'You are right, my love. Marry, it is as if you walk a tightrope.'

'Ay, between the devil of my misguided supporters who will rally to me whether I will or no, and the deep sea of my sister's chancy lenience which may plunge me to my doom through fanaticism and jealousy. Kat, I say I will not go to Mass unless I am forced thereto.'

A day or two after this, on the fourteenth of

September, Kat burst into my chamber gasping with agitation.

'Save us, what is it?' I cried, jumping to my feet and dropping the cards which I was setting into a game upon the table. 'Is my sister ill?'

'Nay, 'tis Archbishop Cranmer. He is arrested and prisoned in the Tower! I cannot believe such a dreadful thing.'

I shook my head. 'I guessed it would come from the moment he refused to leave the country,' I said heavily. 'Mary did give him the chance to do so, and would have given him honourable retirement in England had he but stayed mum. He saw no danger and has no idea of that hateful Renard's ability to persuade the Queen.'

'Ay, he should have kept quiet,' agreed Kat wiping her eyes. 'Yet it was right brave to say that he was not afraid to own that all changes in religion in the last years were made by his means.'

''Twas crazy foolishness!' I snapped, irritable in my distress. 'His fate is sealed. He will die for those words, either by fire or the axe. How damnable useless is his bravery, my poor dear fool of a Godfather.'

'He will wear a martyr's crown,' said Kat dubiously.

'Sweet Jesu!' I cried. 'What canting twaddle! Of what weight is a martyr's crown against the red blood of life and the fragrant earth beneath one's feet?'

'He is old,' said Kat. 'He may prefer his own kind of glory.'

'Well, mayhap you are right,' I agreed. 'Mayhap

he sees no future for himself and could never change his ways to suit Mary. But Cranmer, Kat! Why, my father trusted him above all. He used to call him The Fox for his cunning and devious ways.'

'Perhaps he is tired of deviousness and cunning and the struggle for power,' said Kat. 'I cannot tell; I am not of the stuff of martyrs.'

I sighed deeply. I had known and loved Cranmer all my life and felt sore dismayed. My sister, urged on by Simon Renard, would tolerate no opposition to her obsession to bring England back to the Catholic fold. She had refused to accept the title of Head of the Church of England, saying that the Pope was the only head of any church she knew. As I whispered a prayer for my Godfather, Thomas Cranmer, I knew that I was not of the stuff of martyrs neither. My crown would be of gold, and the Kingdom of Heaven could wait for me until I had ruled mine own — God willing.

★ ★ ★

There was to be a requiem Mass for Ned, but I would not go, though I had loved him with all my heart. I did not wish to be seen at a Catholic ceremony. My prayers for Ned were sincere and said in my own way. God would not think any the less of them for that. I wished to see Mary in order to set matters right between us, but she would not have it, for my refusal to attend the requiem had upset her deeply. At last she relented and gave me audience, but her face was grim and her words hard. She said I was cruel and selfish to hold out against her and make her so miserable. She said that she knew I was jealous of her position and wished to take it from her. She said that she could not trust me.

'Oh Mary!' I cried, much agitated. 'Do keep your heart open for me. Remember our childhood and the happy times we spent together. Do not turn against me!' Before I could stay them, the tears had spilled from my eyes and I began to weep, for I was grievously distressed. Mary started up from her chair.

'Elizabeth,' she begged, 'do but come to Mass. 'Tis all I ask.'

'It is not my fault that I cannot believe!' I sobbed. 'My teaching was not yours. I only know what I was taught.'

'Sister, listen to me,' said Mary, her voice more kind. 'If you go to Mass, belief will come, I promise you. Go, to please me, Elizabeth.'

So I had to go. But on the way to Mass in the Chapel Royal at White Hall I complained loudly of an agonising pain in the belly, desiring one of Mary's ladies to rub it for me, making sure that all round about saw and heard. These doings would all be reported in common gossip, and it would soon be known through all the land that The Lady Elizabeth had gone miserably to Mass.

Afterwards Mary kissed me and gave me a pretty brooch of rubies and diamonds which I liked and a white coral rosary which I did not. A few days later she commanded me to her presence again and asked me about my state of mind in religious matters. My state of mind was in such confusion that I trembled as if with the ague for the effort it cost me to remain calm. My words, such as they were, seemed to satisfy her for the moment. Then suddenly she said:

'How will you like to ride in my Coronation procession, sister? I am to appoint a day at a Council meeting tomorrow. I have chosen the first of October for the Coronation itself. Have you a gown that is suitable?'

I must have looked perplexed, for Mary smiled. 'Why,' I stammered, my pride aroused, 'I can contrive. 'Twill not matter what I wear, after all.'

'Nay, that would cause talk that I keep you in poverty,' said Mary. 'Let me give you a gown, Elizabeth. I have one that is useless for me, but will be perfection on you. It is brand new and has never been worn, so do take it and welcome. Come, give me a kiss and be friends.'

I kissed her right heartily. 'Oh Mary, do believe me. I am your friend, none better, for all said by mine enemies. I will wear the gown gladly. 'Tis more than kind of you.'

Was there ever such a creature of contradictions? She both loved and hated me, and never could I be sure which face she would show me. There was a song being sung at this time which was very popular in the streets and taverns.

'Mary, Mary, quite contrary,
'How does your garden grow,
'With silver bells and cockle shells
'And pretty maids all in a row?'

It was a neat comment upon Mary's efforts to turn England back to the old days of bells, pilgrims and a fully Catholic Court.

Well, the gown suited me admirably and I thought I should do her credit in it. The great procession was to take place upon the thirtieth of September, starting from the Tower, and as we passed slowly through the City on that day, excitement overlaid my worries to such an extent that I enjoyed all with true happiness. Mary spent the night at White Hall, and so therefore did I and all those to follow her on the morrow. The day broke like a day in full summer, and Mary looked upon it as a good omen, being quite unlike October weather. Kat was full of excitement as she dressed me in the new white satin, calling my maids to powder and perfume me, and Blanche to brush my hair which I wore long and loose after my usual custom. Over it I wore a caul of white satin and silver pearled, upon a gilt coronet, and I looked as well as I had ever done, although not like an angel as Blanche would have it.

'Nay,' I laughed. 'My nose is too long and my eyes are too knowing for your 'angel' Blanche. I have not the innocent look, I fear, despite the white which enfolds me.'

'Virginal then,' amended Blanche laying down the silver brush.

'Aye, I'll take that,' said I, 'for 'tis truth.'

So out we went into the courtyard where waited Mary's chariot and mine, with their fidgeting horses all betrapped in crimson velvet, tossing their heads with impatience and striking sparks from the stones with their restless feet. The yard was full of ladies and gentlemen of the Court, soldiers, servants, squires, men and maidens pushing about, calling and chattering as they awaited my sister's coming. At one end arose a commotion as my sole surviving stepmother, the Lady Anne of Cleves, appeared, smiling hugely, full of goodwill as ever, the dear soul, and gabbling an excited mixture of English, Flemish and German.

As I stepped forward 'midst the bowing backs and bobbing heads, the Lady Anne saw me and waved delighted welcome, saying that we were to ride together. I looked at her, and 'fore God, 'twas an effort not to laugh aloud. She was covered in jewels from head to toe and the effect was dazzling. Whether the gems were all real I know not, but it was a brave show. She blazed in the sunlight like some heathen goddess from Cathay. I curtsied to her with great respect.

'Well met, dear Madam,' I answered. 'I am most happy to ride with you. Will you face the horses or have them at your back?'

She insisted that I rode forward, that my rank demanded it, and while we were discussing this, Mary appeared, surrounded by her women. In all, there were seventy ladies, each one in crimson velvet. Mary herself wore a gown of deep blue velvet trimmed with ermine, with a caul of gold on her head. This caul was set in a golden circlet full of jewels and looked most imposing, but the caul was heavy as lead, she told me after, and the circlet had been made for a larger head than hers, so she was in fain to bear up her head with her hand through most of the day. By eventide she had a severe headache. Come my chance, I would not suffer so, I promised myself.

I climbed into my chariot, followed by the Lady Anne of Cleves, and the procession began on its way to Westminster Abbey. The shouts, the clangour of bells, the clatter of the horses' hooves, the colours, the sunshine, all whirled together about mine eyes until methought I was in a dream. We alighted at the Abbey, my sister going on ahead, being met at the door by the old Bishop of Durham and the equally aged Earl of Shrewsbury, both sometime stalwarts of my father's reign, and both in tears of joy as they walked each side of Mary into the dimness beyond.

Inside the Abbey it was cool and the tall carven roof was filled with singing. Stephen Gardiner, black-browed Bishop of Winchester, crowned Mary in place of Archbishop Cranmer, who was in the Tower along with the Bishops of Worcester and London. They were purposely left all unguarded in their prison in the hope that they would escape to the Continent, but they recked not their peril, to their sad and horrible cost.

At last, after five hours, Mary, now truly Queen, wearing a robe of purple velvet furred with ermine and miniver, the Crown upon her head, showed herself at the Abbey door and began her short journey back to White Hall. I lingered a little and the Sieur Antoine De Noailles appeared at my side, full of enthusiasm for the beauty of the ceremony. I spoke a few words about the unexpected weight of the gilt circlet upon my head.

'Have patience,' he whispered, ' 'tis only the preliminary to one that will sit more lightly.'

I made no sign and gave no answer to this piece of daring, for I wished to be drawn into nothing that could harm me.

Two days after the crowning came the first Parliament of my sister's reign, led by Dr. Stephen Gardiner, now Chancellor of the realm and no friend to me. A bill was passed revoking the divorce of my father and Mary's mother, thus rendering me illegitimate. Upon hearing of this, Kat became greatly afflicted.

'It is monstrous, I tell you!' she stormed. 'Such humiliation! Have you not had trouble enough? You, the King's daughter, heir to the Throne, rendered illegitimate by a parcel of fools who prate in Parliament!'

'Kat, 'twas bound to be,' I tried to soothe her. 'You know that Catholics do not admit divorce, and that by their rules, any subsequent marriage must be invalid. So in their eyes I am illegitimate even though my parents were truly wed.'

'How can you be so calm?' she cried. 'Why, here am I in distress, and you cool as snow.'

'Aha,' I said, grinning. 'I am governed by naught but calm reason, as I told you once before. 'Tis a wonderful thing. You should try it. I find it most soothing.'

Her sobs caught on a laugh, turned to a choke, and ended in a fine fit of coughing and whooping to catch her breath. So we laughed about it in the end, although Kat remained touchy upon the subject for many a day.

If I had thought that my troubles had been diminished by my unwilling attendance at Mass, I was wrong. There was to be no lessening of the pitfalls that surrounded me. 'Twas like a stranger stumbling through marshy ground in a storm at night, where there is but one narrow, difficult path, lit now and then by a flash of lightning, and where one small, false step could lead to straight and certain death. My danger increased many-fold when Mary announced her intention of marriage.

She had chosen as her prospective groom Philip, Prince of Spain, thus antagonising all the country to enraged dismay. Not only was he foreign, but Catholic too. In our dear, dogged land, all foreigners are detested. I hold no brief for this attitude, merely knowing it as a fact to be reckoned with when policy at home is directed. Mary chose to ignore it. As to the Catholic religion, most people of middle age had sympathies in that direction, having been raised as Catholics before my father changed all. Most of them had compromised with the New Religion, however, and did not relish changing yet again. All others had been taught that the Old Religion was anathema, and would have none of it; while the reformers and learned men were in a state of anger and alarm at the thought of this Spanish alliance and what troubles it would bring to England, both emotionally and politically. Mary never did have any commonsense or awareness of others in issues large or small. It was an undoubted fact that she thought all should agree with her, and counted as her enemy any who did not.

Worse still, there arose a faction demanding that I marry the silly Edward Courtenay, Earl of Devonshire, who had beauty, charm, noble blood and no sense at all, being an innocent in the ways of the world, having spent most of his life in the Tower. This was bad enough for me, but terrifying to Mary, for I was the heir to the Throne under my father's will, while Courtenay, although Catholic, was pure Plantagenet, of the stock of the old Kings of England. The true Kings, some said. So here was already the excuse for a rebellion. It put me in great danger, but my would-be supporters were unable to comprehend this. To ignore it was my only hope of survival and I knew it.

That autumn, my twentieth, was difficult for me, for although the annulment of my father's divorce had not affected my claim to the Throne, it had vastly diminished my standing at Court. I found myself having to give precedence to Jane Grey's unpleasant mother, the Duchess of Suffolk and to the Countess of Lennox, daughter of my father's sister of Scotland by a second marriage. These dames were my cousins, but there was no love lost between us, for sure. Lady Lennox I particularly disliked. She was a real Creeping Jenny, worming her way into Mary's favour whilst whispering malicious falsehoods about me.

So well did she succeed in her purpose that I was astounded to discover that Mary had chosen this lady to follow her in the Succession instead of me, giving out that she had done this because of my 'heretical taint.' I was near sick with fury and humiliation and broke two earthenware pots against the wall in my passion, besides tearing a favourite gown. It did me good, I swear, and Blanche mended the gown later, so the loss of two pots was no matter. But my sister's action was of great matter. It would cause fresh dissatisfaction up and down the country, for I was much loved all across the realm.

'These place-seekers!' I said angrily to Kat. 'They would sell their souls for favours, crawling like the worms they are. And it is not only my lovely cousin Lennox, mark you, it is anyone who can play on Mary's religious feelings. It is hateful to me here. I shall ask her if I may leave and go to Ashridge. It is well away from London, comfortable, and retired enough to discourage visits from hopeful plotters. Cold, bare December though it be, anything seems preferable to the spites and slights I have had to endure here.'

Well, Mary let me go. I think she was as glad to see the back of me as I was to show it to her. At any rate, she seemed kind, and I took advantage of that to beseech her that whatever she might hear of me, not to condemn me unheard and unseen. The lesson of the Seymour brothers still wrought strong in my mind.

'I am true to you, sister,' I declared passionately, 'whatever some may say and whatever you may think. I pray you to believe this. If aught seems suspicious 'gainst me, I beg you to allow me to speak to you myself. I ask in the name of the blood-bond between us.'

At this, Mary's eyes softened, she raised me to my feet and kissed my cheek, holding my hands in hers as she did so. 'Well, I will, if it should come to that,' she answered. 'But now I have some gifts for you, to sweeten the parting. Take them, Elizabeth, with my kindness. I wish you a safe journey into Hertfordshire. 'Tis an ill time of the year to travel and this hood will warm you on your way.'

She handed me a beautiful hood of sable fur with a shoulder-cape of the same attached to it. Indeed I would wear it on my journey, and welcome. Next, she gave me a long rope of pearls, stones I have ever favoured. I was truly touched and kissed her warmly in return. And so we parted.

In the few days before I was ready to leave, Mary's marriage agreement was signed and England was in uproar. None knew the terms of the agreement, for the stupid Councillors had not made them public, so all believed the worst. It was a good enough agreement, for our country at least. Prince Philip of Spain would get naught but prestige from the match, although he could be called King, by courtesy, while Mary lived. If she died first, he would get nothing. If he were to die first, Mary would inherit Spain, Sicily and other Spanish dominions.

Mary was as full of dreams as a young maiden, creeping to stare upon Titian's portrait of the Prince and fancying herself deep in love, poor thing. The day after the agreement had been signed, her dreams were torn aside somewhat rudely, for into her chamber, smashing the glass of the closed window, was flung a dead dog.

'Merciful heavens, what next?' I enquired of Kat, amazed, as I ticked off the items on a list of possessions to accompany me to Ashridge.

'The Lord knows,' she answered. 'You should have heard the screams as the creature landed amongst the ladies' skirts, right at the Queen's feet!'

'Where were you to hear all this?'

'Just passing by,' replied Kat, innocent as a babe, 'and the door was ajar, so I stayed awhile to watch and listen. It was a nasty thing, I tell you. The creature's ears were cropped, its head shaven and it had a halter about its neck with a label on which was written: '*All priests should be hanged.*' This much I gleaned before I left the doorway,' said Kat.

'Humph,' I snorted. ' 'Tis such shows the blowing of the wind, yet none wishes to see it.'

★ ★ ★

We rode out through Charing and St. Giles, the frost white on meadow and twig, the sun a flaming orb in the blue dome of the sky. The air, though still, was like a blade and I was glad of my fine new hood. The hooves of our horses rang on the hard ground and the harnesses jingled merrily as I was not.

'Thou knowest,' I said to Ascham who rode beside me, 'that I leave behind a very tinder-box of plots and whispers that needs only a spark to roar into a flame that will consume me.'

'Is it so bad?' he queried. 'I know that there is much discontent, but the people love you, Princess.'

'Roger, this stupid talk of marriage between Courtenay and me is like to rouse the country. De Noailles believes that if we married, the whole West Country would rise in our favour and overset my sister. Well, I mislike Courtenay and he mislikes me.'

'Why, I had thought him dazzled by you! He was at first.'

'Ay, before he knew me. But he is Catholic and I am not; also I am too sharp, which scares him. And what if all this did take place and the rebellion failed, Roger? I would be held on a charge of high treason, being thought to have implied consent to these dangerous ideas. Then it would be lawful to imprison me, and there I might stay for ever if I be not turned off in secret by some poisoned draught.' He gasped, turning a shocked face to me as we rode. 'Ay,' I went on, 'we live in parlous times and I am in true peril from those hot-heads who think to serve me by using me against my Queen and sister.'

The weather was fair throughout our journey to Ashridge, but we were glad to arrive there to a loving welcome from my people who had gone ahead to render the house sweet and warm against our coming. It was a pretty place, all amongst the woods, and set upon a ridge of the Chiltern Hills, being once a college of holy men in ancient Norman days. A pleasure awaited me there in the person of my dear friend and lady, Isabella Markham, whom I had not seen for six years, since when I was sent from Chelsea Manor. Her father had recalled her from my service, deeming my presence too scandalous for his daughter. I could not blame him for that, for there is nothing more damaging to the prospects of a well-born and marriageable young lady than to be associated with scandal. So she had left me, but since then, her father had relented, feeling that I had reformed my ways. She was now twenty-five years old and still unwed.

'So, Tib,' said I, teasingly, as we sat with our stitching, feet to the fire, that evening, 'does Sir John, your father, now consider me a fit person to rule a household with yourself in it?'

She laughed. 'Oh Madam, my father fusses over me like a hen with one chick. Ay, he says that you now seem to be the very pattern of the virtues, and one whom young women may safely copy.' She giggled at my raised brows and graciously inclined head. 'Indeed, he thinks that you may have been misjudged at that unlucky time. Anyhap, here I am, and still unmarried.'

'What can be amiss with the young men of Cotham?' I asked, smiling. 'Surely you have had many an offer, so pretty as you are.'

She blushed and shrugged her shoulders. 'As to that, Madam, there were none there to suit my father's requirements or his daughter's fancy.'

'Ha, I'll wager you have a secret lover, which is why you are still a maid,' I jested. 'Who can he be?'

To my surprise, her eyes filled with tears and a look of great sadness overspread her charming face as she gazed down at the floor, fetching a most heart-rending sigh. 'Oh Madam,' said she, 'you are right, but I dare not think of him, nor say his name, he being imprisoned. All I can do is wait and hope.'

'Why Tib, is there aught I can do to help? Perhaps a word from me — ?'

'Nay my dear Lady, leave it go I pray. I would say no more.'

Seeing her distress, I forebore to press the point and we talked of other matters until she smiled.

Yuletide that year was merry enough, yet I was far from merry within. At night in my bed, my fears and anxieties returned anew to chase sleep from my pillow, so that I was forced to call for Kat, or Blanche, or Tib to share my bed and talk to me of light things to ease my mind.

To add to my burdens I received letters from Sir James Croftes and Sir Nicholas Throckmorton touching some wretched plot they were hatching in company with Tom Wyatt, Will Pickering and Will Thomas. They gave me all the names and much of the detail. I read the things and burned them. They were best in flames, those letters, before they blew up of themselves. They contained particulars of a rebellion to be stirred up in the shires by these gentlemen, who would then converge upon London, overcome all resistance, take my sister prisoner and offer the Throne to me and Edward Courtenay. I wished that these rash gents would keep their plot, if they must make one, just to themselves and leave me alone. But my luck was out, for Sir James and Sir Nick had the temerity to visit me to have speech with me upon the subject. They had nothing of me save a warning to be gone, and yarely, afore they were marked and questions asked about their presence at Ashridge.

Then, in early January, I had a letter from Wyatt, unsealed and tied with tapes. In it he advised me to take flight to Donnington Castle immediately. Donnington was one of my own properties and why should I fly there? Why should I fly at all? Reading swiftly on, I discovered that it was thought by the rebels that I might be snatched by force from Ashridge by my sister's men, it being only an unfortified manor house. Snatched by force, fortifications, flight — what was this madness? I had no intention to leave Ashridge, nor would do, except by royal sanction. After I had refolded the parchment and retied the tapes, it presented exactly the same appearance as when handed to me by Tib who had brought it to my chamber but moments before.

Entering the Great Hall, I looked round for the messenger, and saw him, tankard in fist, legs up on a bench. He came smartly to his feet at my appearance with the letter in my hand. I tossed it to him. 'Take this back to your master. Tell him it is unread. I will not accept letters from any disaffected persons. Tell him I want none of it, nor letters, nor messages. Tell him what he does, he does on his own. I will have no part of it.'

But the fellow was taken and the letter too. The messenger's fate I know not, but the letter came into the hands of the Queen to bring more suspicion upon me. I thought that if Mary should have a child by Spanish Philip, my danger would be somewhat lessened, but then England and I would never be one. If she had no child — well, my life would hang at risk until she or I died. So my peace was fled for years, mayhap for always.

In the middle of January the rebellion broke forth indeed. It was led by Tom Wyatt, handsome, hot-headed and with no common-sense worth a groat. He was the son of the poet who had writ sonnets to my mother. The silly, white-faced, chicken-hearted Courtenay was in the plot too. His part was to march upon London from the West, Wyatt from Kent, whilst Jane Grey's father, the Duke of Suffolk, led an army from the Midlands. I verily believe that this Duke was a halfwit, for to have assisted in this enterprise was like running upon his own death, and making his daughter's certain, should aught go amiss.

This was alarming, but worse was to follow, for after the arrival of this news, there came a letter from the Queen. After I had read it, I flung it to the floor and sat rigid as a cornered beast. Tibby darted forward.

'Lady, are you ill? You have turned as white as bone!'

'Ay, I am ill,' I muttered through clenched teeth. 'Get me to bed — call Kat — get out of here! Call Kat quick. Hurry, I say!'

She ran off, alarmed, while my mind whirled. The letter bid me to London to clear Her Majesty's mind upon certain matters affecting me. 'Twas naught but a lure to draw me into the net. Once in London, straight to the Tower, and no more would be heard of the Princess Elizabeth. So Princess Elizabeth would not go.

When Kat entered my chamber, her quick eyes

went at once to the letter lying upon the rushes. 'The Queen,' she said.

'Ay, she wishes me in London.'

'That accursed rebellion,' groaned Kat. 'Does she accuse you?'

'Not in so many words,' I answered. 'She wishes but to ask me some questions as to my doings, my religion, my loyalties — and my proposed move to Donnington.'

'Move to Donnington? What mean you, love?'

'I mean that she knows as much of the plot as the plotters themselves.'

'She thinks you have a part in it?'

'Oh yes, Kat. Yes indeed. Well, I am sick unto death with the fever, the plague, what you will, but I cannot be moved. I am too ill to leave my bed. Send Blanche to tell the messenger of my sickness and then get me to my bed. Quick, Kat, lose no time over it!'

So Mary wanted me in London. Her questions would have to remain unanswered and her desire for my company unfulfilled. I would not go there and put myself in more deadly peril than I was already, should she turn against me. And while keeping to my bed from expediency and nervous fret, I grew truly sick, so that all about me were dismayed. I had severe pains in my back, my body swelled and oft I was wandering in my mind, returning to consciousness of deadly ill-being and much vomiting.

I was not yet recovered when I was told of the failure of the rebellion and nigh relapsed, for the tidings were desperate bad, and I feared, despite all my precautions, that I might in some way be implicated. Kat repeated the news in a hushed voice, glancing at me warily ever and again, afraid that such a tale of such a succession of misfortunate happenings might bring on my fever. She told me that Courtenay had played the coward and remained in the West Country, leaving Tom Wyatt to march alone upon London; that Suffolk had been sniffed out by dogs, while hiding in a hollow tree near Coventry, and had surrendered.

'So, lacking all supporters, Thomas Wyatt was taken in London and sent to the Tower,' she went on. 'The worst of it all is — ' she stopped, uncertain how to continue.

'Worse? There is more? Come, let us have it.'

'Do, I pray, keep calm, my love. I will tell you, sure, but I fear for your health. Promise me that you will not excite yourself.'

I nodded, my eyes fixed on hers in an agony of apprehension.

'Well then, they blackened your Highness's royal name and tried to implicate you to save their sorry skins.'

'Oh Kat!' I gasped. 'I feared it, I did indeed.'

We stared at one another wordless. My mind seemed to spin like a windmill as I realised my plight. I shook my head as if to clear it. 'I shall have to go to London now,' I said at last. 'There will be no gainsaying it this time. They will come for me and I shall have to go. Kat, I am greatly afeared.'

'And I,' she said.

* * *

In early February there arrived two doctors at Ashridge. They were Mary's own and had been sent by her to tend me and to discover when I should be able to travel. They had brought with them the Queen's litter, and if they agreed I could be moved, a Commission would be sent to bring me, in the litter, to London. They examined me and pronounced that I was suffering from watery humours and that these had brought this fever and sickness upon me. After much consultation, they decided that I could go to London if my journey was slow and taken in easy stages.

'Well, my good doctors,' I said, leaning wearily against my pillows, 'I am willing to go, but I fear that I am too weak, for indeed I have been very sick.'

'The litter is comfortable, dear Princess,' fussed little Dr. Wendy, 'and we shall see to it that it travels smoothly. You will be resting upon cushions, wrapped up warmly, and the curtains are of the best leather to withstand draughts.'

When the gentlemen of the Commission arrived, I found that their leader was mine own great-uncle Lord William Howard, now Lord Admiral of England. He strode into my chamber and stood by my bed, looking down upon me in some concern.

'How now, Bess, sorry I am to see you in such a pickle. You look as pale as a corpse, beshrew me you do. What ails you, lass?'

I stared up into his strong, dark face with the

large Howard nose and snapping brown eyes. His once black hair was grey now, but his tall, athletic figure was as upright as ever.

'Watery humours, they say,' I answered. 'I know not what that may mean. Suffice it that I have been grievous unwell and am still so weak that I cannot walk.'

'Listen, my girl,' he said urgently, 'no one is asking you to walk to London, but come you must. For God's sake get your women to put you in the litter and begin your journey. The Queen's blood is up and she will have her way, no matter what you do.'

So on the twelfth of February, Kat and Tib brought me to the litter that stood waiting in the courtyard. It was a cold, bleak day, and I was wrapped in furs from head to foot. So weak was I that the world swung dizzily round me, and for a space, the earth and sky changed places as I reeled against the supporting arms that held me. Once in the litter, still the world swung, my stomach heaved, and thrusting my head swiftly through the curtains, I retched and, perforce, vomited upon the ground. Lord William dismounted from his horse and came over to me as Kat wiped the sweat from my forehead.

'Poor maid, I am sorry indeed,' he said. 'But niece, take heed of what I say. Mayhap if you show obedience and make the journey, undoubted sick though you are, it might stand in your favour. To stay behind will lose you all. Come, I will send a messenger to the Council that you cannot travel more than six or seven miles a day. This much I can do for you, my girl.'

Smiling weakly, I thanked him and we set off. It took us five days to reach Highgate and Mr. Cholmondeley's house, where I rested until I was more recovered. On the twenty-third of February I told Kat to dress me well all in white, with no touch of colour and no jewels.

'Sure, you need none, sick as you are!' she said. 'Who is to look at you through closed litter-curtains and a mountain of furs?'

'Nay, Kat, once we reach London I wish the people to see me and know that I am not come slinking into town like a guilty rat. I want them to see that my body is no longer swollen, that I am not pregnant as some slanderers have said. Oh yes, I know what is whispered,' I said noting her startled look. '''Tis the Spanish Ambassador's doing — mine uncle Howard told me. I wish these lies to be refuted. Now, dress me in the white velvet and the white fur-hooded cloak, and let us be on our way.'

So she did my bidding, protesting that I would catch my death, I was too weak, but I paid no heed. She was right, the weather was cold and raw, the clouds hung low, but I forebore to shiver. I would show no flicker of weakness lest it be taken for cowardice or culpability. My litter rocked on its way between the ranks of my escort. 'Twas early and still grey dawn, so that few people were out, but once we had passed the Charterhouse, I pulled back the curtains and called a brief halt, straightening my back and holding my head high.

''Tis policy, my dear,' I explained to Kat. 'I

would the people see me alive now, for if I were to disappear of a sudden, questions would be asked. It will also be noticed that I am desperate ill and forced to travel, even so. A stir would be made, I am certain of it. So do as I say and argue no more.'

We came in through Aldersgate, and there on the gate I saw many heads and quarters, still fresh, raw and bloody, and fully recognisable as parts of human beings that had been men. I sighed as I realised that these were the remains of those taken in the rebellion. At least twenty gallows were up along the way, all with bodies swinging creakily on the ropes, their garments flapping like unheeded signals in the cold wind, as a warning to others who would essay to rebel 'gainst their Sovereign. It was a melancholy sight.

By this time, many folk were abroad, and the sound of our approach catched the ears of the rest, so they came running to see who passed by. The cheers at seeing me changed to groans and cries of dismay at my altered, pallid looks. Some hot-heads began a cry of: 'Rescue, rescue!' I shook my head and smiled, but said naught, being too weak, yet glad to know their loving temper. I smile now, when I recall that someone described my behaviour on that journey to Renard as 'proud, lofty and superbly disdainful.' How that must have enraged the gentleman, who, no doubt, had hoped to have me reduced to cringing fear, ready to do aught to save myself from a dread fate. Ho, he ever underrated me, as Spanish Philip was to do later! Woman I am, weak vessel I never was; but few knew it then. Now the world knows it, and has done for many a year.

And this brings on my douleur when I misdoubt me that even so much as a year may not be left unto me. I wish I could be as certain of Paradise as my cousin, poor little Jane Grey. She had no doubts at all as to her triumphal entry into Heaven. Will I sleep for ever, remaining only in the hearts of men, or shall I find my sins forgiven me and a wondrous city to dwell in? Oh, but I would wish to rule it! Nay, for there are no rulers in Heaven, only God. Will He shrive me of the sin of the death of Mary of Scotland? That lies heavy as lead upon me, although, for the safety of England, I feel I could have done no less. Will He have forgiven my sister for her terrible sins, seeing that she committed them in His name? But these are grim thoughts which increase my heaviness. I prefer to call to mind my youth, with all its terrors, than to dwell upon my dotage with its worse fears, for hope is absent now. In my young days, it always rose anew.

When I arrived at White Hall I was chilled to find no reception of any kind. Even more apprehensive did I feel when all but a few servants were taken from me. Kat, Blanche and Tibby Markham I kept by me, nor would I let them go. My uncle forebore to answer my anxious questionings, merely bidding me be of good cheer and enjoining me not be down-hearted, before riding off with his men.

'Good cheer, indeed!' sniffed Tib as she and Kat supported me. 'Precious little good cheer there is here, forsooth!'

'Oh, men are all alike,' comforted Blanche as

she trotted behind, carrying my writing desk and jewel casket. 'When the Queen sends for you, all will be resolved.'

'I hear she lately pardoned four hundred rebels, so perhaps she is in merciful mood,' suggested Kat.

'Ay, but rebels! This is her own sister,' protested Tib. 'It is not the same thing at all.'

I could only hope that my sister shared Tib's feelings, but made no comment, being too weary. My chamber was drab and not of the best, but glad was I to fall upon the day-bed while waiting for Mary's summons. It did not come. After several days, came Chancellor Gardiner instead.

I did not like this gentleman. My father had called him a 'wilful, heady man,' and had misliked him ever since he had tried to encompass the downfall of sweet Queen Catherine Parr, removing him from the Council and striking his name from the list of executors of his will. Gardiner and I eyed one another with mutual distrust, he attempting to bully and terrorise me by stamping up and down my room, shouting like a sea-captain and flourishing his arms excitedly.

'Confess your part in this shameful affair Madam, and mayhap your miseries will be over!' he ranted, pausing in his march and thumping threateningly upon a small table.

'Ay, over for ever, you mean,' I retorted. 'I know you wish me dead and out of your way.'

'That is for Her Majesty to say,' he answered. 'She refuses to see you until you show proper regret. You can expect no mercy else!'

'I have told you that I had no dealings with any in this foolish uprising,' I cried. 'I know why you try to intimidate me! 'Tis because no one will say aught against me, for there is naught to say!'

'Indeed,' he said nastily. 'I tell you that if you wish to escape the fate of Lady Jane Dudley, your only chance is to beg the Queen's mercy.'

'What!' I cried scornfully. 'Beg mercy for a fault I have not committed? I will do no such thing.'

He lowered his voice to a sinister growl, glaring at me ferociously. 'Knowest thou,' he said, 'that upon the same day that you left Ashridge, your cousin was executed? Ha!' he cried triumphantly, seeing me flinch, 'that touches you, does it not? Her royal blood did not save her, and she had naught to do with her silly father's plotting. Yet she paid the penalty of a traitor. I heard that she saw her husband's head and body, all bloody in a cart, when she looked from her window too soon after his 'heading.'

'I heard it too, my lord,' I whispered and said no more for fear I should weep aloud.

'Ay, she fainted away,' he went on, 'and was barely recovered when her turn came. When the headsman struck the blow, there was a very fountain, a torrent of blood. 'Twas as if she burst. I saw it, and I tell you I never beheld aught like it and she so tiny and small. Have you thought that this could happen to you if you continue to defy Her Majesty? The Lady Jane's scaffold still stands, mark you, Madam!'

'Sir Bishop,' I said in a trembling voice, 'you have given me sore distress, but I will not do your bidding. I am innocent and refuse to sue for mercy. Mercy is for those who have done wrong, and I have not!'

It was deadlock. He left me to my thoughts soon after, and dark, disturbing thoughts they were . . . In all, I was at White Hall for nigh on a month and never saw my sister. For her part, she knew not what to do with me, hearken though she did to Simon Renard's persuasions. His greatest desire was to see me meet poor little Jane Grey's horrid fate and thus secure all his ambitions for himself, his sovereign and his country. Mary, although she could screw herself up to the point of having Jane killed, could not do the same by me. Jealous, mistrustful, thinking of me as a bastard, even affecting to doubt my father's siring of me, she could not do it. The blood-tie was there and I would have to hope that it would hold, despite Renard's cozenings.

To add to my miseries, there was another annoyance that I had to suffer and it stemmed direct from my cousin Margaret Lennox. My rooms at White Hall were below those given to her servants for a kitchen, and God's death, how they crashed the pans about! 'Twas like suits of armour being tossed to the ground all day long, and near deafened me, giving me no peace. Several times did I send Kat up, first to beg for, then to command quietness, but she wasted her breath for all the effect it had. She told me that one of the Countess's servants whispered to her that they had been bidden by their mistress to make a great noise especially to irritate me. I prayed that plague and misfortunes might fall upon the head of my charming cousin, and that her children would live to cause her sorrow — a good comprehensive curse it was, and the last part came true in full measure in the years to come, for her son, Lord Darnley died of his marriage to Mary of Scotland.

On the sixth of March, the Queen married Prince Philip of Spain, by proxy, at White Hall. The gallant bridegroom had refused to set foot in his wife's country while the people were so hostile to him, and while that jade, the Lady Elizabeth still was not under lock and key.

'God's truth!' I cried to Kat. 'Does she mean to imprison me? If she does so now, then what will happen to me after? Gardiner has told me, most meaningfully, that poor Jane's scaffold still stands.'

'How he dared, the beast!' burst out Kat furiously.

'Well, if I be not killed, then might I not be prisoned all my life? Think of it — never again to be free! Always to live under the shadow of lurking death from those who would find the world safer without me, to be ever confined!'

During these dark days Kat brought me what news she could from outside my rooms, and one morning she came sighing and long-faced.

'Wyatt has spoken,' she said. ''Twas under torture and the hope of a pardon.'

'He brought my name into it?' I asked. Kat nodded. 'Oh God,' I gasped, 'it is the end!'

'His trial is tomorrow, my lamb. Mayhap we shall learn more then. Come to bed now and rest.'

'Rest? I shall never rest again!' I protested wildly, suffering her to lead me to bed as if I were a babe.

Wyatt, at his trial, said that I had never written to him, but ruined that by announcing that he had written to me. I felt that my race was run; indeed, death stared me in the face. Mayhap God would work a miracle in my favour, though I doubted it. I had heard many beseech God for less and remain disappointed.

'If there is a miracle, 'tis because the Lord hath a brave future laid up for you,' said Kat, in an effort to rally me, as she brushed my hair one forenoon a day or two later. 'The Almighty gives nothing easy. As St. Thomas Aquinas said: *Whom the Lord loveth He chasteneth.*'

'In that case, I am His best friend,' quoth I glumly. 'If you have no better cheer than that, Kat, you had best stay mum.'

As I spoke, there came a thumping on the door and Tibby went to open it. There stood William Paulet, Marquess of Winchester, thin, wizened and sour as a lemon, and beside him, big, clumsy Tom Radcliffe, who had served my father.

'Come in,' I said irritably. 'Do not hover in the doorway. What tidings have you brought, sirs? By the look of you, nothing good.'

'That is as may be,' snapped out Winchester, striding forward arrogantly. 'Our mission is to carry you to the Tower.'

'My God!' I cried, springing to my feet. 'Why? What for? What is to be done with me? I am no common criminal! I will not go, I say!'

237

'It is an order, Madam,' answered Winchester. 'The Queen is to Oxford, there to open Parliament, and would have you in safe keeping the while, where you cannot cause disaffection, nor write treasonable letters to His French Majesty. Never look so amazed. One was found in the French mailbag. That alone is enough to condemn you.'

My brain span with terror. I was ringed round with plots. I knew naught of what letter he spoke and cared not to ask. Once in the Tower, I feared that would be the last o' me. I would be left to die within its walls, meeting some secret end.

'My sister cannot know of this,' I protested. 'She would not act so to me. 'Tis Gardiner's doing — I know it. It cannot be Mary. I must see her, gentlemen, I must! Prithee, may I not see her?'

'No you may not,' said Winchester. 'She will not suffer it, so now come your ways.'

I stood my ground, shaking, my fingers plucking my gown. 'I would write her a letter then,' I blurted through trembling lips, 'for she must hear me!'

'I say Nay!' shouted Winchester, suddenly violent. 'Cease this delay, Lady, and come with us.'

But I had seen a flicker in Tom Radcliffe's eyes. He did not move to the door with his companion, but stared at me searchingly, whilst I fixed my anguished gaze upon his heavy, earnest face. Then he turned to the Marquess.

'Wait, my lord,' said he, 'you are too hasty. I say she shall write.' Turning back to me, he dropped upon his knee. 'Lady, write your letter and I myself will carry it to the Queen.'

Winchester demurred, but Lord Sussex was

unmoved. Kat and Tibby hastened to me with pen and paper and I began to write. The agony of my mind was great, but I forced myself to write slowly so that the words would be clear for my sister to read. As my brain searched frantically for phrases that would reach Mary's heart, I heard Lord Winchester say angrily: 'But the tide! If she delays, we shall miss the tide and so lose a whole day.'

I seized on that. I knew well that the waters beneath London Bridge were unnavigable at low tide. So I wrote slow and slower yet, striving to round off my sentences with polished elegance. Over the page, my panic became too strong for the steadiness of my hand, and my thoughts began to race wildly, yet I kept on . . . *'And as for the traitor Wyatt, he might peradventure write me a letter, but on my faith, I never received any from him.'* Not quite true, but true enough for my purpose. *'And for the copy of my letter to the French King, I pray God confound me eternally if ever I sent him word, message, token or letter, by any means. And to this my truth will stand to my death.'*

I had writ all I could. There was no more to say, and yet most of the second page was empty. To foil a possible forger, who could wreak my death by writing a confession of guilt in a hand like mine own in the empty space, I scratched several heavy lines across the sheet to fill the emptiness left, and at the very end I wrote: *'I humbly crave but only one word of answer from yourself. Your Highness's most faithful subject that hath been from the beginning and will be to my end, Elizabeth.'*

Lord Winchester snatched the letter from me,

anxiety writ angrily upon his face. 'We shall be in trouble for this!' he railed. 'We cannot move her now, it is too late. 'Tis your doing, my lord, and I shall say so!'

'I shall say so myself,' retorted Sussex. 'Now, give me the letter and let us go to Her Majesty.'

So they left me and I heard their voices arguing as they hurried down the passage. Alone, I fell almost hysterical. The strain of long waiting, the shock of the threat to me following upon my illness was too much. I paced and flung about my chamber, crying out and weeping distractedly. I was certain that those who were mine enemies were intent to push me into the Tower, despite all, and there let me rot or worse. It had happened before and for less reason. Besides, how had that letter, purporting to be from me, got into the French mailbag? What was more, who had got it out? I had writ no letter to the French King or to anyone else; I was not such a fool to put pen to paper upon such a dangerous business that could well be the death o' me. Nay, that was the work of spies in my household, Satan's curse upon them! I would have to rely on God and my wits to steer me through this valley of shadows. I was frantic all day, nor could I sleep that night.

The next morn dawned dim and rain-soaked. Palm Sunday it was. There would be no palm-hung church for me this day, and no merry Easter-tide to follow. I would be prisoned in the Tower with the good folk of England led to think ill of me. My lords Sussex and Winchester came to my door at nine of the clock, sore at the memory of high words from my sister who had professed herself

240

amazed at their insolence and defiance, and had called upon her royal father's name to witness her great annoyance at such disobedience from her servants.

'So my lords, why now, in the rain?' demanded Kat furiously. 'Would not the night's tide have done as well? 'Twas dry then, and my princess has been sadly ill, as all seem to forget.'

'There is fear of a rescue at night,' said Winchester crossly. 'So come now, and be quick.'

'I see!' cried Kat. 'We go now, in the rain, while people are at church or indoors, and by river too, so that folk who are abroad in the streets cannot see her and so raise the alarm. It is wicked!'

'If you wish to accompany your mistress, you will do well to hold your tongue, Mrs. Ashley,' remarked Winchester unpleasantly. 'She has other ladies besides yourself.'

Kat, thus silenced, put my cloak about me and we hurried forth. With me came Kat, Blanche, Tibby and two tiring women; we scuttled after the men, huddled in our cloaks and bowed against the rain. Our way led across the wet garden, below which lay the river, grey and tumbling, the Surrey bank a mere blur of misty shapes, the river stairs where our barged rocked, so slippery with the rain that we were forced to clutch at one another for support as we trod down the wooden steps. Once in the barge, we crowded into the covered cabin, where waited a gentleman attendant and young Tom Cornwallis who drew the leather curtains against the down-pour. We shot the rapids under London Bridge, sitting tense as usual, for this is

241

always a dangerous undertaking, even for such long experienced watermen as were ours. When the barge tied up, I came out of the cabin with my head held high, but when I saw where we had got, I stopped and refused to go, for I was to enter the Tower through the Traitor's Gate. I stared, horrified, at its grim grille and crossbars; at the low arch under which it hung.

'Nay, I will not,' I said sharp and clear. 'This place is not fit for me to enter and I will not use it.'

'Lady, you cannot choose,' said the Marquess of Winchester. ''Tis here you must disembark, so go you forward.'

So forward, perforce, I went, up over my shoes in water. He offered me his cloak, but I thrust it furiously aside and turned my face up to the teeming sky.

'Here lands as true a subject as ever landed at these stairs,' I shouted loud, so that all could hear me. 'Before Thee, oh God, do I speak it, having no other friend but Thee alone!' And up the steps I went. At the top, I declared I would go no further and sat down plump on the wet stones. Those men were all amazed and knew not what to do. I stared up into their perplexed faces, and as God is my Judge upon the Last Day, I near burst out a-laughing, although I did not feel merry. For the first time, but not the last, I held the Council upon my will, and mighty confused were its members thereby. Sir John Brydges, Lieutenant of the Tower, stood by the gate in a very ill mood, his fine crimson velvet soaked, and all for a green girl who would not do as her elders bid her.

Then I heard cheering, and I saw that the Yeoman Warders, drawn up to guard the gate upon my entrance, had broken ranks and some were on their knees to me, waving and shouting: 'God preserve Your Grace!' which moved me deeply. It moved Tom Cornwallis, who stood anxious at my side, so much that he fell a-weeping for sympathy. That fired me as naught else could have done. I jumped to my feet and clapped him on the shoulder.

'Come Tom, hold your noise. Be of good heart, man. By heaven, 'tis your place to support me in my hour of need, not mine to support you!' I said bracingly. Then, swinging my dripping cloak about me, I turned towards my fate. 'Since there is no help for it, let us go in,' I called. 'My truth is such that I thank God my friends have no cause to weep for me, so Tom, be of good cheer.' And in we went bravely.

My apartment lay upon the first floor of the Bell Tower. It struck upon me like a tomb at first sight. Stone-walled, stone-ceiled and vaulted, stone-floored it was, with a great fireplace like a cavern, empty of fuel. Opposite this gaping fireplace were three tall, pointed windows, deeply recessed, with stone window seats. Outside the door was a small passage with three garderobes shielded by stuff curtains. They stank. It was cold. 'Jesu,' I said grimly, 'this place has the chill of death.'

'Sweet my Lady, 'twill not take us long to render it more cheerful,' Tibby encouraged me. 'A few cushions and some curtains — '

'And a fire in that great fireplace,' added Kat, trying to smile.

I nodded. 'See to it,' I replied briefly, and sat me down on a window seat which struck cold even through my gown. The lords of the Council stared about the chamber, seeming somewhat disconcerted at its chill bareness.

'Do you mean to share my imprisonment, gentlemen?' I enquired sardonically. 'I need to change my wet gown and would have privacy to do so.'

At once, they began to murmur apologetically and shuffle towards the door, glancing back uneasily, as if loth to leave me. I looked at my lord of Sussex and saw him regarding me gravely and sadly.

'My lord,' I said to him, 'I give you thanks for what you have tried to do for me.'

He made as if to speak, but thinking better of it, bowed low before turning to follow his companions. As they hesitated in the passage, I heard him say: 'Let us take heed, my lords, that we go not beyond our commission, for she was our King's daughter.'

The echoing slam of the outer door drowned any reply made by the others, and we were left to manage as we could. I wept no more; I had done my part of that. But oh, I wondered if I should ever again breathe the air of freedom which none find so precious 'til they lose it. I sat on, silent and despairing. Presently Kat came to me.

'Hey my love,' she said, taking my hand, 'how you are cold! Come, we have a bed for you and a fire just lit. Rouse you, dearest, for a posset is warming and all will seem better on the morrow.'

'But you,' I murmured at last, 'where do you all sleep?'

'Why, we have mattresses on the floor for the present,' she answered brightly, 'and each day we shall do more to make this apartment meet for us to live in. Come now, to your bed, we would not have you ill again.'

After that first night, Kat and my women were quartered elsewhere, whilst all my meals were brought in by the guard, for mine own cook was not allowed to work for me, 'case of messages brought in from outside. I had no books, no writing materials and wellnigh no companionship, for my ladies were kept from me. During that week I felt utterly lost for the first time in my life. I became deeply melancholy and filled with the dire certainty that Mary meant to kill me. So depressed were my thoughts that I decided to ask my sister to allow me to be beheaded by a French swordsman, even as my mother had been. Indeed, I thought much upon her ending as I sat alone in that grim chamber. I felt I was destined to follow her fate and that my family was peopled with murderers.

Then, one dark morn, as I lay doleful abed, having no reason to rise, there came a hammering at my door. Wrapped in a bed-gown, my hair in a tangle, I opened the door myself. There stood Bishop Gardiner and members of the Council, all unannounced, to catch me unaware. At first, I thought that they had come to take me to the scaffold and felt the blood leave my limbs weak for sheer dread. But their first words reassured me, though 'twas cold comfort enough.

'Lady Elizabeth,' quoth Gardiner, tramping over the threshold, 'We come to question your doings in the Wyatt plot.'

I could not collect my wits, for it had been a shock, and I was woefully conscious of my weak and dishevelled appearance. I all but fell on to a stool, my heart beating wildly, waiting for what Gardiner had to say.

'We are somewhat put about,' he went on, 'upon the suggestion to you by the traitor Wyatt that you move to Donnington. Have you aught to say to clarify this?'

Wyatt's letter! Should I confess that I knew of its contents? Nay, better not. Panic-stricken, I spoke at random. 'Donnington?' I faltered. 'I know naught of Donnington. I do not know of it, nor have I visited there.'

'Come, come, Madam,' blustered the Bishop, 'this will not do. Perhaps this gentleman will serve to aid your memory as to your own property — ' and in through the door was hustled Sir James Croftes; he who had visited me at Ashridge. He was pale from imprisonment and ill-usage, but his appearance served to collect my scattered wits.

Striking my hands together, I said: 'Indeed, I do remember that I have such a place, but I never lay in it in all my life. And as for any that hath moved me thereto, I do not remember.'

Sir James went on his knees before me. 'I do assure your Grace,' he said, 'I have been marvellously tossed and examined touching your Highness, and I swear to God before you all that

246

I know nothing of that crime which you have laid to my charge. To the death I swear it, if I should be driven to such a trial!'

These brave words put fresh heart into me and I pressed his hands gratefully, lifting my head and allowing my eyes to rove haughtily over the persons of the Councillors as my thoughts began to marshall themselves. 'My lords,' said I, steadily, 'touching my removal from Ashridge to Donnington, I do remember that Mr. Hoby of my household and you, Sir James, had some trifling talk about it. But what is that to the purpose? Might I not, my lords, go to mine own houses at all times?' Ha, I had them! They shuffled their feet, cleared their throats and turned their heads one to the other as if seeking the answer to my question. Swiftly I went on: 'Well, my lords, you sift me narrowly, but you can do no more than God hath appointed, and so may He forgive you all!'

I drew a deep breath and caught the eye of the Earl of Arundel, who was regarding me with a look compounded of compassion and surprised admiration. I allowed the corners of my mouth to tremble into a tiny, wistful smile, whilst holding his eyes with mine own — and down on his knees he tumbled. 'Fore God, it was almost worth all the trials I had yet endured to see the faces of his companions! Utterly chop-fallen, were they, even my lord Bishop. 'Twas as good as a play, I swear. As for me, I kept my haughty look and dignity, forgetting my uncombed hair and dragged-on bedgown, and listened to Lord Arundel's words.

'My lords,' he exclaimed, 'her Grace speaks truth. I am sorry to see her troubled by us all and by so vain matters. Madam, so help me God, I hope for my own part, never to trouble you more!'

It was as if the sun shone in that bleak room. I rose, smiling upon him and proffered my hand, which he kissed most fervently. What made the miracle more profound was that he was an ardent Catholic and counted upon by Gardiner as strong support. Surely God wrought for me that day. When they had taken themselves out in great haste, I fell upon my knees to give thanks to Him who made me and for His intervention in the shape of mine enemy.

Right soon did I feel the effects of Lord Arundel's words, and my life became a little easier. My uncle, Lord William Howard, took up my cause, and I was allowed to walk in the Queen's own apartments. When I complained of the lack of fresh air, the erstwhile disdainful Sir John Brydges came, full of apologies and bowing nose to knees.

'Dearest Madam, I do regret to be compelled to refuse your request to walk in the garden, but this reverse will be but temporary, I do assure you. 'Tis contrary to mine orders, you understand, but I will lose no time in speaking to the Council, and sure, the lords will grant your wish. We would not wish to keep the roses from your cheeks!' So spake Sir John, very fulsome and ingratiating.

I hardly believed him, yet permission was granted and I was allowed to walk in a small enclosed garden. The fleeting April sunshine and scudding clouds, the damp, rain-filled air seemed to me as a foretaste of Heaven. What mattered it if a certain dour Mrs. Coldeburn was constrained to accompany me and spend the time pacing behind me, or standing at the gate jingling a bunch of keys? I cared not; the trees were well on in bud, the small hedges were greening and herbs and lavender springing up in the beds. This garden lay beneath the Beauchamp Tower and the apartments that held Edward Courtenay and Lord Robert Dudley — my Rob — the friend of my childhood. Oft I glanced up at the panes, yet beheld no one.

'Your Grace will see no one, neither,' said Mrs. Coldeburn. 'They have been ordered not to look from the windows while your Grace walks abroad. 'Tis truth,' she insisted, seeing my look of disbelief. 'The Council fear that the sight of you will set them mad to have speech with you, and then what plots might not be hatched?'

'Good God!' I cried. 'Am I a magician that the mere sight of me will send them to a frenzy?'

Mrs. Coldeburn's hard face creased into a reluctant smile. 'Your Grace is very beguiling and mighty like your great father,' she replied.

Yet I did see Rob, but a few days later. Scanning the windows as usual, I noticed a movement behind one. I did not start, nor check in my steady pacing of the paths, but my eyes remained alert for I was near enough to distinguish the dark hair and the flutter of a kerchief. Quick-thinking, I asked Mrs Coldeburn to pluck me some herbs to ward off the stink in my chamber of the latrines. While she was doing this I waved my hand and was rewarded by the throwing of a kiss, which I returned, my

249

heart beating high. My spirits rose excitedly and the blood leapt in my veins. It was good to realise that I was young and desirable after so long without any such feelings. Indeed, I envied Tibby Markham who was all afire with love and romance, she having found her sweetheart within the very walls of the Tower. Her lover was Sir John Harington whom she had met some years agone. Here was the reason of her unwed state. She had been in love with him since Tom Seymour's downfall five years before, when she had been ordered from me. He, as a friend of Tom's, had been imprisoned and had been in the Tower ever since. I had never known of their love, for Tib had been sent off too quick, Sir John taken so sudden, and all in the middle of my grievous trouble and misery when I had little thought to spare for anyone save myself.

Sir John was much older than Tibby and a widower, but handsome, merry, well-looking and of comfortable means. He was also a relative by marriage of mine, in a left-handed way, for his dead wife had been a red-haired, bastard daughter of my father, the King. 'Twas not spoke of, for she was of a low-born mother and was passed off as the child of my father's tailor, though all knew the truth. Etheldreda was she called, and brought Sir John a fine house at Batheaston and a handsome dowry, before dying young. So, through this twisted link, I had a kindness for Sir John, as ever I had for those who were connected with my family. I wished Isabella and he very happy; sure, they deserved it for waiting so long and true.

Oft did they contrive to meet, so Tibby told me

upon one of the few times that I was allowed to see my ladies. 'Ay, Madam,' she smiled, all rosy with love, 'sure we meet. It can be managed and why not? Sir John cannot stay here for ever; he did no wrong and the Lord Admiral is dead this many a year.'

'Certes,' quoth I, very dry, 'I am not like to forget.'

'Well, but your Grace, if I can contrive to meet Sir John, mayhap he and I might contrive aught for you.'

My heart jumped, but I held myself cool as water. 'So,' I answered with careful blankness, 'you might contrive aught. What, and with whom, pray?'

'Why, with Lord Robert, your Grace. He worries my John night and day for a meeting with you. John says he is near mad for love of you and watches you each day as you walk in the garden. He says you are like a lodestone, a snare, to drive a man crazed, or so John tells me.'

I raised my brows. ' 'Deed, he is far gone then.' Suddenly dropping my pose, I said eagerly: 'Oh Tib, tell me, what did he say else?' So we giggled like the silly maids we were, and, each day as I walked in the garden, I contrived to distract Mrs. Coldeburn and greet Rob who stood at his window.

Then one day came little Harry Martin. A sweet little manikin of five summers was he, and round-eyed to see a real Princess.

'Son of the Keeper of the Queen's Robes,' murmured Mrs. Coldeburn, ever at my side. 'Harry, make your bow to her Grace,' she said aloud, and the child executed a very tolerable obeisance.

'Are you in truth a Princess, Madam?' he asked.

'Indeed so,' I answered gravely. 'I am Princess of England.'

'I told you!' he called triumphantly to one yet hidden. 'Come from that bush, Susannah, and do not be silly!' Turning to me again he endeavoured, most earnestly, to explain. 'It is my friend Susannah who hides there, for she is shy, being but four years old to my five. Oh, I will get her, for she longs to see you.' He ran behind a hawthorn bush and reappeared dragging by the hand a tiny girl, whose head was firmly cast down and whose free hand tightly grasped a bunch of primroses. Urged by Harry, she made a bob and held out the flowers, eyes still bent on the ground. As I took the little nosegay, she gave me a quick glance from under long, black lashes, and whispered to Harry.

'What does she say?' I enquired, amused.

'She says, where is your crown?' repeated Harry. 'But you would not have it here, would you, Princess? 'Twould be at home in your palace, would it not?'

'Surely,' I replied. 'It is at my home with all my jewels.'

Susannah whispered again and Harry hastened to explain. 'She says why do you wear such a dull dress? But that is because you are prisoned here. You would not wish to wear your best gowns in prison, would you?'

I laughed. 'Nay, indeed. I have no use for the

fine gowns and jewels here and so must appear dull and plain.'

'But your hair is pretty,' suddenly spoke up Susannah in a deep, gruff voice.

'Will you have your crown and jewels one day?' asked Harry.

'If God so wills,' I answered.

'Mama says,' he went on, 'that we must pray for what we want, and if God thinks it fit for us, He will allow it.'

'Your Mama is right.'

'I will say prayers,' said Susannah. 'I will ask God to let you out of your prison and make you into a great big Queen.'

Again I laughed. 'It is in His hands, Susannah. Princess though I be, I must bow before God's will. Come, walk awhile with me, both of you. I would be with you, for you have made me laugh twice in a short space, when for a very long space, I have not laughed at all.'

At this, little Harry's rosy face beamed and his blue eyes lit with pride and pleasure. Taking each a hand of mine, the children walked beside me, chattering hard the while, until it was time to go in. As the children left me I waved a quick salute to Rob at his window and went to my chamber more light-hearted than I had been for many a long, dreary day.

'Twas at about this time that I heard the news that Tom Wyatt had been 'headed. He exonerated me, and Courtenay too, on the very scaffold. It was bravely done, for he could have gone to his end silent, and done naught to save me, but he was a true and honourable man. I thank God for such, and have done all my days. Yet Wyatt's words availed me little, for I was kept in durance while Courtenay was released and was allowed to walk abroad. Bitter felt I about this, for Courtenay had been in the plot whilst I had kept out of it by my own choice. Kat did her best to soothe me when she was allowed to see me.

'My love,' she said, 'mayhap Wyatt's words did not serve to release you, but perhaps they served to save you from death. If nothing be proved 'gainst you, what can they do? You are heir to the Throne by your father's will, and well the Council knows it.'

'Ay,' I cried, 'and Gardiner and Renard know it, and they know too that they would get naught from me, should I inherit! What of poison, Kat, and secret means to put me away? To kill me, have me sped before my sister discovers it — why not? If I can think of that, be sure so can they.'

'Ah,' whispered Kat, hands to mouth, 'then we must watch and care night and day.'

'Hast thought,' I said, after a moment, 'that having heard Wyatt's words, the people will not like my continued prisoning? There will be unrest about it, I tell you.'

'That will do you no good, I think.'

'Just so,' I answered, swift. 'It may serve to irritate Bishop Gardiner further, and irritate Renard to use poison upon me. It may cause my sister to prison me straiter yet. I see little good coming of any of it.'

''Cept you are still alive, God be thanked!'

'May He allow me to reach my natural end, Kat.'

'Amen to that!' breathed Kat very solemnly.

* * *

So the dull days rolled on, one much like another, but for the starry time when Rob and I met through the stratagems of Tibby and her John. 'Twas for but twenty minutes, I should guess, and those fraught with fear of discovery. How Rob ever got to my chamber I know not, but Tibby cozened Mrs. Coldeburn into her room, with Kat and Blanche for company, and kept her chattering there.

When my door opened and he slipped within, all the breath seemed to rush from my body. For a moment we stood mum as statues, then he ran across the stone floor and I was in his arms. Ah, I gave him kiss for kiss and held him close as he held me. 'Twas sheer good fortune that our time was short and we in a panic of excitement and tension, or I and my maidenhood had been parted then and there.

'I love you!' he said, kissing, kissing. 'I adore you and will until I die. We belong to one another. I love you, beautiful, wild, red-headed witch that you are! Do you love me, Bess? Do you? Do you?'

I said I did and it was the truth. It was something I could neither understand, control or deny. My blood flamed at the sight of him; in his arms I scarce knew what I did. Yet, when John Harington scratched at the door, and we fell apart, silent and apprehensive, I knew a certain relief.

After he left me I saw him no more for five long years, and then all was changed, for my star was high in the heavens and I had ascended to my rightful place in the world. Well, I loved him all my life, and many the tear he cost me, and I him; but never would I have been without him, my dear, my Gipsy, my Eyes, my heart's darling.

The next day, when I walked in the garden, Harry Martin and Susannah came with a little friend, smaller even than Susannah. She hung back shyly and would not speak, but Harry more than made up for her silence. 'See Princess!' he cried. 'I have brought another friend. She has something for you, but she is bashful. Come, Jane. Come, tell the Princess.'

I bent towards her, touched by their sweet innocence. 'What is it, Jane?'

She held out a dimpled fist, smiling trustfully. 'Help you to 'scape,' she said, opening her hand in which lay a small bunch of keys. I took them from her, swinging them on my finger.

'Why Jane, this is kind indeed,' said I, smiling in return. Before I could do aught with the keys Mrs. Coldeburn swept among us, skirts a-flap and hands upraised in horror. She snatched the keys from me as if I were an erring serving-maid, holding them away from her as though they bore some deadly contagion.

'What is this? What are these?' she spluttered, her eyes large with indignation. 'How came these keys here, I say?'

'Mrs. Coldeburn,' I said, as little Jane set up a dismal howl, 'where are your manners that you rail here in this wise? How dare you snatch from my very hand, Madam!'

'Well — but — ' she stammered, ' 'twas the keys, your Grace. Where did the child get them? What will they unlock?'

'Mere small boxes, I should say, from their size. You surely did not think I could unlock my prison with them?'

'Nay, your Grace, it seems to me that if a child could bring you keys, she might bring something else. A message, perchance, or plans for escape. Who knows?'

'Such nonsense!' I snapped. 'The children but come to me for company and because I am Princess. The little one here thought to help me. A childish whim only.'

Yet I realised the truth of her words and guessed that I should see my young friends no more. The next day I walked alone, and thereafter. Mrs. Coldeburn told me, with righteous bridlings and head-tossings, that the child Harry Martin had been brought before the Commissioners for questioning. The poor mite could say naught, of course, but that he had brought flowers for the Lady. Stoutly did he maintain this in the faces of those men, who finally told his father to keep the crafty young knave at home and to keep better watch upon him for the future. Dear Harry, I made him my knight in after years, and a fine, staunch fellow he proved to be.

My time in the Tower was almost done, had I but known it, for upon the fifth of May I heard the clatter of horses, the shouts of men and the clash of arms in the courtyard. Rushing to the window, I could see little but the glinting of sunshine upon the points of pikes. My heart began to beat loud with fear, and swift did I send for Sir John Brydges.

'Sir John,' I said, without preamble, 'is the Lady Jane Grey's scaffold yet removed?'

'Why yes, Madam,' he replied with an astonished look. 'It is taken down.'

My whole body relaxed with such relief that I almost fell from my chair. Trembling, I said, striving for calm: 'I ask because I had thought those soldiers were to guard me upon my way there.'

Sir John gave me a look of the most speaking sympathy. 'My dear Princess,' he said warmly, 'it is no such thing, believe me. You are to be taken from here to Woodstock in Oxfordshire in the company of Sir Henry Bedingfeld of Oxburgh Hall in Norfolk, a most worthy gentleman. The men-at-arms you glimpsed out there are but to guard you upon your journey.'

'This gentleman, he is Catholic, is he not?'

'He is so, but true and honest, your Grace. He is also a Privy Councillor, Vice-Chamberlain of the Queen's Household and Captain of the Guards.'

'I would know,' I said slowly, 'if Sir Henry Bedingfeld were a person who made conscience of murder if such an order were entrusted to him.'

Sir John was emphatic. 'Nay, your Grace, he is not. He is of a most tender conscience in all things.'

I was to discover the extent of Sir Henry's conscience for myself soon enough, but knew naught of it at that time. I shook my head, full of doubt and dismay.

'Princess, I am sorry that your abiding here has been so discomfortable for you,' said Sir John. ' 'Twas my orders, you understand, not my will. I have come to feel much sympathy for you. 'Tis best you leave here, for there are those who would destroy you. If I were removed from office I could protect you no more, but Sir Henry is the Queen's own choice. He will do naught but by her own express word. You will see.'

'Have you protected me?' I asked, after a moment. 'How so?'

Then he told me that he had lately received a warrant from the Privy Council for my immediate execution. Upon handling this document he had seen that Mary's signature was not upon it. I stared at him, wordless. The Wings of Death had brushed me indeed. 'Yes,' declared Sir John, 'and I refused to carry out the order until I knew the Queen's exact wishes. 'Twas fire and lightning with me and the Chancellor for hours, but I would not give way. I could not, Madam.'

The tears came to my eyes and I took his hand. 'Good Sir John,' I said. 'How can I thank you? I shall not forget this, rest assured.'

Kneeling, he kissed my hands. 'Would I could do more for you, but I cannot, Lady. However, I say to trust Sir Henry Bedingfeld. You will be safe from sly attack whilst in his charge.'

So we parted and I had to be content. Later, I saw the Marquess of Winchester and asked if I would be able to walk abroad at Woodstock Palace.

259

He replied that this would be certain. I hoped that it would be so, for fresh air and exercise were as necessary to me as food and drink.

My leaving the Tower was fraught with drama. Tibby Markham, so docile and meek, became a very lion of resolution, and declared, with stormy tears that she would never go from the Tower whilst Jack Harington remained within it. Her Jack, thereupon, wrote to the Council for leave to marry her, and Chancellor Gardiner, so harsh to me, gave way laughing, calling Jack's letter a saucy sonnet. 'Twas reported that Gardiner had chuckled that Jack Harington should serve a year less than his sentence for such a letter. Moreover they would be allowed to marry, even though Tibby was a staunch Protestant and refused to hear Mass. Would that I had possessed such a magic hand with the pen! Such magic as I had wrought not at all with Bishop Gardiner.

★ ★ ★

The first part of our journey was to be by barge to Richmond, and as I trod down the grey stone steps to the wooden landing stage where my barge was tied, I looked about me, breathing deep of the sweet air. Ah, 'twas wonderful to see beyond a few yards with no high wall to break my vision; wonderful to witness the river water flowing where it listed, untrammelled and free, even as I was not. I hoped that Rob might have watched my leaving, but he was not at his window, and I feared that I had seen the last of him — mayhap for ever. I knew a piercing pang of regret for my youth and the gaieties of youth that were passing me by. I felt cheated, and resolved to make up for all as soon as Fate made it possible. So I stood upon the boards of the landing stage, gazing across the river to the trees and thatched roofs of Southwarke, with the great silver-grey tower of St. Mary Overy rising solid from the clustering green, the sun glinting on coloured window and golden weather-vane. Suddenly I became aware of Tom Cornwallis and dearest Kat at my side. I gave Tom my hand and Kat my kiss as she embraced me tight.

Once away upon the water, I glanced at Sir Henry Bedingfeld, my appointed guardian. By my faith, a rock-visaged gentleman; serious, I judged, and humourless, very likely deaf to persuasion. I sighed, but at that moment a roar of cannon broke out from the wharf where the office of the Hanseatic League lay. It was the Hansa saluting me as a royal Princess, even though I was being whisked away all unknown to my own countrymen. It warmed my heart, and I glanced again at Sir Henry, noticing that he was looking worried already at such preference on the part of a foreign power to a lady who was in official disgrace. He gave the order for more speed and we fairly raced upstream, the guards trotting along the north bank, until we reached Richmond Palace, all glowing red brick, its many roofs and cupolas winking in the sun, small glass window panes flashing here and there, caught by a stray sunbeam. We shot past the great gatehouse lying athwart the path and tied up at the steps. Here, I learned,

I was to spend the night and see my sister Mary.

'Immediately,' said Sir Henry. 'Come, your Grace, the Queen wishes no delay.' I demurred at such haste. I must change, rearrange my windswept hair, wash my face and hands. 'Immediately,' reiterated Sir Henry. So, perforce, to my sister I went.

She was lying on a cushioned day-bed by a western window in the light of the afternoon sun, looking ill, fretted and old. She gave me her hand to kiss. 'So you have come,' she said irritably. 'I wish to sound you upon a certain matter. 'Tis of your betrothal to Philibert of Savoy that I speak. This cannot be news to you, he has offered for you before, as well you know. I hear he is mad in love with your portrait and all he has heard of you.'

'All?' I queried sardonically.

'So he says,' she replied, with equal irony. 'Would you not find freedom with him preferable to a life here in prison?'

This was naught but a ploy to get me out of the country, poor, without power, in subjection to an exiled foreign prince. The union would also remove any shadow of injustice hanging over her treatment of me. 'No, sister,' I said. 'I will not have him.'

'And why not, pray?' cried Mary. 'Why will you not? He is not good enough for you, eh? He will stand in the way of your ambitions, is that it?' Her voice rose. 'I know you. You think to be Queen. You, with your sly eyes, your white face and slinking ways, you covet the Throne. *My* Throne it is, remember, and goes to my child after me.'

'I do not wish to marry,' I said, low.

'Oh God, send me patience! You expect me to believe that lying nonsense? A man-mad thing like you? You must think me fool indeed.'

'Nay, sister, 'tis truth. I wish not to marry.'

I felt wrung with sorrow to see her thus, and with fear of what would become of me also. She longed for Philip of Spain who would not come to her until I was safe out of the way; exiled, married, or under lock and key. Wedded she was, but by proxy only, and afire with desire for all that her womanhood had missed.

'So, you refuse!' she shouted hysterically. 'You refuse the chance I give you, you force me to imprison you, to make myself seem cruel and unjust in the eyes of all. You wish to spoil my marriage, kill the people's love for me and take my Throne! False, scheming creature, I know you! Well, imprisonment you shall have. Double guards you shall have, ay, and your lying, spying servants shall be taken from you. I order it! I command it! Guard, guard, hither to me! At once, I say, at once!'

Her ladies hustled me outside and I was hurried to the room allotted me. I sat there upon the bed, alone and unattended, shocked and trembling. Never would I grow used to being thus abused by mine own; her treatment of me hurt like a wound. Also, I feared that at last she meant to have me killed. God, I feared to die in my youth, having not experienced life, for all my living of it. Oh Mary, what was to become of you and me? I felt most bitter anguish and burst into a wild storm of tears, calling for someone, anyone, to come to me. Tom Cornwallis came and tried to calm me. I wept upon his shoulder, formalities forgotten, his comforting hand patting my back, his voice uttering agitated but soothing sounds.

'Oh Tom, oh Tom!' I sobbed. 'This night I think I must die. I am in such despair. Oh God help me!'

'Sweet Princess, weep not!' he cried emotionally. 'I will die with you if death should come to you. I swear it.'

At this cold comfort I wept the louder, and Tom rushed frantically from my chamber straight to Sir Henry's friend, Lord Williams of Thame, blurting out his fears, calling that if the Princess were in danger of death that night, he and his companions wished to die with her. Lord Williams, horrified, scurried back with Tom to my room, where they both swore dramatically to defend me from harm, or to die for me, with all their men and companions, then and there. At this, a watery smile escaped me, I fetched a deep sigh and began to wipe away my tears.

Lord Williams went at once to speak with Sir Henry on my behalf, and he sent Kat to me, but sleep came not to us that night. We were glad enough when morning dawned, but more misery came later with the order to leave. Blanche and Kat were wrested from me, Kat's arms being dragged from around my shoulders by force, amid screams and tears. I was hustled away to the waterside, where I was told that the ladies awaiting me there were Catholic ladies of my sister's and were now to attend me.

'I want them not!' I cried. 'I will not have them!'

'You have no choice, Madam,' said Sir Henry Bedingfeld. 'Come now to the barge.'

But it was torment, for all my servants were wailing on the bank, Kat and Blanche weeping uncontrollably among them. I knew not where to turn, so bemused was I. I became aware of Sir Henry at my elbow urging me forward, despite my pleas for time to make my farewells.

'Come, come,' he said nervously, 'we must be off; there is no time for lingering. Quickly now.'

A flame of defiance lit in me and I stopped. 'Hark ye, my dears!' I called. 'Look to yourselves, for I can make no farewells. I say to you '*Tanquem oris*,' — which is: '*Like a sheep to the slaughter*', for so am I led!'

Then we were rowed away to Windsor, where we spent that night at the lodge of the Dean. On again next day by road we went; the Queen had sent her own litter to bear me, for 'twould not do for her own sister to be seen travelling in discomfort as well as disgrace. There was even an escort provided of sixteen servants, all in tawney coats, in order to preserve the illusion of wealth and friendliness, as if I were on a happy journey with the Queen's blessing. So, shrugging my shoulders, I settled myself in the litter, resolving upon ease of body if not of mind.

My heart lifts yet at the memory of that journey. By God, I learned the temper of England and her people that day. As we passed through Eton, the townspeople and scholars shouted, cheered and crowded around me so that my cortège could not get along, and the bells never stopped ringing. The good folk followed my litter to the edge of the town, throwing flowers, Latin verses and messages of goodwill into my lap.

'Floreat Elizabeta!' cried the boys, and 'God save our Elizabeth!' cried the townsfolk. 'Long may you live!'

Ay, and they hung gay cloths from their windows as if 'twere for a true royal progress and not the path to prison for a disgraced Princess who had been declared illegitimate and who went in fear of her life. Sir Henry, shaken to the core of his being, was helpless to stem the tide. I began to fear lest he should report such behaviour to the Queen or Council and so bring trouble upon these dear and devoted people. Half-laughing, half-horrified, I heard them begin to sing a version of a Coronation song writ for my brother and sung for my sister, substituting my name for that of the Sovereign: 'Joy in Elizabeth who *will* wear the Crown!' Loud they yelled and loud they sang, each taking it one from the other. It was purest treason, bless their hearts, but what would you?

'Floreat Etona!' I shouted back. 'I will return to you one day!'

'Ay, come back when you are Queen, God save your sweet Grace!'

And so it went on, all through the small villages on our way. By what I could see of Sir Henry's face, he was utterly confounded.

That night we lodged at Lord Williams of Thame's house of Ricote in Buckinghamshire. Lord Williams provided entertainments and music for me and a goodly feast withal. The fare was excellent and my lodgings luxurious; there was merriment and dancing, much to Sir Henry's unease, and my secret amusement, for he had desired somewhat more discreet. Whilst staying here I had begun to make a friend of one of the Catholic ladies forced upon me. Her name was Elizabeth Sands, a forthright, merry girl she was, sympathetic to me from the first, looking to my comfort and seeking to cheer me as best she could. I liked and trusted her, while she became greatly attached to me.

When, after some days, it was announced that I must go on to Woodstock, all was consternation, for none knew the way. In that remote country, few knew far in any direction from their own villages, but at length a farmer was found who undertook to guide us to Woodstock, and a goodly fee we had to pay him for it. We left at last, with many thanks and Godspeeds, to begin the last part of our journey, and a horrid one it was, over vile tracks, with ruts nigh up to the horses' knees; the mud still not dried out from the spring rains. Without our guide, the Lord knows what would have become of us. Mayhap I and my whole meinie would have fallen into a bog, never to be seen again, thereby making life easier for Her Majesty and the Council.

After a parlous journey we reached Woodstock. At first, I refused to believe that this was where I was to stay, for the place looked as if it had remained untenanted since Fair Rosamond's day, three hundred years before. Even Sir Henry looked taken aback at the grim prospect. As for me, all I wished to do was to lie down and rest. A shed would have sufficed, I was so weary. Part of the mechanism of my borrowed litter had broken and the resultant painful jolting had rendered me near dead with exhaustion. Thus it was that I did not notice the particulars of the four small and shabby rooms assigned to me in the Gatehouse until the next day, when, after a long sleep, I arose much refreshed and looked about me.

Lord, what a sight! The rooms were dark, dilapidated, badly ventilated by windows stuck open or jammed shut; there was a clutter of worn, dusty hangings and a muddle of furniture upon filthy floors. Some of the furniture was mine own stacked up, the rest consisted of some ancient, unwanted pieces of the Queen's left about higgeldy-piggeldy. 'I cannot stay in these rooms!' I exclaimed decisively. 'I will look over the rest of the palace and see if there is better accommodation.'

I could have saved us all the trouble. We marched all over the small palace and found it to be worse than the Gatehouse. There was nothing left but to make the best of it. In the whole place there were but three doors that could be locked, and this caused even my new ladies disgust and shocked comment. Such a scrubbing and cleaning as went on was never seen. Lizzy Sands and the rest of the ladies worked like kitchen-maids, with my five servants setting to with a will to assist them. In the Gatehouse I had two rooms downstairs and two up, all dirty, but the larger apartment upstairs had a fanciful kind of ceiling, it being groined, painted blue and powdered with gold stars.

'Forsooth,' I sniffed, glancing up at its grubby splendour, ' 'tis the nearest I shall get to heaven while I am in this place.'

However, I decided to use it as my parlour and receiving room, for it was the best of a poor lot and commanded wide views over the Great Park, which was some consolation.

Tom Parry had followed my retinue, determined to be near me and to see that I got fair treatment. He was enraged at my latest residence and took Sir Henry to task, demanding that he refuse to lodge me in such a place. Their voices rose, chiding, until with a final bellow, Tom turned and stamped away, red-faced and swearing. I called him to me, asking what was the matter.

'God's death and damnation — save your Grace — I am dismissed! He has no right!' Tom waved his arms, almost choking with fury. ' 'Tis for you to dismiss me, your Grace! Well, so I may leave this shoddy palace, but no further than the village will I go. There is the Bull Inn and there will I stick fast. He called me a 'suspicious person,' may he rot! To the Bull I go, and not a yard further, though he torture me with hot irons!'

So, breathing fire, Tom Parry took rooms at the Bull Inn in Woodstock village, no doubt telling of my wrongs to all who would listen. Sir Henry was desperate fussed about this and wrote at once to the Council to learn what he should do upon the matter. He also wrote to the Queen for further advice upon my care. The Council sent word that Parry must remain at the Bull, for he was in charge of my finances, and it was my money that would pay for all who lodged in or near the palace in my name. Sir Henry feared that Parry might cause trouble and fretted over this by the hour.

The Queen wrote that she wished me to be honourably used, and specified that I should be allowed to walk in the garden as long as Sir Henry would accompany me. She added that I must not speak with suspected persons out of his hearing, nor must I send or receive any messages, letters or tokens to or from any person. 'And as I understand that, Madam,' said Sir Henry, looking up from the letter he had been reading aloud to me, 'it means that I must forbid the use of pens, paper and ink.'

'What!' I expostulated. 'No writing materials at all? Oh, this is too much. I must have pens and paper.'

Sir Henry shook his head, frowning in perplexity. 'The Queen, as I see it, refuses. I cannot allow them, your Grace.'

'Well, but what must I do? If I may not set pen to paper, what of books? I have so few with me and I wish to read. I must exercise my mind somehow.'

'As to that,' fretted Sir Henry, 'I know not what to say, or what the Queen would wish. I will write to her about it, your Grace.' I struck my hands together and turned away in exasperation, while he bowed punctiliously and went off to write to my sister.

The next day, Lizzy and a servant girl were struggling to put up my cloth of state, which must be raised in every place where resides a royal personage, when in bustled Sir Henry. 'By the Cross, what do you both there?' he cried agitatedly. 'What hanging is it that you put up? Who gave you leave to do so?'

'We need no leave,' answered Lizzy pertly. ' 'Tis the Princess's cloth of state, and sure, it must be up where'ere royalty dwells, as well you know.'

'I have received no instructions about it,' said he. 'You must take it down.'

'I shall do no such thing,' retorted Lizzy. 'You might as well tell the Queen to put aside her crown.'

'Insolent!' exclaimed Sir Henry. 'I insist that you remove it until I receive instructions about it.'

'Well, I will not!' snapped Lizzy, climbing down the ladder, leaving the cloth half-hung. 'The Princess shall hear of this!' she cried threateningly, as she pulled the servant girl after her through the door. I did hear of it, but what could I do? Sir Henry wrote yet another letter to my sister and eventually received the required permission to hang the cloth. And so it went on. Everything, no matter how trivial, seemed to need permission before it could be done.

'God save us!' expostulated Lizzy one day. 'I wonder he does not write to the Queen for permission to pass water, indeed I do!'

Yet he was not cruel or unkind, poor gentleman. He was naturally good-hearted and not one to put himself forward, also devilish feared to make a mistake. The charge he had got in me was too much for him; he had no wish to be held responsible for the safety and well-being of royal blood. Several times did he cross swords with Lizzy, who found herself irritated beyond all bearing by all the palaverings. At last the blow fell. In June, a letter came from the Council ordering her dismissal and appointing another lady to replace her. The storm over this raged long and loud. First, Lizzy refused to go, and then only with much weeping and hard words, whereupon I refused to accept the lady sent in replacement. Deadlock upon this was reached, with all of us in tears, including Sir Henry. Distractedly, he tried to soothe me, saying that he only wished to act for my good and also do the Council's bidding in all things. His unwished-for appointment was a trust, he said, and he could only do his best. Wiping my eyes, I accepted his explanation with as good a grace as I could muster, but 'twas not easy, for I ached for freedom.

Walking tamely in the garden soon was not enough for me who loved hard exercise, and I recalled that the Marquess of Winchester had mentioned that I could walk in the Great Park. I took this up with Sir Henry, who at once began a long, agitated debate as to whether or not, culminating in a fresh series of letters to my unlucky sister. Poor Sir Henry, I could not truly dislike him. Indeed, as time went slowly on, though my nerves were tried unbearably and my health broke down, I grew to respect him and even to feel a certain irritable affection for him. I am sure he grew to feel an affection for me, for all that I was captious and difficult while I was at Woodstock. Kind though he was, I felt desperate unhappy for my ladies were all of the Queen's choosing, staunch Catholics, hung about with beads and rosaries that clanked at every step and crossing themselves night and day. Now that Lizzy was gone, I had no one to whom I could be close.

Kat and Blanche were staying in the village, I heard, and it was heartening to know that my dears, so loyal and so loving, had come as near as they could to me, but I needed their presence right sorely in my loneliness. 'Twas cruel hard to have no one to turn to for comfort, and heavy with sadness I grew.

I longed to write to Mary, and Sir Henry penned a letter to the Council on my behalf. Back came a note refusing permission for me to address the Queen, but instead, granting me an English Bible to read. 'Twas not what I needed. I became loth to rise in the mornings and sluggish and heavy-hearted during the days. I lost my appetite and swellings began to appear upon my face and body. Sir Henry came to me one day, expressing much concern when I refused my usual walk with him.

'I am ill,' I snapped. 'Look at my face. My body also is so puffed up that I cannot lace my gown. My head aches, my ears ache, my teeth ache, and worst of all, my heart aches. There is naught you can do for me. Leave me alone!' And I turned my head away so that he should not see the tears which had begun to flow.

'Oh, your Grace, speak not so I pray you. Try

to keep your heart up if you can.'

'Ay, 'twould not look well for you if I were to die in your charge, would it?' I flashed. 'Or,' I went on, still more unpleasantly, 'mayhap that is the plan, hey? Mayhap you are party to it?' I knew he was not, and if I had not known, his shocked face and saddened eyes would have told me. I felt immediate compunction and held out my hand to him. 'Nay, Sir Henry,' I said more gently, 'my temper runs away. I meant it not. I must have a doctor, one whom I know, to see me and devise a remedy for me. Would you write to my sister and beg her to send me one of her own doctors? I am not well.'

Good fellow, he wrote at once and received a reply from the Council recommending me to take two learned men who had studied at Oxford, and who, they assured me, would cure me. I did not want them. I was ill and frightened, needing someone familiar who knew and understood me.

'Well, I will not have them,' I said stubbornly to Sir Henry, 'for I am not minded to make any strangers privy to the state of my body. Rather will I commit it to God.'

When he had left me and I heard the sound of his footsteps dying away down the spiral stair, I turned my face into the dark softness of a cushion and wept. It was not mere whimsy causing me to refuse the doctors, it was deadly fear. How could I tell but what these two professedly learned men from Oxford might not be Spanish spies, paid to put me to death by a so-called remedy?

The next day I was worse, and the next. Almost did I wish to die and cease troubling all around me.

I lay in a bed-gown all day, staring at the wall, but deep within I remembered King James of Scotland, and did not quite relinquish my hold on life, for even at its darkest it was sweeter than death, and so have I always felt. I grew worse. It was caused through sickness of the spirit, as I guessed even then, for always with me my mind has wrought powerfully upon my body. Sir Henry was nigh distracted at my state, and fairly besieged the Council with letters on my behalf. At last he was able to tell me that permission had been granted me to write to my sister, and I spent hours composing a letter in which I tried my utmost to make her believe that I was her friend and would do naught against her. When I had finished it, I sealed it up and gave it to one of my ladies who was to attend the Queen's wedding. Mary had requested this lady's presence, so I made her promise to give my letter to the Queen, and this she swore to do.

Then I had nothing to do but fidget and wait for a reply. This arrived twelve days later from Farnham Castle, but it came in a letter to Sir Henry. When he had read it, he did not show it to me, waiting another week until I should seem stronger, for still I stayed in my room, refusing to see any doctors but those of the Queen's.

I was constrained to hear Mass at Woodstock, but judged it better to make no fuss about this. No doubt God would hear my prayers, an He willed, whether in Latin or sweet English, and heartily did I pray for deliverance. One day at the beginning of July, Sir Henry came to hear Mass with me as was usual, but he looked worn with anxiety and, after the service was over, I turned sharp to him. 'Is there aught from my sister? Sure, there must be by now.'

He hedged, looking as if he wished himself elsewhere, saying that there had indeed been a letter, but writ to him and that he would read it to me later. With a sinking heart, I told him I would hear it now. He had not it with him, so I had to kick my heels while he bustled away to find it, returning letter in hand and looking as sick as a pauper.

'Come, read it, man,' I urged. 'Let me know the worst.'

So he read it aloud, most unwilling, as if he did not wish to say the words which made plain that Mary still believed I was privy to Wyatt's plot. When he had done, I stared at him, white with rage and disappointment, my heart filled with frustration.

'Does she want me to lie to her, then?' I shouted. 'Ay, 'twould suit that snake Renard's book, would it not? They all think to force me to confess to complicity in that woundy plot, even though I speak plain truth as I desire to be saved before God Almighty! Oh, I am sick of it all.'

'If your Grace would be patient — ' began Sir Henry. I cut him short.

'Patient! I have been a very Griselda. What can I do, stuck here with an old Papist to spy on me? Oh, I know you do not — I am overwrought. You must write to the Council yarely, and get them to give me better comfort than this, or I fear my brain will turn.'

The next day, Sir Henry persuaded me to walk in the garden with him. I leaned on his arm, for I was weak from my sickness and remaining so long indoors.

'Have you written?' I badgered him. He said he had not. 'Well, you must!' I said wildly, stopping short. 'How can I continue this hopeless life? My cause is true, and I am the Queen's true subject as I have ever been during my life.'

Sir Henry shook his head gravely and returned no answer. He gave a deep sigh, looking sorely perplexed, coaxing me to walk a little more. But after a few steps, some drops of rain fell and I snatched my arm from his. ' 'Tis of no use to dawdle here,' quoth I ungraciously. 'It waxeth wet. You may walk; I am going within.' And so I did, swinging round with a fine flurry of skirts. Without turning my head, I marched in and up the stair to my chamber, where I slammed the door, fell upon the bed and wept like the rain outside my window. 'Twas vile unmannerly to my poor guardian, but my heart was too low for ceremony and I could not feign any.

That evening, Sir Henry came to my parlour with pens and paper. I gaped at seeing him with such articles. 'Good God!' I cried, halting my nervous pacing of the floor. 'Writing materials! Do I dream?'

'Not so,' he answered, serious as ever. 'Mayhap you and I could contrive a letter to the Council between us, your Grace. Perhaps they would give more heed to both our voices together. What think you?'

'What think I? Why, I think you are a dear, good soul with a kind heart, despite your grimly visage.' I pressed his hands in mine own, and the grimly visage turned a dull, brick-red. 'Let us write. Come, to it!' and I pulled the chairs out from the table, bidding him sit.

It was a good letter. In it, I begged Council to tell me of any special matters to be answered, or why was I prisoned here? I entreated the Lords who knew me well to see the Queen for me, so that I would not be forced to think myself utterly desolate of all refuge in this world. To this, Sir Henry added words of his own, asking the Lords who had been privy to my father's will to further my suit in this matter.

'Excellent,' I said. 'That will remind them that I am a King's daughter and if my sister should marry but bear no child — ?'

'It was thus in my mind,' nodded Sir Henry. 'It is necessary that they should remember it. Moreover,' he went on, 'I will take the opportunity to remind them that this roof leaks, as well as we all know, and that somewhat of repairs should be made to the windows in the way of glass. I dare not imagine winter here.'

'Perhaps 'tis intended I should die of cold,' said I, 'for sure, unless aught is done, we shall freeze to ice-blocks or perish of rheums and stiffness. Lord, there must be an answer to this letter, if only to mend the windows!'

We had no answer. My sister's wedding day

came and went and still no word, while I fretted myself to fiddle strings. 'Glad am I that I am not at the wedding,' I chafed to Sir Henry. 'I would not be there an I could. 'Tis odd to hold it at Winchester. I'll wager the London folk would not suffer it. Well, and I too would be sickened to see that Spanish manikin posturing at my sister's side, calling her Wife and himself King! And should she have a child, 'twill be more than half Spanish and wholly Catholic. Pah! It would be a midget I daresay, with her so small and him so dwarfish. No ruler for England, for sure. Now report me to the Council, Sir Henry. I have spoken treasons. Do you write one of your letters and say that I have spoken against the Queen, her little husband and hoped-for child to be!'

He glanced at me nervously, then smiled. 'Your Grace will have her jest,' he said. But it was not all jest, and he knew it.

★ ★ ★

I heard no more from Mary for many a weary day. Her Spanish bridegroom had put the thought of all else clean out of her head. I heard she was mad for him and would not leave his side. The Latin part of her nature boiled over at sight of him, it seemed, and it was as if she had regained all her lost years, for she bloomed like a late rose, 'twas said. One lady told me that she had shed ten years of her age since her marriage. I reflected, sourly, that even so 'twould still leave her older than her husband, but I kept my thoughts to myself as I moped about,

279

having heart for naught but worry and repining.

In a sorry state was I, that August of 1554, with fits of rage and frustration alternating with black and desperate depression. I became so that I cared little or wrought little for those about me, for the sore heaviness of my spirit blinded me.

One day, the sound of singing from outside drew me to the window.

'What is that stupid din?' I cried crossly. 'Such a caterwauling as I never heard! Who is it?' Looking from the casement, I beheld a milkmaid, a yoke across her shoulders, bearing pails brimming with milk. She was walking through the park, signing as if she had no care in all the world. I slammed the window shut and rounded on Sir Henry. 'Hear you that? 'Tis the song of a girl who is happy. I tell you, Sir Henry, that a very milkmaid's lot is better than mine, and her life merrier. Hark how she sings!' And I flung my book on the floor, half-sobbing. He attempted words of comfort, but words would not do, and I commanded him to take himself off, which he did, poor good gentleman.

Amongst my collection of jewels I had a ring with a good diamond in it, and I began thoughtlessly to scratch upon the window with it, my heart being too full to realise what I did. Of a sudden, a rhyming sentence came into my head and I repeated it aloud:

'Much suspected of me,
'Nothing provèd can be,
'Quoth Elizabeth, prisoner . . . '

'I could die here, alone and unregarded,' I said to myself, 'and none would care. Posterity would never know of me, and I would be forgotten before remembered. Merely Mary Tudor's bastard half-sister would I be.'

Perhaps to ensure that posterity should indeed know of me, I took the ring and scribed my little rhyme upon the window glass with the diamond therein. Then I retrieved my book from the floor, half-thinking to stitch a cover for it, to beguile the time away. This stitchery was to prove a solace to me in the times ahead, and I began to take a positive pleasure in unpicking my mistakes, for it made the work last longer.

★ ★ ★

The day of my birth passed almost unnoticed. I received no gifts and no letter. I had no word of my dears in the village, for the summer weather had been too bad and too wet to allow the ruts in the lanes to dry out, and each new rainfall turned them into quagmires, so that I and my people were temporarily marooned. Moreover, money was growing short, and it seemed to me that I could not afford to remain prisoned much longer. I could not support those at the Bull, nor the servants and cooks at Woodstock, nor the soldiers eternally on duty there. Were we all to starve, I wondered? My love-stricken sister had forgotten me indeed. Opening the door, I called down the winding stair to Sir Henry, who came puffing up to see what I wanted.

'Sir Henry,' I began, 'my funds are low, are they not? I keep my own books and reckon well how all is spent. We are nigh destitute. A pretty state of affairs, eh?'

'Indeed, your Grace. As we have had no word, I feel that someone must be sent to lay your case before the Council. I will seek out messengers and send them, whatever the roads be like. They will have to make their way across fields as best they may.'

So messengers were sent, and, as a result, I got permission to write in my own hand to the Lords of the Council, but it was ruled that my letter must be enclosed in one of Sir Henry's own and taken to London by one of my servants. I chose Francis Verney of Claydon, who was lodging with Parry in Woodstock, to take the letter from Sir Henry and me, but when I came to write I had no heart for it. I had the headache and my eyes watered. I felt weary and sad.

Upon the next day, taking Sir Henry's advice, I washed my head. He told me that his mother regarded it as a sovereign cure for pains in the head and tired eyes, besides being soothing to the nerves. I ever preferred to be clean, and bathed my whole body every month, though many looked upon this as a short way to the grave. I found it pleasurable and calming, assuaging violent humours as they rose to the head. 'Twas nigh impossible to bathe at Woodstock, but as my head was risen full of violent humours, I resolved to wash it and discover if it would indeed soothe me besides cleansing my hair. The operation took most of the day, and when it was done and my hair dry, it had grown too dark and I too sleepy, to write.

When the next day came, I declared I could not write without a secretary, so Sir Henry must do it. I liked not to say that I still had the headache. He wrote at last, from my own words, adding at the end a pathetic plea for repairs and pay for the soldiers who had received no wage for a month or more.

And so it went on. The slow days crept by, the restrictions grew more irksome and I more fretful and chafed by them. A letter came to Sir Henry from Mary, written in a moralising strain as to my conduct, but giving no further instructions. Finally Sir Henry paid the soldiers four hundred pounds from his own pocket, so that they, at least, were happy. I grew to hate and detest my small, shabby rooms, the constant restraints serving to render my temper shorter still, oft near to hysterical tears on many occasions.

One day in September, as I went to walk in the park, the sight of my guardian locking and unlocking six pairs of gates as I passed through each pair tried my nerves so severely that I felt near mad with irritation. Clutching my head, I whipped round upon the unlucky gent, my feet stamping, my face twisted. 'Gaoler!' I shrieked. 'You are nothing but a gaoler, you, with your locks and your keys!'

Before I could draw another breath, he had fallen upon his knees at my feet. I halted, astonished, the breath panting in my throat. His eyes were full of tears, his voice when he spoke, harsh and broken with emotion.

'Oh, my dear lady, I beg you not to give me that hard name, for I am but appointed to save you and guard you from the dangers by which you are beset!' Stiffly he got to his feet. 'Thou knowest I feel your trials as if they be mine own. Your free spirit chafes at this way of life. I am truly sorry dearest Princess, but what can I do? I must discharge my office as I see fit, and what is more, while you are here with me, you are safe from spies and slinking death, which things I know to have been in your mind.'

The water rushed to my eyes and would not be stayed. 'Sir Henry, good friend,' I sobbed, 'you make me ashamed. I have so lost my wits, my spirits and my manners that I cannot tell my allies from my enemies. Dear sir, forgive my churlishness and know that I count you comrade. I feel that my youth is slipping away and this sits heavy upon my heart.'

He gave me his arm and I leaned gratefully upon it. Though fussy and pernickety, he was indeed my true knight and my friend.

My health did not improve, and after a week or so, I desired to be bled, but for safety's sake, only by doctors known to the Queen. I wanted Dr. Wendy and Dr. Huick, whom I knew and liked, and Sir Henry sent a letter to the Council to this effect. Well, they came, and with them they brought a surgeon, so I was bled in the arm in the morning and in the foot during the afternoon in Sir Henry's presence. My persistence was thus rewarded, and certainly I did seem to mend somewhat after that visit. I asked the doctors to take a message to my

284

sister, and this they agreed to do.

'For see,' I said, 'could not Council be persuaded to allow me to a place nearer to London, or even to dwell in mine own house there, remaining at the Queen's pleasure?'

'It should be so,' agreed Sir Henry. 'I will scarce answer for her health if she stays here throughout the winter.'

The doctors shook their heads dubiously at this, glancing uncertainly at one another. 'Well, we will try,' announced Dr. Wendy, 'but by my faith Madam, I think you will get but little from the Queen, her head being turned by her husband.'

And so it fell out. We stayed at Woodstock throughout that winter, and miserable damp and cold it was. For months we were never free of coughs, rheums and pains in the head. Before the cold weather fairly set in, the news came that my sister was pregnant and expecting to be confined in late April or early May. So be it, I thought, my chance is gone and I am to be left here to lose my youth and bloom; my wings clipped, sans hope, sans pride, while Mary finds motherhood and happiness.

A mere day or so after the tidings of Mary's pregnancy, I heard my ladies chattering together and demanded to know their talk. They were reluctant to say, but I insisted and learned that upon my sister's gate had been nailed a scurrilous notice. It read, I was told: *'Will you be such fools, oh noble Englishmen, to believe that our Queen is pregnant, and of what should she be but a monkey or a dog?'*

Upon hearing this, I let out a crack of laughter. ''Fore God, it seems that the people have but a poor opinion of my sister's breeding abilities and worse of her husband's siring!'

They were scandalised, of course, and rolled shocked eyes, crossing themselves as devoutly as if I had the Evil Eye.

After a miserable Yuletide and an icy January, we tried to look forward to spring, but in February the burnings began and we had no more care for spring. This fiery consumption of human flesh was to burn and blacken my sister's name for ever. No matter what good she did before or after, no matter her very real personal kindness and sensitivity, all were forgot in the crackling of flames and the columns of smoke which continued to rise for nigh on the next four years. She could not hope to escape the blame, for others in England did not see these deaths as did she and her Spaniards. To her, the deaths were necessary and to the glory of God. To the people of England, they were a series of murders. The nickname of Bloody Mary was first heard in this year of 1555. It will follow her bewildered ghost through time, through history, through hell.

I heard it all in my prison. There were John Rogers, canon of St. Paul's, John Hooper, Bishop of Gloucester, both burned. There followed Hugh Latimer, Bishop of Worcester, and Nicholas Ridley, Bishop of London, whose deaths were nightmares of horror. And my Godfather, dear Cranmer, heard and saw all, may Jesu watch over his spirit. He was forced to stand upon the leads of the Bocardo Prison, watching until his friends had screamed and writhed and settled into crumbling, glowing ash. Oh, I heard it all, and sweet Christ, could do naught save weep.

At Easter-tide Cranmer himself was sent to his Maker amid the crackle of wood and leaping flames. Before his death he had signed a paper recanting, acknowledging that he was a foul blasphemer and deserved eternal damnation, in a desperate bid to save his life. I did not blame him for that. Life is sweet whatever one's age. I thought so then, I know so now. His efforts were no manner of use, and when all hope was gone he faced his horrible death with high courage. Standing amidst the wood of his funeral pyre, between those who guarded him, he spoke his true mind aloud.

'I refuse and renounce those papers I signed in the hope of prolonging this miserable life,' he had called out, lifting his right hand, 'and here is the hand that wrote my name to them. Before my body dies, I condemn that hand to suffer just punishment for its coward deed!' and he thrust his hand into the new-kindled flames, holding it there without a sound, until it fell black and shrivelled and the crowd groaned and cried for pity. And when he was chained to the stake and the fire rose up all about him, his voice could be heard, loud and clear in prayer, high above the sobs and wails of those who watched in grief and horror. So another martyr was made for the Queen, another soul was lost to the Catholic heaven.

We had heard that Mary had retired to Hampton Court in late April to await the birth of her child. Good luck to her, thought I, for she will need it at her age. And then came a shock, for messengers arrived in wild haste at Woodstock, bidding me straight to Hampton to be present, as heir presumptive, at the birth of the Queen's baby. Oh, the excitement as we rushed about making ready to leave. I could scarce believe that I was about to go from my hated prison. Woodstock could fall ruinous and crumble away, for all I cared, and I would not give a snap of the fingers. I laughed for joy as we scuttled about, all in a commotion of pleasurable agitation. Indeed, it would look strange to the world if the heir-presumptive, heretic and bastard though she might be, were absent at the birth of the heir-apparent.

We made good speed to Hampton Court through a countryside bright green with spring, all free and beautiful under a clear blue sky. And I too was free, for the nonce. I saw water in the ditches catch gleams from the sky as if little hidden mirrors lay in the long grasses, and the air was main sweet after Woodstock.

Yet it was all illusion. I was not free. When I drew rein at Hampton on the last day of April, it was at the entrance to a back courtyard and there was no reception for me. I was hurried indoors to my room and guards were stationed outside. I had expected to see Mary, but it was made full clear to me that no matter what my position with regard to the coming heir, I was still 'the red-haired brat' of doubtful parentage in Mary's eyes. I had to watch from my window while the sun shone unwinking through the days. Between the trees I could catch glimpses of the river and the boats upon it. I could hear the voices of those who called to one another in the sunshine. It was all colour, sparkle and movement; it lay within a stone's throw of me, but I was still a prisoner.

One day, I was cheered by the visit of my uncle, Lord William Howard, who burst energetically through my guarded door, chaffing loudly with the soldiers there.

'Marry!' I cried pertly. 'Visitors, by my troth. So I am not to moulder solitary after all!'

He laughed boisterously, clapping me upon the shoulder. 'Ha, niece, 'tis easy to see that your spirit has not mouldered. Thou'rt as mettlesome as ever. Give me a kiss and tell me what is in your mind.'

'Indeed I will!' I answered. 'Why am I brought here to be shut up like a criminal? If I am good enough to appear at the birth of Mary's child, I am good enough to appear now. I would see some Council lords and put my case before them.'

'God's truth, and so you shall!' he roared heartily. 'My lass, you are a fighter. I wish you success in all you do, by my faith!'

He was as good as his word, for a few days later came Dr. Gardiner, Lord Arundel and Mr. Secretary Petre to my room. I greeted them haughtily, favouring Lord Arundel with a wintry smile which he returned with anxious eagerness. Gradually I allowed my haughty look to sink into one of saintly pathos and fixed my visitors with mournful eyes. Then I spoke and my voice was low and gentle.

'My lords,' I murmured, 'I am glad to see

you, for I have been kept a great while from you, desolately alone. Would you, I implore, be a means to the King and Queen's Majesties that I be delivered from my imprisonment? I have been kept thus a long, sad time.'

There was a pause while they glanced at one another. 'Well, Madam,' answered Gardiner at last, 'it seems to me that you must confess your fault and put yourself on the Queen's mercy.'

Instantly I forgot my woebegone air and sprang to my feet. 'God's death!' I yelled. 'I would rather lie in prison all my life then! I crave no mercy at the Queen's hand. I tell you, the law shall decide if ever I did offend her in thought, word, or deed! If this is the best you can do, get out and take your henchmen with you!'

Startled by the change of meek maiden to raging virago, they turned and made for the door. Furious, I snatched off my slipper and hurled it after them, swearing as hard as I knew how. Yet Gardiner did go to the Queen and returned with Arundel and Petre the next day to tell me that my sister marvelled at my boldness.

'What boldness?' I shouted.

'Why, in your refusal to confess.'

'Jesus, how can I confess when I have done no wrong?' I screeched, stamping my feet and waving my fists like a wild hellion from the fishmarket.

'Her Majesty feels that this refusal might seem as if she has wrongfully imprisoned you,' he pursued stoutly.

'Well, so she has, and I care not who hears me say it. I will scream it from the windows if I feel so inclined!' A look of alarm passed over his face and those of his companions, and they glanced apprehensively at the windows as if I would put my threat into practice then and there. I tossed my head angrily and we glared at one another like furious beasts. 'Ah, what can I do?' I cried at length. 'If the Queen insists upon my guilt after all, I suppose she must punish me as she thinks fit. She is Queen and I am but a subject, helpless and alone.' I turned my back on them. 'I am sick of it and you. Get you gone.'

'There is more,' said Gardiner, but less truculently.

'Oh speak it, for God's sake. What now?'

'Her Majesty willeth me to say to you that you must tell another tale of religion and beliefs e'er you are set at liberty.'

I drew a deep breath and swung round to face him. Did I dream it, or was there a spark of uncertainty in his fierce old eyes?

'Sir Bishop,' I said, 'it seems to me that we are at deadlock. This has been reached because of the Theory of Transubstantiation, I think.'

'Just so, Madam. Am I to take it that you now admit that the Holy Bread and Wine change into the Body and Blood of our Lord when the Host is elevated?'

I intended to admit no such thing, but what to say I knew not. I sent up a silent prayer to God for words that would deliver me from this coil. Then I spoke, and my voice seemed to come from my lips of itself, as if my brain had no part in it.

'His was the Word that spake it,
'He took the bread and brake it;
'And what that Word doth make it,
'I do believe and take it.'

Gardiner gaped, and we stared at one another, I almost astonished as he. 'Go and tell my sister that,' I said, recovering myself as swiftly as I could. 'I shall say no more upon the subject.'

There was a long pause as a look of reluctant respect appeared upon Gardiner's dark face. His words came slow and halting: 'Then your Grace has the vantage of me and these lords for your wrong and long imprisonment.'

For a moment I scarce understood him; then it was like a blaze of light in my head. Christ! I had done it. I had won. 'What advantage I have, you know,' I answered mildly, gesturing round my small chamber. 'I see no vantage that I have had at your hands for so dealing with me — but God forgive you, and me also.' I raised my eyes heavenwards in saintly but injured innocence as I spoke these angelically magnanimous words, and, looking down, beheld them all kneeling at my feet, desiring me to forgive and forget. Although my heart was pounding fit to leap out of my somewhat worn bodice with triumph and exultation, I managed a faint, sweet smile. 'You do but your duty,' I said gently. 'I cannot blame you for that.'

They babbled of my generosity, of my forgiveness, until such a note of concord was reached that almost did I expect to see the Dove of Peace appear bodily before mine eyes. It would have been no bigger miracle than that which had already taken place. The door closed behind them and I laughed aloud. Flinging my arms wide, I danced round and round my room like a madwoman, laughing and weeping together. Then, when the fit had passed, down on my knees did I go to give thanks to Him who had brought me safe through another trial.

5

SUNRISE IN VIRGO

1557 – 1558

During the evening of the day of my deliverance, I received a message from my sister and the guards were withdrawn from my door. The message was to bid me wear my richest gown, for the King desired to see me. I laughed derisively.

'My richest gown, says the Queen? I have no rich gowns, you may tell her. None of my gowns are fit to wear, as she must know very well.' Susan Clarencieux, the lady who had brought the message, hastened to reassure me, saying that, in such case, Mary wished me to accept a gown from her. 'Indeed I will do so,' said I, 'if it suits me, and if it fits.'

Exceeding ungracious, but again I was assured that the Queen had had a gown especially made for me, feeling that I might have none suitable of mine own. After near two years of dressing plain and acting meek, it was full exciting to wear a Court gown and hold my head high and proud as a Princess should. When my long red hair was brushed and combed and the green velvet jewelled caul set upon it, I saw the looks of admiration upon the faces of the ladies who dressed me, and my heart lifted in my breast. I was sent for at ten of the clock and led by Susan Clarencieux, Mistress of the Robes, through the dark gardens and up the torch-lit privy stairs to my sister's chamber. The door was flung open, and there was Mary standing alone in the candlelight by a window, clutching the crimson draperies with one hand and her jewelled crucifix with the other, looking pale and ill, with a great belly. I collapsed in the prescribed triple curtsey.

'Rise, sister,' she said, her deep, husky voice echoing round the empty chamber. 'So you are come. I trust you are now in good health.'

I felt the tears rush to my eyes. I had not seen her for over a year, she looked sick and feeble and, despite all, I loved her. I knelt and the tears burst forth unrestrained. 'Oh, Mary,' I sobbed, 'I pray you, do believe me. I am, and have always been, your loyal subject. I pray you, do think well of me.'

She shrugged her shoulders, staring past me to the wall-hangings. '*Quien sabe?*' she said, clapping her hands twice.

I sprang to my feet. Spanish? A signal? Where was Philip? The hangings quivered, were pulled aside, and out stepped the little Prince of Spain. Again I curtseyed, and he raised me up, calling me 'Sweet sister,' in his blurred Spanish-English. A pretty, neat little fellow was he, a very cock-sparrow, although I topped him by almost a head. Dressed all in white and gold, he looked as fresh and pert as his wife did not. I was glad when the interview was over, for Mary was silent and watchful as if she feared he would make love to me on the spot. He was as fulsome as his limited English would allow, and finally I was given to understand that all was forgiven and that I would be treated with love and friendship thereafter.

I slept well that night, with a light heart and easy mind for the first time in near ten years. I was made much of in the weeks that followed, for the Court, seeing the way of the wind, flattered me greatly, the young men in particular. And my brother-in-law was the particularest of these, though in secret. He left no chance untaken to catch me alone, to press his embraces upon me. Constantly was he patting my hands and clasping my waist, while his kisses grew ever less fraternal, but my sister saw none of it, such was his care. Attractive he was in his way and very masculine withal. Yet even now a spurt of laughter comes to my lips when I recall how swift he would be to have me seated so that my height would not o'ershadow him and render him ridiculous in his own eyes.

The weeks went by and Mary, though swollen, did not give birth. No child, thought I, remembering the notice on the palace gate, nor a monkey nor a dog neither. Sure, it could not be a child in her womb; no human was ever so long gestating. By August, 'twas plain that she was not nor ever had been pregnant. Indeed, the size of her belly began to decrease with the increase of her tears and lamentations. Moreover, her little husband showed a marked desire to be anywhere but at her side, at last pleading the necessity of his presence in Spain to leave her as soon as he could. I spent many hours with Mary at this time, attempting to soothe her, for at last it was cruelly obvious that he had never loved her but had married her only to obtain power and prestige in England.

'He would rather have you,' she groaned once. 'Ay, he would! His last words to me were: 'Do not quarrel with your sister'. He charged me with it. He hopes to gain you when I am gone. He would put me away if he could!' she burst out, sobbing anew. 'What a fool I was, old and ugly as I am, to dream that he could have loved me.' She gazed at me mournfully, her brown eyes red and streaming tears. 'Yet I was not always ugly, was I, Elizabeth? You remember, do you not, that once I was passing fair?'

'Indeed I do,' I answered warmly and with truth. 'You were most pretty and good to look upon.'

'Nay,' she cried, shaking my hand off her arm, 'I have had a bitter, hard life, an ugly life, and it has wrought its work upon my person and my heart. Yet I love him still!' She wept, covering her ravaged face with her poor hands, knotted and twisted with rheumatism. 'It is a madness that persists and will not leave me.'

★ ★ ★

Sir Henry Bedingfeld was soon discharged from his governorship of me, declaring that God Almighty knew that this was the joyfullest news he had ever heard. I laughed when this was told me, saying that I wagered the joyfullest part was to be rid of such a hellcat as I! My new governor was to be Sir Thomas Pope, who was pleased to accept the charge, and no wonder, for he was not required to keep me as a state prisoner, but to act as friend and advisor merely. He had founded and established the new College of Trinity at Oxford the previous year, and spoke to me of it. He had a high opinion of my wit and learning and also called me beautiful, which made right pleasant hearing.

In September came my twenty-second birthday, and in October Mary allowed me to return to Hatfield. I left London in an uproar of love and loyalty that sounded like the bellowing of a thousand storms. There were such scenes of excitement that I was forced to send some gentlemen from my company amongst the crowds to keep order. I made my way through the City, beneath old, crumbling Aldersgate, past St. Bart's Priory and away upon the Hatfield road, leaving the glad sound of bells echoing behind me.

At Hatfield waited my sweet Kat, dear Tom Parry and Blanche, and many of those who loved me well. All was a whirl of emotion as we laughed and cried together. A few days later, Roger Ascham arrived.

'What!' I cried. 'I had thought you Latin Reader to the Queen. How come you here, Roger-man?'

He gazed at me with devotion plain to see. 'The Queen has ordered me to resume my reading with you, sweet Princess,' he said. 'I am the happiest man in the world.' Now we were no longer master and pupil, but fellow-scholars reading and learning together.

'Marry,' he said to me one day, 'but I learn more from you day by day, Madam, than you do from me, for although I may teach you words, you teach me things. Things about statecraft, of politics, of men and their ways, life and living. You are wise as any judge in the ways of the world. I have writ as much to John Aylmer.'

'Heyday,' said I grinning. 'You would have my head grow as big as your heart, my dear.'

In London the burnings continued until even the most hardened were sickened, while Mary became more and more unpopular. To my dismay I became again the centre of plots to put me on the Throne with Courtenay. The French Government and a band of English refugees were the instigators of one, which was terrifying enough, but no sooner had the alarm of this subsided than a young fellow arose in Essex, announcing that he was Edward Courtenay. It seemed he had a Plantagenet look which gulled the simple country folk into believing him, and they proclaimed him King and me Queen as far as Yaxley.

I became ill with fright, and even after Mary's messengers had come twice to Hatfield assuring me that the Queen exonerated me utterly, still did I feel very poorly with spasms of breathlessness during which I gasped for air like a felon taken by the hangman. Then I contracted the Jaundice, or Yellow Disease, and full sick was I for many a se'ennight, recovering but slowly. While I was still weak I received a message from the French Ambassador De Noailles promising the eager support of his King if I would entrust myself to his royal care. I had heard this often enough before, but my troubles and sickness had so undermined my spirits that I scarce seemed to know my own mind at this time. However, I sent Lady Sussex to London, secretly, to speak with De Noailles upon the subject.

By God's goodwill, the Ambassador was recalled to France before Lady Sussex arrived in London, his place having been taken by his brother, the Bishop D'Acqs. This gentleman told Lady Sussex that it was imperative that I should not leave the country, for if I did I would never return. Simon Renard would see to that, he said. When my Lady came back to Hatfield and gave me the good Bishop's words I was loth to believe them for of a sudden I felt I knew not whom I could trust, the Bishop's counsel being so opposed to that of his brother. So I sent her off again to demand stronger reassurance, and back she came, straight, with a repetition of the Bishop's words, adding that if ever I meant to be Queen, not to leave England now. That stiffened my back. I realised that I must resign myself to retirement, and possible poor health, until my day should come. I longed for my release from this half-life, but 'twould only come by the death of my sister and this seemed inexpressibly sad to me.

Pleasant indeed it was at Hatfield, but I knew well that all I said or did was known to the Queen, and all who came and went. Her spies were in my household; it was understood and accepted, although friends and dear ones were around me and my sister seemed friendly towards me. Fierce old Gardiner was dead, all was easy and pleasant enough, but it was a strange time, as if the whole of England waited. So matters went on for over a twelvemonth, when Mary's errant husband returned to her side, and not for reasons of love. One was to get me wed and out of the way, the other was to bring England in as his ally in the Spanish-French war. So in the February of 1557 I came to Court again, and a wonder it was that I caught not my death on the way, for the weather was foul.

Philip lost no time in seeing me and putting a marriage proposal before me, telling me of a prince nigh dead of love for me and ardently desiring my hand.

'God's death!' I cried. 'So fiery a suitor and I not know of it? Who is this lovesick gentleman?'

Motioning me to be seated so that I could look up at him, he perched himself upon the edge of a table gazing at me thoughtfully.

'I tell you, sister,' he said suddenly, 'I would you were mine.' I held his stare questioningly with mine own, and he went on hurriedly, 'A dream only, but you could be my cousin if you wed him who asks for you. 'Tis Prince Philibert of Savoy who begs for your hand.'

'Again?' I smiled. 'A persistent fellow, since I have refused him oft before.'

'But now you will make him happy, will you not?'

'I will not,' said I.

'How is this? Do you not wish to wed? Indeed you must wed. All women must wed, especially Princesses. And I wish it.'

'Sad am I to disappoint you then, brother,' I replied, 'but I will not have him.'

'Why not, by Heaven? He is not ill-favoured, he

is my cousin, he is faithful to his love for you, and it is my wish.'

'It is not mine,' I answered calmly. 'I will not have him.'

My little brother-in-law leapt off the table and stood before me, quivering with indignation, the firelight catching the diamond buttons upon his black velvet suit so that he twinkled like a constellation in a patch of night sky. 'You are headstrong, you are wilful!' he cried. 'I am a man and your King, and yet you gainsay me. In my country we have ways of forcing women to obey their masters!'

'Then I am fortunate, Sire, that I dwell not in your country.'

He blustered and fumed for a short while before dismissing me, and 'twas no secret that he and Mary quarrelled mightily over this; he insisting that it was her duty as his wife to command my marriage, she in tears protesting that it was not in her power to do so. She knew well that the people of England would not suffer my leaving; she was unpopular enough already.

Although Philip was unsuccessful in his efforts to get me wed, he did better in his attempt to bring England into his fight with the French, for our government had been greatly upset by the endeavours of certain English refugees to make an armed invasion of England from France. Nervous ears listened to Philip's persuasions and promises of safety against France so long as we joined Spain in the fight, and English aid was pledged to Spain. I felt this to be a great mistake and productive of nothing but trouble, which was how it turned out later. After having made sure of English committal, little Philip returned to Spain, deaf to his wife's frantic pleadings.

At Easter another suitor arrived for me in the shape of an envoy from King Gustavus of Sweden to propose his son, Prince Eric, for my hand. This was entire unexpected and threw Mary into a nervous fret for fear of Philip's displeasure at such an occurrence, but I sent word to her that I had no wish to change my state and would write to the Swedish King to tell him so. Mighty popular had I become of a sudden and had to endure all manner of roguish teasings from many who were sure that my refusal of the Swedish proposal was mere coy maidenliness. At first this amused me, then, when I had come into my own, it enraged me. Nowadays all know that I truly meant my words, but so contrary are the ways of women that I would give much to be sought after as I was years ago.

★ ★ ★

Before many weeks were out my sister, lonely in her Queenship, unpopular with her people, and with no husband by her side, sent word for me to come and bear her company at Richmond. Right glad was I to do so, for dearly did I wish to be close to Mary. Now that Renard had been recalled to Spain and his place taken by another, I felt that my place at Court would be more comfortable. Never could I hope to influence Mary, nothing I could do would stop the burnings which continued to the grief and horror of all English folk, but she was my sister, notwithstanding, and the feeling I had for her was deep and enduring. It has ever been so once my affections are given.

I travelled down to London with a large number of my household, leaving servants behind to sweeten Hatfield Palace against my return. Upon reaching White Hall I found that Mary had sent a barge to convey me and my ladies with all honour to the turrets and weather-vanes of Richmond. I remember that barge well. It had a canopy of green silk all broidered and fringed with gold, ruffling and swinging in the light breeze. The barge itself was garlanded and hung with fresh flowers. This delighted me, for I love flowers and keep them about me whenever possible in garlands or posies; fresh in the spring and summer, or broidered and jewelled in the winter. As we cast off, the musicians in the prow struck up a fashionable air and so we swung on our way, singing, over the bright water under the blue sky.

Mary wept happy tears to see me and I to see her. My joy was tempered by distress at her appearance, for she looked mortal ill and much aged. 'I must tell you a secret,' she said, after the greetings were over and we sat by the open window watching the sun shining upon the rippling waters of the Thames. 'If I am right, it will not be a secret for very long, but I wish to tell you first, Elizabeth. I believe myself to be pregnant again.'

My mouth smiled but my heart sank. Could she be right this time? I felt part glad and part dismayed; my heart was torn in two. If she were pregnant it would be a disaster for England. Would she get through the birth, even? If the child lived and she did not, the way would be open for Spain. If both lived, my hopes were dead. If Mary lived with no babe, would she survive such a disappointment long, and could I bear to live as I was now doing, with my sister at once a block and a stepping-stone to my emergence into power and all I wished? It was a hateful position to be in and caused me much anguish of mind.

'Sister,' I said, 'truly am I happy for you. I will make you some baby-clothes if you would like that.'

'A sweet thought, dearest,' she answered, her tired, lined face brightening. 'I would like it indeed. It gives me much pleasure to have you here with me, Elizabeth. All has not been well between us, I know. It is all so mortal difficult. I had thought it would have been easy once I was Queen, but truly, things have been worse. No one is like they seem, and I begin to see spectres and ogres where none exist. I feel I can trust no one, sister, no one at all; not even you, as no doubt you have realised but too well.'

I bowed my head, feeling that she had said all that was necessary upon that tricky and heartbreaking subject. But she continued to talk, moving restlessly up and down the sunlit apartment. 'I fear I may have been unfair to you,' she went on. 'I have tried to be impartial, but so much has been done and said in your name that in the end I knew not what to believe. At times I almost hated you, knew you that?' I nodded, not wishing to say a word, for I realised that she wished to talk some of her heart out to me. 'Ay, of course you know,' she said. 'How could you not? But great were the pressures upon me, Elizabeth.' She paused in her fidgeting walk and swung round upon me, the jewels winking on her crimson satin gown, her greying auburn hair haloed in the sunlight. 'Some there were who wished me to have you put to death. My own sister! Yet, I was so eaten with jealousy of you, of your youth, your looks, your air of certainty and your popularity, that almost I listened. I could not have you near me, Elizabeth. I was afraid of myself.'

'Dearest Mary, dearest sister,' I said urgently, seizing one of her restless hands and prisoning it in mine own, 'fret yourself no longer, I pray you. 'Tis all past and done. You must keep yourself as calm and merry as you can for the sake of the small one within you, so that he be not harmed by violent passions and flurrying of the nerves.'

Nodding in agreement, she lowered herself awkwardly on to a day-bed, for already she was swollen and heavy-looking. 'Philip did not want me!' she cried out, after a moment. 'He looks upon me with dislike and repulsion, for all I am Queen. Dost remember how we used to say: 'All Queens are beautiful?' ' She gave a harsh laugh that was more like a groan of pain. 'Such fools as we were then! All my beauty vanished years ago; wasted, unwanted, unseen. Now it is all too late.' She paused and stared at me. 'It may yet happen to you,' she said broodingly.

'I know it,' said I hardily, 'but I will not think of

it. Rather will I think of you and your peace
happiness. Come, I will play you some music u
the clavichord. 'Tis a piece I have writ myself and
you shall say how you like it.'

So I played to her for above an hour, and
watched her face grow more peaceful and her
eyes less despairing. When Kat came to take me to
change my gown for the evening, Mary kissed me.

'You are a good girl,' she said. 'I am glad you
came.'

★ ★ ★

Kat found me a length of white satin and we cut
out tiny patterns from it. I sewed industriously
thereon, and before I left Richmond for Hatfield.
I had completed a baby's bonnet, a smock and a
pair of minuscule shoes, wrought in my smallest
and most even stitches. Mary was delighted and
vowed that the work was the best she had seen,
even from her own broidery woman.

We spent a happy time that summer, she and I.
Even the new Spanish Ambassador, Don Gomez
De Feria, spared no pains to show me that Spain
had decided to court me these days. He was mighty
enamoured of little Jane Dormer, one of Mary's
ladies; indeed, it was whispered that he intended
to wed her and make her his Countess — all very
romantic, especially as she doted upon him. Sad it
was for Mary that her own Spaniard had not felt
the same for her. She wept when I had to leave,
but I comforted her, saying that she was to follow
me to Hatfield.

Well, she came, and merry were we. Whilst at Richmond, I had sent messengers back to Hatfield to prepare all kinds of fantasies to entertain the Queen. There was bear-baiting, dancing by torchlight in the garden, and upon one evening a flower-battle. Ay, it was a good time and I am still glad of it, for that was the last happiness the poor soul was to know.

Soon after Mary had returned to London, the news came that in our ill-starred alliance with Spain against France we had lost Calais, our last French possession. The whole country was enraged at this, feeling it a slight against England's supremacy and power — shaky enough in all conscience — and furiously censured the Queen for being so led by her Spanish husband into a foolish and humiliating war. Poor Mary was driven near hysterical by this reverse and the roars of disapproval it engendered. It was told me that she sobbed like a child for its mother, crying that the name of Calais was engraven upon her heart, so deeply did she feel the loss and disgrace.

'Ay, the disaster of Calais, coupled with her own personal loss, has driven her into a deep and settled melancholy,' reported the messenger who had brought these tidings.

'Her own loss?' I queried sharply. 'Why, what mean you?'

'Madam, there is to be no child,' announced the young man with gloomy relish, staring up respectfully from where he knelt before me.

'No child! Did she then miscarry?'

'Oh nay, Princess. There was no child of which

Her Majesty could miscarry. The doctors say now that she was never pregnant.'

I drew a long breath. No child. Then I was but a step away. I felt an extraordinary surge of elation, tempered immediately by distress. 'My sister the Queen, is she ill besides being melancholy? Tell me, fellow, quickly.'

'She is very ill, Madam. She has dropsy they say.'

'Dropsy? Sweet Jesu, are you sure?'

'Madam, the doctors think it to be dropsy, but they are not truly certain. The Queen is very feverish and very sick. The doctors are dismayed at her condition, Madam.'

'Well, get you gone, lad. My people will give you some refreshment. And — keep me informed.'

'Oh surely, Madam, indeed you will be kept informed. 'Tis all arranged by the Council,' he finished significantly.

Left to myself, I remained upon the window seat as still as a stock. I stared at the sunshine, at the trees softly waving, at the late roses blooming in the neat parterres of the formal garden. I stared as if I had been struck blind or turned to stone. It was coming. My sun was rising and even now began to glow over the horizon of my future.

I recall that one day there was a false rumour of Mary's death when all was a whirl of excitement and conjecture. I tried to keep calm, for it was necessary for me to have positive and certain confirmation of such an event. It would not do to be so eager to assume the mantle of Queenship that I was seen to grab it before my sister had fairly cast it aside. Glad was I of my foresight when I received a message from Sir Nicholas Throckmorton, ever my friend, to tell me that the Queen still lived, but enclosing in the letter various helpful instructions and tactics to follow in order to succeed happily through a discreet beginning.

Soon, messages of loyalty began to arrive from all over the Kingdom. Even while I thrilled, it sickened me. There lay my unhappy sister in London, in pain, dying; gradually being deserted by all. I instructed Throckmorton to bring me the Queen's black and gold betrothal ring at the end, for I knew it would never leave her finger until she lay dead, God rest her soul. I told Tom Parry to keep in touch with Sir John Thynne who could promise me a stout following in Wiltshire should trouble arise on my claiming the Throne when the time came.

De Feria had arrived in London from Brussels, all in a ferment to see Mary and receive her last instructions in case of her death. News was brought me that he had called a meeting of the Privy Council, and in Philip's name, had approved the choice of the Princess Elizabeth as heir to the Throne of England, and that Mary had rallied enough to agree. Oh God, it was coming. My poor, poor sister, it was coming; the end of your hopes and the fruition of mine. It was coming as surely as day follows night.

These last tidings I heard from Mary's own Comptroller and her Master of the Rolls, they having hastily left the Court and ridden hard to Hatfield to inform me of it. There they stood, fawning and fulsome, hoping for favours like two placatory dogs begging for tasty scraps. I hearkened to their words politely enough, but within me my stomach turned with contempt at their crawling. They were followed rapidly by De Feria himself, who arrived almost upon their heels, ready, I was amused to discover, to take command.

All my people were in awe, for they realised full well what was about, as I sat silent in my chair of state under its crimson canopy, while he bowed to me with as many a flourish as if I were already the Sovereign. I sat quiet to hear his words.

'You must realise, Madam, that you owe your Throne to your brother-in-law my master's intercession,' he began pompously, but I cut him short.

'Nay sir,' I answered him swiftly, 'sing me not that song. It will be the English people to whom I owe the Throne when it is time for me to take it. 'Tis they who will place me there — no foreign prince, I promise you!'

He stared at me, nonplussed. 'But you are full young for such a position. And a woman. And all untried! Who is to guide you? How will you contrive?'

I held up my hand to silence these protestations, my eyes agleam. 'Wait sir, and you will see. Now I have said enough upon a subject which I mislike while my sister still lives.'

Looking most thoughtful, he stepped back whilst I called my servants to arrange a night's lodging for him. Ay, thought I, and you will have still more to ponder on later, Don Gomez De Feria!

Those last days at Hatfield, they were like a dream. Cecil came and went, quiet and busy, with written proclamations and plans for taking over the government in my name. Every corner, every doorway was full of eager, low-voiced whisperers, their eyes following me with a mixture of suppressed excitement and reverence in their darting glances, wherever I went. I turned in revulsion from the sight of the London road. It was thronged with horses and riders; place-seekers hurrying to ingratiate themselves with me. My sister lay dying in sickness and misery at St. James's and all were deserting her as she lay. Then and there I vowed that this should never happen to me, should I live to be a hundred. I would keep my Court about me until my last breath. On the soul of my father, I swore it.

* * *

Daybreak on the seventeenth of November 1558. I was twenty-five years old, two months and ten days. I arose betimes, feeling an uneasy heaviness in my breast. I had known this sensation before, when my brother had passed. I felt a shortness of the breath and a fluttering of the heart that would not let me rest. My sister had died, I was sure of it; I felt it in my blood and bones. I was alone now, with my future in my own hands. Calling Kat and my women to dress me, I said I would walk awhile in the garden.

'Tis a pleasant day and the sun shines, Kat,' I exclaimed. 'Give me my hat and a cloak. The cloak will keep me warm and the hat will shade my eyes.'

Wrapped in a fur-lined rose-coloured velvet cloak, my pink, broad-leaved garden hat upon my head, I went outside into the chill air. I wandered about scarce knowing what I did, my life opening out before me like the dawn. I stood beneath a great oak, its few remaining leaves shrivelled now and autumn brown; its branches dark and knotted against the clear sky. As I stood, I saw them coming. The Lords of the Council were coming to me to tell me that the reason of my birth was upon me, that I was the first in the land. My sister was dead and I was Queen. On they came and knelt to me.

'Majesty,' they said. 'Sovereign Lady.' Then, looking up into my face as I stood, 'The Queen is dead. Long live the Queen.'

They kissed my hand, they waited for my words. As they knelt, so I knelt also, before the only One now higher than myself.

'*A domine factum, est et mirabilis in oculis nostris!*' said I. 'This is the work of the Lord, and it is marvellous in our eyes.'

I was Queen. Queen Elizabeth of England by the will of mine own dear English people, who wanted me and no other. I would be their mother, their father, their leader, their all-in-all. For this had I been born, rendered motherless, endured terror, loneliness, misery and hardships. The stone that the builders had refused had become the headstone of the corner.

I was Queen.

ELEVEN WEEKS MORE TO LIVE

White Hall, January 1603

It is enough. I am aweary. I can recollect no more, this Twelfth Night. See how the Queenly spectre hags back at me from between the alabaster pillars of my clearest mirror; old pointed chin on delicate jewelled hand, hooded eyes glimmering from under sunken brows. See the hollowed cheeks, their wrinkles filled with fucus, that white paste compounded of hog's bones ground powder-fine and mixed with white poppy oil. If laid on with white of egg, thick and solid, it will last smooth for an hour or two if one remains solemn-faced. A smile, and 'twill break into a thousand cracks like shattered porcelain.

See the thread-like lips of that old mask; a line of painted, sticky cochineal drawn up like the edges of an empty purse. Toothless. Ah, hideous! Why did I look into this cursed glass? Why did I torture myself thus? Yet many ancient dames look worse than I, and some not so old, neither. Ha, but that is no comfort to me, who am always stared at where'ere I go. There is but one of me.

I will call my women to cleanse my face of the paint, remove my wig, comb and plait my white hair and lay my finery by until tomorrow. So now, all is a-bustle and my thoughts are taken away from my hateful mirrored image, as warming pans are plied and garments lifted and folded; while coverlets are laid back and aged Sovereignty slips beneath. A night's rest will do me good and clear my mind for further memories and recollections, since now I have begun, I wish not to stop. It is like the unrolling of an endless tapestry of moving pictures, if such a thing could be. Ay, I will continue tomorrow, there is more living to do yet; so come, old Bess, stretch out your tired limbs, close your weary eyes, compose yourself to sleep, to dream, until the sweet light of morning, when you will dwell upon the past glories and excitements of your young Queenship . . . of power . . . of Rob . . . of glory . . . of Cecil . . . of Rob . . . of England, of England, of England . . .

THE END

Other titles in the
Ulverscroft Large Print Series:

THE GREENWAY
Jane Adams

When Cassie and her twelve-year-old cousin Suzie had taken a short cut through an ancient Norfolk pathway, Suzie had simply vanished . . . Twenty years on, Cassie is still tormented by nightmares. She returns to Norfolk, determined to solve the mystery.

FORTY YEARS
ON THE WILD FRONTIER
Carl Breihan & W. Montgomery

Noted Western historian Carl Breihan has culled from the handwritten diaries of John Montgomery, grandfather of co-author Wayne Montgomery, new facts about Wyatt Earp, Doc Holliday, Bat Masterson and other famous and infamous men and women who gained notoriety when the Western Frontier was opened up.

TAKE NOW, PAY LATER
Joanna Dessau

This fiction based on fact is the love-turning-to-hate story of Robert Carr, Earl of Somerset, and his wife, Frances.

McLEAN AT THE GOLDEN OWL
George Goodchild

Inspector McLean has resigned from Scotland Yard's CID and has opened an office in Wimpole Street. With the help of his able assistant, Tiny, he solves many crimes, including those of kidnapping, murder and poisoning.

KATE WEATHERBY
Anne Goring

Derbyshire, 1849: The Hunter family are the arrogant, powerful masters of Clough Grange. Their feuds are sparked by a generation of guilt, despair and ill-fortune. But their passions are awakened by the arrival of nineteen-year-old Kate Weatherby.

A VENETIAN RECKONING
Donna Leon

When the body of a prominent international lawyer is found in the carriage of an intercity train, Commissario Guido Brunetti begins to dig deeper into the secret lives of the once great and good.

A TASTE FOR DEATH
Peter O'Donnell

Modesty Blaise and Willie Garvin take on impossible odds in the shape of Simon Delicata, the man with a taste for death, and Swordmaster, Wenczel, in a terrifying duel. Finally, in the Sahara desert, the intrepid pair must summon every killing skill to survive.

SEVEN DAYS FROM MIDNIGHT
Rona Randall

In the Comet Theatre, London, seven people have good reason for wanting beautiful Maxine Culver out of the way. Each one has reason to fear her blackmail. But whose shadow is it that lurks in the wings, waiting to silence her once and for all?

QUEEN OF THE ELEPHANTS
Mark Shand

Mark Shand knows about the ways of elephants, but he is no match for the tiny Parbati Barua, the daughter of India's greatest expert on the Asian elephant, the late Prince of Gauripur, who taught her everything. Shand sought out Parbati to take part in a film about the plight of the wild herds today in north-east India.

THE DARKENING LEAF
Caroline Stickland

On storm-tossed Chesil Bank in 1847, the young lovers, Philobeth and Frederick, prevent wreckers mutilating the apparent corpse of a young woman. Discovering she is still alive, Frederick takes her to his grandmother's home. But the rescue is to have violent and far-reaching effects . . .

A WOMAN'S TOUCH
Emma Stirling

When Fenn went to stay on her uncle's farm in Africa, the lovely Helena Starr seemed to resent her — especially when Dr Jason Kemp agreed to Fenn helping in his bush hospital. Though it seemed Jason saw Fenn as little more than a child, her feelings for him were those of a woman.

A DEAD GIVEAWAY
Various Authors

This book offers the perfect opportunity to sample the skills of five of the finest writers of crime fiction — Clare Curzon, Gillian Linscott, Peter Lovesey, Dorothy Simpson and Margaret Yorke.

DOUBLE INDEMNITY
— MURDER FOR INSURANCE
Jad Adams

This is a collection of true cases of murderers who insured their victims then killed them — or attempted to. Each tense, compelling account tells a story of cold-blooded plotting and elaborate deception.

THE PEARLS OF COROMANDEL
By Keron Bhattacharya

John Sugden, an ambitious young Oxford graduate, joins the Indian Civil Service in the early 1920s and goes to uphold the British Raj. But he falls in love with a young Hindu girl and finds his loyalties tragically divided.

WHITE HARVEST
Louis Charbonneau

Kathy McNeely, a marine biologist, sets out for Alaska to carry out important research. But when she stumbles upon an illegal ivory poaching operation that is threatening the world's walrus population, she soon realises that she will have to survive more than the harsh elements . . .